Tonino Benacquista, born in France of Italian immigrants, dropped out of film studies to finance his writing career. After being, in turn, museum nightwatchman, train guard on the Paris–Rome line and professional parasite on the Paris cocktail circuit, he is now a highly successful author of novels and film scripts. Bitter Lemon Press introduced him to English-speaking readers with the critically acclaimed *Holy Smoke*. *Someone Else* won the RTL-Lire literary prize in 2002.

SOMEONE ELSE

Tonino Benacquista

Translated from the French
by Adriana Hunter

BITTER LEMON PRESS
LONDON

BITTER LEMON PRESS

First published in the United Kingdom in 2005 by
Bitter Lemon Press, 37 Arundel Gardens, London W11 2LW

www.bitterlemonpress.com

First published in French as *Quelqu'un d'autre* by
Éditions Gallimard, Paris, 2002

This book is supported by the French Ministry for
Foreign Affairs, as part of the Burgess programme
administered by the Institut Français du
Royaume-Uni on behalf of the French Embassy
in London and by the French Ministry of Culture (Centre
National du Livre); publié avec le concours du Ministère
des Affaires Etrangères (Programme Burgess) et
du Ministère de La Culture (Centre National du Livre)

ii institut français

© Éditions Gallimard, Paris, 2002
English translation © Adriana Hunter, 2005

A CIP record for this book is available from the British Library

ISBN 1–904738–12–5

Typeset by RefineCatch Limited, Broad Street, Bungay, Suffolk
Printed and bound in Great Britain by Bookmarque Ltd,
Croydon, Surrey

For Alain Raix

Prologue

That year, for the first time in ages, Thierry Blin decided to play tennis again, with the sole purpose of confronting the man he had once been: a competent player who, without ever earning a place in any official seeding, had given a few ambitious players a run for their money. Since then the cogs had ground to a halt, his shots had lost their edge, and the simple act of running after a little yellow ball no longer seemed so instinctive. Just to be clear in his own mind, he took out his old medium-headed Snauweart racket, his Stan Smiths and a few other relics, and made his entrance cautiously at Les Feuillants, the club closest to him. Having paid for his membership, he asked an attendant whether he knew of anyone who was looking for an opponent. The attendant pointed to a tall man who was playing alone against a wall, returning the ball with pleasing regularity.

Nicolas Gredzinski had been a member of the club for two months now, but he still didn't feel confident enough to challenge a seasoned player, or sufficiently patient to restrain his shots against a beginner. Gredzinski was actually refusing to admit to himself that his perennial fear of confrontation was being demonstrated yet again, in these weekly two-hour tennis sessions; he had a way of seeing hawkish tendencies in the most peaceful situations. The fact that a stranger had come and suggested knocking up for a while, or even playing a set, was his one opportunity to get onto a

1

court for real. To gauge his opponent's skill, he asked a few questions to which Blin gave only guarded replies, and both men headed for court number 4. From the first few warm-up shots, Blin rediscovered forgotten sensations: the felty smell of new balls, the sprays of rust-coloured grit on his shoes from the clay surface, the creaking sound of the strings as they slackened with the impact of the first returns. It was still too early to talk about the rest: the feel of the ball, the gauging of distances, his position, the suppleness of his leg movements. The priority was to return the ball. To return it, come what may. He had to launch into this dialogue and remember how to use the words, even if his first sentences were not those of a great speaker, let alone epigrammatic.

Gredzinski was reassured by the eloquence of his forehand, but felt that his backhand was talking gibberish. There had always been something forced about it; he avoided using it as an attacking shot and preferred taking his chances and lunging – at his own risk – in order to end up playing a forehand. He had actually succeeded in integrating this weakness into his game, paradoxically creating a style. It only took a few balls for him to make up for that slight delay in the attack, and his backhand rediscovered that little flick of the wrist which was far from a copybook move but which usually proved to be successful. He surprised himself by suggesting a match; however wary he was of competition, he could already see himself emerging from the trenches as a hero and striding towards the enemy lines. "It was bound to come to this," they both thought, and it was actually the only way that Blin could be absolutely sure, and that Gredzinski could break free of his fatalism, which meant he didn't see tennis for what it really was: a game.

2

The first exchanges were courteous but unremarkable, each of them wanting to review his argument before the great debate. With his long straight shots which kept Blin behind the baseline, Gredzinski was trying to say something like: *I could go on chatting like this for hours.* To which Blin replied with a succession of precise, patient *as you please*s, alternating forehands and backhands. When he lost his service, which put him 4–2 down in the first set, he decided to get to the point by coming in unexpectedly for a volley, which clearly meant: *How about stopping this chitchat?* Gredzinski was forced to answer *yes* by serving an ace, taking him to 15–love. And the conversation became increasingly heated. By systematically coming straight up to the net after the return of serve, Blin threw all of his opponent's suggestions back in his face, flinging down a *Not a chance!* or an *Onto the next!* or even a *Hopeless!* or a *Pathetic!* with each definitive volley. It was a good tactic and it saw him win the first set 6–3. Gredzinski never seemed to think of things until it was too late; it was while he was mopping his forehead as they changed ends that he realized how he should have replied to such peremptory attacks. He thought he might demonstrate for the two or three onlookers who had come to hang on to the wire mesh round the court. He now started serving into the middle of the service box to give his opponent as little angle as possible, then he had fun sending his drives one way then the other, playing Blin back and forth to the point of exhaustion as if to say: *You see . . . I too can . . . pick up the pace . . . you madman . . . or you poor ignoramus . . . who wanted . . . to make me look . . . like an idiot.* The madman in question fell into the trap and missed a fair few opportunities as he ran out of breath and failed to follow his shots through properly. Some of his net-skimming volleys warranted a bit of attention and issued a strange request, a sort of *Let me get one in, at least.* The second set was beginning to look like a summary execution, and the members of the Feuillants club, whether they were players themselves or just there to watch, were pretty sure which way it would go. There were now almost a dozen spectators to applaud the risks Gredzinski was taking and the rare replies from Blin, who lost the set. Even so, Blin had a psychological advantage that Gredzinski had always lacked, a profound conviction of his own rights, a belief in his own reasoning which forced him to play within the lines, as if the principle was self-evident. Gredzinski couldn't help but be affected by this and it wasn't long before Blin was giving the questions and the answers, taking the lead 5–2 in the third with victory in his sights. One of the elementary laws of debating then came to poor Gredzinski's aid: a debater of limited skill can't bear having his own arguments thrown back in his face. Accordingly he started using long shots with maximum spin as if deciding to resume control of a conversation with an inveterate talker. Strange though it may seem, Blin lost a game at 5–3 and was quickly overwhelmed, eventually letting Gredzinski re-enter the set at 5–5 with his service still to come. But Blin still had a few lines of argument in his racket; he had a perverse way about him, he was the sort who would never lie but just wouldn't tell the whole truth. Now for the first time he played several magnificent backhands straight down the line, and this saw him break the service of Gredzinski, who turned to stone between the tramlines. The latter had been prepared for anything except for this show of bad faith from an opponent who, from the very beginning of the match, had had the good grace to proceed quite openly. Where had these backhands straight down the line come from? It was dishonest! He should have declared them at the outset, just as you pronounce some profound truth to show exactly what sort of man you are. The third set ended in a painful tie-break which brought both men right back into the match, and proved what each of them was capable of when he felt threatened. Blin came up to the net to volley three times in succession, and the last of these was too much. Gredzinski replied with such a high lob that you could clearly read the message in its parabola: *This sort of reasoning will always be way over your head.* That showed he had misjudged the other man, who wasn't afraid of sending drop shots from the baseline just to see his opponent run: *You have no idea how far you are from the truth.* Gredzinski ran as fast as he could, sent the ball back onto the court and planted himself in front of the net: *I'm here and I'm staying!* And he stayed, towering, waiting for a reaction from the man who'd just made him run flat out, the man who hated using lobs, even in the direst straits – to him they were a cheap trick, cowardly shots. He delved to the depths of his racket to come up with a superb passing shot which meant: *I'm cutting you off at the knees.* The beginnings of a tear fogged over Gredzinski's eye; not only had he run several miles to get the drop shot *in extremis*, but now he was floored by the most humiliating rejoinder known to this demonic sport: the passing shot down the line. The *coup de grâce* was dealt by a handful of spectators who had become fascinated by the quality of their game: they started clapping. One of the longest standing members of Les Feuillants climbed up onto the umpire's chair to pronounce coolly: "3–0, change ends."

Gredzinski could see himself cracking his Dunlop over the poor devil's head; but all he did was change ends, as he had just been reminded to do. Like any other shy person who feels humiliated, he trawled through his darkest feelings for some residual energy. Blin, on the other hand, was celebrating the fact that he had found himself again, the man he had been, the man he might be again for some time, always agile, mischievous and sure of himself when it really mattered. He just managed to win the fourth point and then lost the next with just as much effort. When one of them said: *I'll be here to the end,* the other would reply: *And I'll be right there beside you,* but neither of them had managed to edge ahead. At five all, the two players exchanged a last look before the final showdown. A look which said the same thing, a feeling almost of regret that they couldn't find a gentleman's agreement or some way of pulling out, each with his honour intact. The moment of truth had come, they were going to have to go through with it. Gredzinski eased the pressure and lost the next point, then the match, delivering tired shots devoid of malice. As if to tell Blin that *victory comes to whoever hungers for it the most.*

*

When they came out of the changing rooms they bypassed the sodas and the club's garden chairs to take refuge in a bar near the Porte Brancion. They needed somewhere worthy of their match, a reward for so much effort.

"Thierry Blin."

"Nicolas Gredzinski, pleased to meet you."

They shook hands a second time, sitting on two tall stools, facing hundreds of bottles of spirits lined up in three rows. A barman asked what they would like to drink.

6

"Vodka, ice cold," Blin said without thinking.

"And for you, sir?"

The fact was that Gredzinski never knew what to have in cafés, let alone in bars, where he hardly ever set foot. Fuelled by a sort of complicity engendered by the match, he looked at the barman with obvious delight and said: "The same!"

Now that "the same" needs some consideration because Gredzinski, despite distant Polish origins, had never drunk vodka. He sometimes sipped at a glass of wine with a meal, or a beer to freshen up when he left work, but you could say he didn't have a personal relationship with alcohol. Only the enthusiasm and the euphoria of the match could explain that "the same" with which he surprised even himself.

Tennis was not truly a passion for either of them, but no other sport had given them so much pleasure. Leaning on the long wooden counter, they ran through all the players who had made them dream. They very quickly agreed: whether or not you were susceptible to his game, Björn Borg had been the greatest ever.

"And his extraordinary list of wins is only the tip of the iceberg," said Blin. "You just had to watch him play."

"That silence the minute he walked on the court, do you remember? It hovered in the air, it didn't leave room for any doubt about the outcome of the match. He knew it, you could see it in his face; but his opponent would still try his luck."

"Not one spectator ever asked themselves if he was having a good day, if he'd recovered from the previous match, if his shoulder was hurting or his knee. Borg was just there, harbouring his secret, which – like any real secret – shuts everyone else out."

"Borg didn't need luck. He even denied the whole idea of chance."

"The one unexplained mystery is his gloominess, that little something in his features which was so obviously sad."

"Oh, I wouldn't say there was sadness but, quite the contrary, serenity," said Gredzinski. "Perfection can only ever be serene. It shuts out emotion, drama and, of course, humour. Or perhaps he had a sort of humour, which involved robbing his opponents of the last weapons they had left to defend themselves with. When people tried to dismiss him as a machine returning balls from the baseline, he'd retaliate by playing extraordinarily cruel volleys."

"Put Borg up against the biggest server in the world? He'd start by inflicting a love game on him, all in aces!"

"Did Borg sniff out their weaknesses? Did he wear them down? If he wanted to, he could step on the accelerator and save more than an hour for an audience keen to go and watch a less monotonous match."

"As soon as he lost just one game, the journalists started saying he was on the way down!"

"Whoever the other finalist confronting Borg was, he could be a hell of a tournament winner. Being number two to Borg meant being the best in the eyes of the world."

They stopped talking for a moment to bring the small chilled glasses to their lips. Blin automatically took a good swig of vodka.

Gredzinski, who was not prepared for it and had no experience of the stuff, kept the drink in his mouth for a long while to let it express itself completely, swirling it round so as not to miss out a single taste bud, creating a cataclysmic response all the way down his throat, and closing his eyes until the burning passed.

"There's only one shadow on the picture of Borg's career," said Blin.

8

Gredzinski felt ready to take up a new challenge. "Jimmy Connors?"

Blin was amazed. Gredzinski had responded with all the confidence of someone who knows the answer. And it wasn't *the* answer but *his* answer, just his opinion, a quirky idea intended simply to rock the so-called specialists.

"How did you guess? He's exactly who I was thinking of!"

And, as if it were still possible, the very mention of Jimmy Connors inflamed them almost as much as the vodka.

"Are we allowed to love something and its exact opposite?"

"Absolutely," replied Gredzinski.

"Then you could say that Jimmy Connors was the opposite of Björn Borg, don't you think?"

"Connors was a destabilizing force, the energy of chaos."

"Borg was perfection, Connors was grace."

"And perfection is often lacking in grace."

"His constant willingness to pin everything on every shot! His exuberance when he won and his eloquence in defeat."

"The sheer audacity of his despair, his elegance in the face of failure!"

"How can you explain that he had every audience in the world on his side? He was adored at Wimbledon, adored at Roland-Garros, adored at Flushing Meadow, adored everywhere. People didn't like Borg when he won, they liked Connors when he lost."

"Do you remember the way he used to launch himself into the air to strike a ball before it had even had time to get there?"

"He made his return of service into a more deadly weapon than the serve itself."

"His game was counter-intuitive, it was even counter to the rules of tennis. As if, ever since he was little, he'd made a conscious effort to contradict his teachers in every lesson."

"We love you, Jimbo!"

They drank to Connors, and then drank again, this time for Borg. Then they fell silent for a moment, each lost in his own memories.

"We're not champions, Thierry, but that doesn't mean we haven't got a bit of style."

"Sometimes even a bit of panache."

"That backhand down the line, have you always been able to do that?" Gredzinski asked.

"It's not what it used to be."

"I'd really like to have had a shot like that in me."

"Your turns of speed are much more impressive than that."

"Perhaps, but there's something arrogant about that backhand that I've always liked. A thundering reply to anyone with any pretensions, a trick which would freeze the feet of the most insolent opponent."

"I stole it straight from Adriano Panatta, Roland-Garros, 1976."

"How can you *steal* a shot?"

"By being pretty conceited," replied Blin. "At fifteen, you have a lot of nerve."

"That's not enough, unless you're exceptionally talented."

"I didn't have that sort of luck, so I just had to sweat blood and tears. I neglected all the other shots to concentrate on that down-the-line backhand. I lost most of my matches, but every time I managed to place one of those shots I'd floor my opponent against all expectations and, for those five seconds, I was a champion. Now it's disappeared from lack of use, but it's still quite a memory."

"It can reappear, you know, and when your opponent least expects, trust me!"

Gredzinski was surprised to find his glass empty just as a strange feeling came over him, relaxing his whole body. A sort of bright gap in the foggy sky that hovered over him all the time. Without actually being unhappy, Gredzinski had adopted a sort of restlessness as his natural state. He had accepted a long time ago now that every morning he would come across the cold monster of his own anxiety, and nothing succeeded in calming it except for feverish activity, which meant he could never live in the present. All through the day Nicolas struggled to stay one step ahead of it, right up until those sweet few moments before he fell asleep. This evening, though, he felt as if he was where he wanted to be, the present was enough in itself, and the little glass of vodka exhaling icy mist had something to do with that. He surprised himself by ordering another, and swore that he would make it last as long as possible. The rest followed on from there; the words he was uttering were certainly his own, his thoughts were freed of any interference, and a peculiar memory came back to him, like an echo of the one Blin had just described.

"There's something beautiful and tragic about the story of those five seconds; now I understand the *stealing*. I had a similar experience when I was about twenty-five. I shared an apartment with a piano teacher, and most of the time – thank God! – she taught while I was out. That piano was in the middle of everything, our sitting room, our conversations, even our timetables, given that we organized them around it. Some evenings I actually hated it and, paradoxically,

I sometimes felt jealous of the pupils who laid their hands on it. Even the worst of them managed to get something out of it, but not me. I was useless."

"What was the point in battling on with this piano if it annoyed you so much?"

"Probably to insult it."

"Meaning . . .?"

"Playing it myself was the worst revenge I could find. Playing when I'd never learned how to, when I couldn't tell the difference between middle C and a B flat. The perfect crime, really. I asked my flatmate to teach me to play a piece by memorizing the keys and the position of my fingers. It's technically possible, it just takes a lot of patience."

"Which piece?"

"That's where the trouble started! I aimed high and my friend tried everything to stop me, but I stuck to my guns: Debussy's 'Clair de Lune'."

Thierry didn't seem to know it so Nicolas hummed the first few bars; they sang the rest together.

"In spite of everything, she was tickled by this impossible task, and she set me to work on 'Clair de Lune' and, like a performing monkey, I eventually did it. After a few months I could play Debussy's 'Clair de Lune'."

"Like a real pianist?"

"No, obviously, she'd warned me about that. Yes, I could create the illusion with a bit of mimicry, but I'd always be lacking the essential ingredient: heart, a feeling for the piano, an instinct which only comes from a proper apprenticeship, a passion for music, an intimacy with the instrument."

"But, there you are, when you're twenty you've got nothing better to do than impress those around you. And you must have done that a couple of times."

"Only a couple, but each time it was an extraordinary feeling. I'd play 'Clair de Lune' and adopt a brooding expression. The piece was so beautiful that it kindled its own magic, and Debussy would always turn up at some point between two phrases. I was treated to cheering, to smiles from a handful of young girls, and – for a few minutes – I felt like someone else."

Those last words hung in the air, just long enough for their resonance to be felt. The bar was filling up, people heading off for supper were being replaced by new arrivals, and this melting movement brought a new quality to the silence between Thierry and Nicolas.

"Well, at least you can say we've been young."

Caught up in a surprising surge of nostalgia, Thierry ordered a Jack Daniel's, which reminded him of a trip to New York. Nicolas was negotiating his vodka with all the patience he'd promised himself but it was an effort; several times he nearly downed it in one as he had seen Blin doing, just to see how far this first inkling of drunkenness might take him. Without knowing it, he was experiencing the beginnings of a great love story with his glass of alcohol, a story which was unfolding in two classic movements: allowing oneself to be overrun by the effects of that first thunderbolt, and trying to make those effects last as long as possible.

"I'm thirty-nine," said Thierry.

"I was forty a fortnight ago. Can we still think of ourselves as sort of . . . young?"

"Probably, but the apprenticeship's over. If you think that life expectancy for a man is seventy-five, we've still got the second half to go, perhaps the better half, who knows? But it's the first half that's made us into who we are."

"What you're saying is that most of our choices are irreversible."

13

"We've always known we wouldn't be Panatta or Alfred Brendel. Over the years we've constructed ourselves, and we may have thirty years ahead of us to see whether we've got ourselves about right. But we'll never be *someone else* any more."

It fell like a verdict, and they drank to the certainty of it.

"Anyway, what's the point in wanting to be someone else, to live someone else's life?" Gredzinski went on. "Or to feel someone else's joy and pain? If we've become who we are, then the choices can't have been that bad. Who else would you have liked to be?"

Thierry turned round and swept his arm over the room.

"Why not that man over there, with the gorgeous girl drinking margaritas?"

"Something tells me the guy must have a complicated life."

"Wouldn't it appeal to you to be the barman?"

"I've always avoided work which involved contact with the public."

"Or the Pope himself?"

"Not the public, I've already said."

"A painter whose work gets exhibited at the Pompidou Centre?"

"That's worth thinking about."

"What would you say to being a hired killer?"

Nicolas raised an eyebrow in silence.

"Or just the man in the apartment next door?"

"None of the above, but why not me?" said Nicolas. "The other me that I dream of being, the one I've never had the courage to become."

He suddenly had a sense almost of nostalgia.

For the pleasure of it and out of curiosity, they each described this *other me* who was both so close and

14

hopelessly inaccessible. Thierry could see him wearing particular clothes, doing a particular job; Nicolas exposed his great principles of life and some of his failings. Each of them had fun describing a typical day for his other self, hour by hour, in such abundant detail that they found it worrying. They were so thorough that, two hours later, there really were four of them there, leaning on the bar. The glasses had proliferated to the damning point where the very idea of counting them was almost indecent.

"This conversation's becoming absurd," said Nicolas. "A Borg can't become a Connors or vice versa."

"I don't like myself enough to want to stay as me at all costs," said Blin. "I'd like to spend the thirty years I've got left as this other me!"

"I'm not used to this," said Gredzinski waving his glass, "but do you think we might be a bit drunk?"

"It's up to us to go and find this someone else. What is there to lose?"

Gredzinski, captivated, had buried his anxiety somewhere in a desert and was now dancing on its grave. He fished about for the only answer that made any sense to him: "We might lose ourselves along the way."

"That's a good start."

They clinked their glasses together under the jaded eye of the barman who, given the time, was not going to serve them anything else. Blin, who was far more lucid than Gredzinski, suddenly affected a conspiratorial expression; without even realizing it, he had steered the conversation to arrive exactly here, as if in Gredzinski he had found something he had spent a long time looking for. His victory in the match now egged him on to play another kind of match in which he would be both his own opponent and his only partner, a competition so far-reaching that he would have to gather all his forces together, to reawaken his free will, remember his dreams, believe once again and push back the limits he was beginning to sense around him.

"I'll need time – say two or three years to fine-tune the tiniest details – but I'll wager you that I will be that someone else."

This was a challenge Thierry was putting to himself, as if Gredzinski was reduced to a pretext, at best a witness.

". . . It's June 23rd," he went on. "Let's meet in three years' time, three years to the day, in this same bar, at the same time."

Far, far away, intoxicated by the momentum of what was happening, Gredzinski let the drink guide him, a form of autopilot which left him free to concentrate on what mattered.

"If we meet . . . will it be the two of us or the *other* two?"

"That's what gives the challenge its spice."

"And what's at stake? If by some extraordinary chance one of us manages it, he'd deserve some incredible reward!"

For Blin, that was not the question at all. Conquering this other him was the greatest stake in itself. He wriggled out of it with a flourish. "On that evening, June 23rd at 9 o'clock in exactly three years, whichever one of us has won can ask absolutely anything of the other."

". . . Absolutely anything?"

"Are there higher stakes in the world?"

From where Gredzinski was right then, nothing seemed eccentric any more; everything and nothing vied for attention. He was discovering his own capacity for elation, a rare sensation pervading both his head and his heart.

It was time for them to part, something indicated the moment when they should leave. Neither would have been able to say what.

"This may be the last time we ever see each other, Thierry."

"That would be the best thing that could happen to us, don't you think?"

Thierry Blin

He got up without stopping to re-evaluate the decisions taken the previous evening; by setting himself this impossible task in front of a stranger the day before, he had also started a countdown.

On the refrigerator door there was a note from Nadine reminding him they were meant to be having dinner with their oldest friends that evening. Making himself a coffee would have made him late opening the shop, so he settled for the dregs of a lukewarm cup of tea abandoned on the corner of the table by his partner, and went into the bathroom to have a quick shower. He felt unusually energetic for first thing in the morning, and he made the most of this to trim his thick beard, which was beginning to overrun his cheeks. When people asked him why he kept it, Thierry would tell them he loathed shaving. That was partly true, but he did not tell them how much it bothered him looking himself in the face.

Whenever he found himself looking into a mirror above the seat in a café, he would suggest changing places with Nadine so that he was facing into the room; it was second nature to Thierry to avoid his own reflection. When the encounter proved necessary, he resigned himself to it and eventually accepted what he saw, but it did not mean anything to him. A round face with thick eyebrows, lacklustre eyes, slightly protruding ears, an upper lip which formed a tiny V in the middle of the mouth, a terrible lack of chin. That was the damning detail, the nerve centre of his entire being, hence the bushy beard. Some people curse the fact that they are short, others cannot bear going bald. Blin would have given anything to have a strong, square jaw. When he was very young a boy in his class nicknamed him "the tortoise", and he had not known why. A few years later, during a slide show at a holiday camp, Thierry had heard a girl whispering to her friend: "Don't you think he's got a profile like a tortoise?" He had started asking some of his friends but no one had really been able to explain; he had to wait until he was a fully grown man to understand. He was washing his hands in the toilets of a restaurant where the completely mirrored walls created a kaleidoscope effect, when he saw it close up for the first time: his own profile, his contours and how they moved in space. He finally made out the convex curve which ran from his forehead to his nose and his nose to his lower lip, and saw his eyes, which drooped over his cheeks – the whole thing reminded him irresistibly of a cartoon tortoise, a sad tortoise making painfully slow progress.

If only he could have been ugly, literally ugly, but true ugliness is as rare as beauty, and Blin was no more qualified for that category. He might have liked himself ugly. His tragedy was to have an exceptionally bland face, as insignificant as one could get. His features were *pointless*, that was the word he used. He could see himself ageing in a very strange way: with the tortoise getting increasingly sad, increasingly slow, filling out and hunching over at the same time, with flaccid skin and limp limbs. And it would not have made any difference if, even just for one summer, he had felt he was beautiful. He would have believed in it without being taken in by it: people who are physically pleasing are well aware of the fact. Everyone goes to great lengths to keep telling them so when they are children, and once they are adults, they have their memories refreshed from time to time. Blin had never caught a girl's gaze lingering on him as he passed, and the women who had given themselves to him had never mentioned his physique. They liked him but not one of them found him beautiful; the more honest amongst them had admitted as much. On the rare occasions when he touched on the subject, Nadine referred awkwardly to his *charm* to gratify him briefly.

"At your age, you make do with the face you've got. And I like it. Your face, I mean."

But why the hell should he have only one face in this bloody life? You should be able to change it in the same way you can break up a marriage that you thought was for ever.

He left the apartment and disappeared into the Métro station at Convention, re-emerged at Pernety, ordered a coffee to take out in his usual bistro, and opened up his shop, The Blue Frame, where a series of lithographs were waiting to be framed by the end of the week. He let his brain construct a complex scaffolding to flesh out the challenge thrown down the previous day, while his hands set to the task without needing any guidance.

Had Blin ever liked his work? He had chosen to be a craftsman because he wanted the independence and not because he loved paintings, framing or even wood. He had found himself a vocation in the same way you stumble into an affair that's bound to come to an end sooner or later. While he had been doing a stint of research work in the graphic arts rooms of the Louvre, he had met a man who had perfected an ingenious system for checking drawings and pastels without having to touch them; works by Degas, Boudin,

Fantin-Latour. One thing led to another, and he had learned everything you needed to know about framing; one exam later and he had a professional qualification. After contacting Musées de France to ask for work, he was offered a job at the Musée d'Orsay, and the game was won. A brand new workshop which he shared with a restorer, the most beautiful views in Paris, and a specialization in early photography. Nadar, Le Gray, Atget and a few others have him to thank to this day for their eternal rest between two sheets of Plexiglas. Some of his colleagues had an almost sensual approach to the materials, the varnishes, the paper, the gold leaf and, most importantly, the wood. Experts, lovers of wood whose senses were awakened by some piece of sycamore. He gradually came to face the fact: he was not one of them. His first memory relating to wood dated back to the sword thrown together by his father (a disastrous DIY man) from two rough pieces of wood, which gave him a good many splinters. In the years that he spent at the museum, he had done his work without putting a foot wrong, but without a hint of inventiveness. He resigned on a whim to grapple with another medium, an art which was no more sacred but was living. He took out a lease on an old grocery in a quiet street in the Fourteenth Arrondissement and set up his workshop: a paper guillotine, a shelving unit for the lengths of framing wood, harsh strip lighting and a few frames in the window. He did a bit of advertising in the area, relying on the goodwill of neighbouring shopkeepers, and opened wide the door of The Blue Frame, happy to be a craftsman, intoxicated by his brand new freedom, and flattered by the people who saw nobility in his craft and authenticity in his every gesture.

That was when *they* came.

The restaurant owners with their watercolours, the kids with their pictures folded in four, the film-lovers with their posters eaten away by the acid in the Scotch tape, the enlightened amateurs with their nudes, the ambitious amateurs with their hyperrealist nudes, and a few collectors of foxed engravings found at the Saint-Ouen flea market. Next came the artists themselves, with their pure abstracts which dared to use oil but overdid the siccative, the pastorals with their kindergarten pastels, the recent winners of various competitions, including the Fourteenth Arrondissement's Golden Palette, and to cap it all Mme Combes's self-portraits in charcoal. Blin had nothing to complain about; he wasn't inundated by work and the shop was doing well enough to make a living.

Eight years later, he no longer derived any pleasure from taking care with his work. In the name of what? Beauty? Art? After the Louvre and the Musée d'Orsay, the word *art* had a different resonance when he heard it in his little workshop. One of his first clients had been that little woman with her "twelve Klimts" to frame.

"Twelve Klimts! Gustave Klimt? Are you sure?"

"Yes, twelve drawings."

"Originals?"

"I don't know."

"Are they signed? Are these works on paper?"

"No, on a calendar."

With a little experience, he got used to translating. A *Gauguin drawing* was usually a poster from an exhibition, and *I've got an original* heralded a few tricky moments.

"I've got an original Bourrelier, a seascape."

"Who?"

"Romain Bourrelier! From his best period. I didn't

22

know my grandfather had one. Can you imagine: a Bourrelier, in really good condition!"

". . . I'm not really up on my history of art . . ."

"His best period! Straight after the war! That's what they told me at Villebonne – that's where he was from. I want to have an estimate done but I don't know who to ask. Would you know anyone? A specialist?"

"I'd have to find out . . ."

"Did you know there was a Bourrelier hanging in the Hôtel de Ville in Corcelles in Burgundy?"

"I'll see what I can do."

"Discreet, I see."

The prize had to go to the *pure abstract* from the studio opposite, a local artist, destitute naturally, very late with his payments, but his status as a painter gave him the right to be. He entrusted his framer with his strong opinions and his furious shouting – all these civil servants from the ministry who don't know anything! – and felt that exhibiting his canvases at La Tavola di Peppe (a pizzeria on the Rue de l'Ouest) was beneath his talent, which did have the advantage of leaving that opportunity to someone else.

At first Blin was very kind to them. He accepted their touch of naivety, he even envied them for daring to do what he did not: it was his way of paying homage to them as the first person to view their work. Now he no longer felt even curiosity for the creative accidents in the area; whoever came into the shop immediately inspired boredom. He became embittered by this and no longer respected their freedom of expression. Some mornings he felt like venting his general anger on one unsuspecting customer, waxing lyrical about his pathetic lack of style, denouncing him to the committee for the protection of good taste, howling with derision. What he actually did was to stay affable and complimentary – he did have a living to make. Not a hope of opening up about it to Nadine, she was one of them. That was how they had met. A big photograph she was very proud of, you could see it in her eyes when she took it out of the portfolio; it was of an avenue with greyish silhouettes passing each other in complete indifference, and an empty bench in the background. Metaphor, allegory, modern life, uncommunicativeness, intimist-style under-exposure, etc.

"It's very good. It's a good print, too."

". . . Thank you. What would you recommend?"

"What's your home like?"

A question he asked frequently, not maliciously though, but this time he allowed himself an amused little smile, a strangely ambiguous smile, almost disturbing.

"What I meant was . . . what sort of colours are there?"

She was a little more conniving. He even glimpsed the point where she might invite him to come and see for himself.

"It's all black and white, like my photos."

She was speaking the truth and he very soon had an opportunity to check; that was five years ago. They now lived in a two-bedroom apartment in the Rue de la Convention. She was an assistant to a cardiologist, and Thierry was still framing her photos for an exhibition which the gallery kept putting off by another month. Over time, he had come to have more respect for her than for her work, without daring to admit as much to her. The pleasure Nadine derived from it herself should have been enough, but Thierry had trouble facing up to this idea: she was not a true photographer in the same way that he was not a true framer.

He could have perpetuated the illusion for the rest

of his life by providing a setting for the talents of the man in the street, but this uncomfortable dichotomy in his existence cost him dearer and dearer as time passed and the prospect of retirement no longer seemed to be some wild futuristic imagining.

He was not the best administrator. He would have closed shop a long time back if he had not met the woman who managed to put some order in his books, do his year-end accounts and fill in his tax return. Brigitte could handle figures the way some people knit; she could rattle away on a calculator at the same time as taking notes and talking about the last film she had seen. When she got to the bottom of a missing ten francs she would heave a sigh of relief as if she had won a chess final. She always used to say that she "didn't know anything about painting", but would speak about Matisse in her own particular way and Thierry would learn something new every time. He was very fond of her, he found her funny, without artifice. He particularly liked teasing her about her old maid image, which she played on without realizing it; for the first few years he had called her Mademoiselle Brigitte, then just Mademoiselle, which had created an odd intimacy between them. But, despite her Chinese satin dresses with slits up the side, which drew some risqué remarks from Thierry, he never really looked at her as a woman. He would occasionally feel that she regretted this; he saw her only as an ally.

"Haven't you ever been tempted by painting or découpage, Mademoiselle?"

"My only talent is for percentages, that's my strong point. If I'd had even the tiniest urge to paint, I wouldn't have hesitated, because my thoughts about that sort of thing are exactly the opposite of yours. The more people there are expressing themselves, painting, writing, making ripples in the water, the better equipped we'll be to cope with the inevitable apocalypse. Everyone's an artist, some just have the nerve to believe it more than others. When I see some little man coming into the shop carrying all the agonies of Van Gogh on his shoulders just to have his cauliflower in gouache framed . . . I find it touching."

"I do too, I even worry he'll cut his ear off one day."

"You play tennis, don't you?" she said with a shrug.

"So what?"

"How would you rate yourself next to McEnroe?"

"Do you know who McEnroe is, Mademoiselle?"

"Don't treat me like an idiot and don't change the subject. On a scale of one to twenty, what would you give McEnroe?"

"Seventeen, eighteen."

"And yourself?"

"Oh, between a half and one."

"And that hasn't made you give up? Do you realize that Madame Combes with her self-portraits is much closer to Rembrandt than you are to McEnroe? And do you know why? Because she's never seen a Rembrandt self-portrait. She acts spontaneously, she works really hard, there's a sense of necessity in what she does. Rembrandt had a big nose and a double chin, he wasn't just reproducing his features, he was looking for another truth. Good old Madame Combes is working in exactly the same direction, she's not motivated by some sort of narcissism, she's just using the only subject she can lay her hands on: herself. Would you really have the cheek to tell her she's wasting her time?"

On the days when she came to work there, he liked knowing she was in the shop while he worked; nothing could go wrong while she was in the building.

Halfway through the afternoon he felt he had done

enough for the day, and undertook a little tidying up in the workshop. The bookseller from across the street came to have a cup of tea and the remains of a chocolate cake with him; still absorbed by the plans in his head, he merely punctuated the woman's panegyric on the village atmosphere to be found in the heart of Paris. A customer came and broke up their little ritual, and Thierry took a new order: a prize-winning architectural design to be boxed in glass within two days.

Most of the time, when his customers would leave him in peace, he would sit alone at the back of his workshop, settled in an armchair doing nothing except thinking about all the dreams he had not yet buried. Only the most ordinary things, a bit of excitement in his life, a day-to-day existence which might allow for something unexpected, was that asking too much? The thought that, at barely forty, the rest of his life should be doomed to resignation terrified him. Although he did not know exactly how, he would have liked to devote his cherished independence to something other than his tools and his wooden frames, to tackle some more human material (the samples that came into his shop cannot have been representative of the race as a whole!), to penetrate the secrets of his kind without being granted permission. For a few months now he had been haunted by the memory of a blond girl he had seen playing tennis in the Jardins du Luxembourg. She had so thoroughly aroused his curiosity that he had done everything he could to sit close to her when she came off the court. With some clever manoeuvring he managed to sit at a nearby table in the almost empty little café. He had taken some pleasure in playing the small-time spy, in order to see her up close, to hear her. As he caught snatches of her conversation with her opponent, he experienced strange and completely new sensations, and eventually got what he wanted: to steal a little glimmer of her intimacy. He imagined what could follow on from his intrusion into this woman's life and the discoveries he could have made, and the more his imagination was carried away, the stronger his feeling of shameful and, in his own eyes, suspect jubilation. Everyone on earth must at some point have wondered what the person next to them might be hiding, but Blin found the question sufficiently stimulating to take it seriously.

Going further back into his past, he liked remembering the heat wave of 1976, a whole summer spent under the sloping roof of the little house in Rugles in Normandy. Right from the start, the teenager he had been then had suffered much more from the boredom than the heat; he had not been able to forge friendships with the local children, the television had stayed in Paris, and cycle rides were only conceivable in the late afternoon with the first breath of air, when the village took on some semblance of life again. This torture began as the clock struck nine in the morning, and lasted all through the afternoon, in other words a daily eternity which made him curse the holidays.

Until he was saved by a miracle.

He was usually someone who read the strict minimum prescribed by his teachers, but his curiosity nudged him to open a collection of Georges Simenon short stories which he found in a cardboard box. He could see himself now, lying sweating in the shade in his red dungarees, his head resting on a rolled up blanket, the book on his chest. He had read the thirteen *Petit Docteur* novellas at a rate of one a day, and had kept himself going until the end of July by re-reading them, hoping for a new miracle for the month of

August. The little doctor in question was a young GP in the country who had fun playing amateur detective rather than treating his patients, and each story thrust Thierry into an adventure which fired his imagination more than anything he had ever known. What fascinated the young Thierry was the way the character's vocation was suddenly triggered, right at the beginning of the book, by a mysterious telephone call which set in motion some unknown mechanism in the little doctor's mind. Working on a simple clue which he deciphered thanks to sheer common sense rather than any skill, the intrepid Jean Dollent pieced together an argument which made him increasingly curious to know more, and increasingly reckless in the face of the unknown. He felt suspense and adventure breaking into his simple doctor's life; nothing would ever be the same again. Thierry had grasped that this was a pivotal moment which would go on to reveal a formidable need to unravel the true from the false. What made the story so exciting was the very fact that the doctor was an amateur; Thierry followed his logical reasoning one step at a time, and sometimes foresaw those steps because they were nothing like the convoluted deductions of serial sleuths. During the course of the novellas the good doctor became so taken with the game that he would jump at the first opportunity to get out of his consulting rooms, much to the delight of Thierry, who saw this as an irrepressible sign of fate. Doctor Dollent, more seasoned from one novella to the next, started making his clients pay and thought of abandoning medicine to become a professional police investigator. What could turn a doctor away from his vocation in that way, apart from something more powerful still?

Twenty-five years had passed since that love affair

with a book. Like all youthful passions, it was unforget-table. He even felt that, with the passing of time, it had found a disturbing way of coming back to visit him, as if forgetting simply closed a loop and the lapses in memory produced by ageing were just a roundabout way of getting back to what really mattered. Behind the sum of his job-related doubts and the choices he had made, the fantasies of his youth came back to haunt him and, among them, there was one that imposed itself like an injunction, hiding behind two words which had a magical and yet very real ring to them in his mind: private detective.

Before he could even dream of what he might become, Thierry was going to have to shake himself off. Every epic had to start by turning a corner, the rest was just a question of stages to reach and obstacles to overcome. He had to start with a symbolic gesture.

At 7pm he still had time to close up shop, nip to Les Feuillants and get back home in time to attend to Nadine as she stepped out of the bath.

"My name is Thierry Blin, I joined yesterday, do you remember?"

"You played a wonderful match for us. If Monsieur Gredzinski had got a few more first serves in, he would have had a chance. Would you like a court?"

"No, I came to rescind my membership."

*

Nadine and her bath-time ceremony. Very hot, almond-scented bubble bath. A wooden shelf in front of her, a little altar where she laid out a magazine, an aperitif, a mirror and a towel to wipe her hands. Thierry was a part of the ceremony: he simply had to sit on the side of the bath, kiss Nadine on the lips, exchange a few words with her about the day and pour her another drink, usually a dash of whisky with lots of sparkling water. He automatically looked at her breasts, half submerged, at her tiny nose, her serious eyes, her slightly dusky skin. Her imperceptibly sad smile, her slim body. He had always liked things to be little in women. Feet, breasts, stomachs. It didn't matter so much now. He had reviewed his criteria since coming across the blonde in the Jardins du Luxembourg. Little white knickers revealed for all to see at the least acceleration, firm tapering legs which put her navel exactly on a level with the strip at the top of the net. She was about forty-five, with the smile and wrinkles of a woman who still enjoys life just as much, skin accustomed to terribly expensive creams, a coarse voice, a way of wielding the subjunctive similar to her sliced backhand, and breasts too big to appeal to his emotions, but Thierry didn't give a stuff for emotions that day, all that mattered was the feeling of greed. Opulent breasts restrained by a cropped bra fit for a champion, sculpted by thousands of forehands, backhands and winning serves, not one muscle spared; in the long run it had its rewards. He would play with Nadine's, make them into shapes they were not meant to have, then move on to other things. Thierry Blin had imagined spending a bit of time with a woman like that, a great big creature who could cope on her own and would know how to make him laugh. Nothing like the sweet-faced little brunette who could only think of snuggling up for safety. Nadine pitched her voice delicately, but more often than not let everyone else do the talking. Over the years, Blin had started to loathe her discretion; he sometimes even found her gentleness unbearable.

"Thierry?"

"Yes?"

"Shall I put on some make-up and we can go out to this dinner?"

"Take your time."

Nadine had only ever called him by his name. Sometimes he would have liked to have been her sweetheart or her poppet, anything, even something ridiculous, but not her Thierry. His friends also called him Thierry but no one, not even his parents, had appropriated his name to make a familiar, natural sound of it. No woman had sighed a *Thierry!* while they made love, a heartfelt cry, a gasp. He could remember no diminutives derived from Thierry, no nicknames derived from Blin, and God knows there could have been thousands. He did not loathe his first name in itself, but there were others that suited him so much better. As a child, he had never tried to become a Thierry, to live like a Thierry and yet he had known real Thierrys, quite at home with their two syllables, wearing Thierry smiles on their lips. As time had passed, things had not improved. He got worse and worse at being Thierry and he used the name as he might have done, say, Bernard: the problem was the same, he was no more suited to Bernard. Not satisfied with just calling him Thierry, his parents had not deigned to give him any other names he could clutch onto. If only he could have chosen from Thierry Louis Bastien Blin, he would have imposed Louis on everyone and the problem would have been dealt with. He felt much more like a Louis than a Thierry. So he was in fact a thwarted Thierry. An unworthy Thierry. Or unworthy of being a Thierry.

The question of his surname had never been a problem, there was so little intimacy in the family name. He had known dozens of Blins, starting with his aunts and uncles, old people and children, nothing but Blins; he

32

did not feel any more or less like a Blin than anyone else. And in this instance, it was true, it was just to do with how it sounded. *Ah, Blin, I'd like you to come and see me in my office.* In the end, like everyone else, he had grown accustomed to it, and yet he felt sure that surnames are not inscribed in our hearts or our souls, just our memories. Even a dog who has been called Sultan all his life can respond to *Cafetière* or *Versailles* within a week. There was no reason why a human being should be so very different.

All the other questions stemmed from the issue of names. *What did the Public Record Office mean, anyway?* he asked himself. *Why exactly do I exist legally with a social security number and an obligation to do national service?*

Simply his father's affirmation when he had set off one fine morning to declare his birth to an employee at the registry office? Did it all really lead on from there? And if on that fateful day his father had been too happy and too busy celebrating the child's arrival, would that child exist today? They say no one slips through the net but do the rare exceptions come out and show themselves?

He had not been born to unknown parents in some distant country where the archives could have been burned in a civil war. He really was Thierry Blin, he had an identity card, a passport, a voting card, a private health plan and account books, taxes to pay and an official partner. What could he do to retrace his steps, to shout out loud that there never had been this Thierry Blin that everything referred to? Cross it out? Strike it off? Burn it up? Go back to the registry office in Juvisy and rip the relevant page from the great founding document? Even if that were possible, it would not be enough. He would have to find definitive ways of shrugging off Thierry Blin.

With one eye on Nadine as she grappled with her wardrobe, he lay down on the sofa with a calendar of saints' days in his hand.

"You made fun of me when I bought that thing," she said, amused.

As he ran through the names of all the saints on each successive day of the calendar, he made instant, unconscious and instinctive summaries of the thousand connotations, reverberations, references and prejudices attributed to each of them. It was a pleasing exercise and the choices imposed themselves. By the end he had ticked:

Alain, Antoine, François, Frédéric, Julien, Jean, Paul and Pierre.

He liked plain, elegant names, the ones that had always been there but were not given to everyone. By the same token, he felt a certain admiration for those who bore them. Discreet, well-bred people who had the delicate task of being the umpteenth variation on the theme of Pierre or Paul. The man he would be from now on could very well be called Pierre or Paul. He liked the hint of ruggedness in Pierre, the fact that it was the word for a stone counterbalanced its biblical resonance. Blin would have loved to have been spoken to with a: "*What do you think of it, Pierre?*"

Or to have been told: "*Oh, Pierre, you'll always know how to please me.*"

No one had ever told him: "*Oh, Thierry, you'll always know how to please me.*"

If he had been called Paul for forty years, he was in absolutely no doubt that his trajectory would have been different. Perhaps he would have painted pictures instead of framing them, who knows? A Paul was bound to have an artist's soul, or perhaps even the stuff of an international spy. On the women front, his whole life would have been littered with *Take me wherever you want, Paul* or *Paul, do that thing again in the small of my back!* The tall blonde at the tennis court would unquestionably dream of coming across a Paul in her life.

He could not explain it to himself, but Blin felt he was becoming a Paul. He must have been famous as a Paul in a previous life, perhaps he had even been the apostle in person. In a few minutes Paul had definitely won over Pierre.

"Two more minutes, and I'll be ready!"

He put the calendar down and, pen in hand, stretched out his arm to reach the telephone directory without getting up from the sofa.

What surname was perfect for a Paul? After running through whole columns of names, he realized that Paul went with everything. Nagel, Lesage, Brunel, Rollin, Siry, Viallat, the list was endless. Paul was no longer a criterion for selection, which made the choice even more dizzying. Blin no longer knew how to proceed and very soon felt out of his depth. He tried to cling to a few principles which he felt were rational, to help him move forward. Prerequisite number one: the name must have a minimum of two syllables, ideally three, to put paid once and for all to this scarcely audible *Blin* which had been belittling him since his childhood. Besides, *Paul* called for a longer name with a slightly Nordic but still gentle ring to it, something undulating and peaceful. Prerequisite number two: the first letter had to fall between R and Z. A belated revenge but a just one. All his life he had been one of the first on the register, every teacher's designated victim, the first to be given chores, the volunteer who does not even have to step forward. *Blin, to the blackboard!* How often he had loathed that capital B! The time had come for him to be at the bottom of the list, safe and warm. He leafed through a few pages of the directory again, waiting for a miracle which did not come, then, still lying on the sofa, he cast an eye over the bookshelves. In amongst those dozens of books, those encyclopedias and the heaps of reference works he no longer consulted, there must have been, squeezed somewhere between two pages, a Nordic sounding name with three syllables which began with U, V or even W – or why not Z? He intuitively made for his dictionary of Flemish painters, opened the last third of the book, and quietly pronounced names that had always struck him as elegant while still familiar. Rembrandt, Rubens, Ruysdael, Van der Weyden, Van Eyck, ending up with the most prestigious of all, a name which on its own conjured harmony itself: Vermeer.

No one was called Vermeer, but it was a good starting point. He set about making variations on the name by distorting it, combining it with different suffixes and trying to find a different ring to it. At last it became self-evident.

From now on he would be called Paul Vermeiren.

Nadine was ready, pretty, perfumed, smiling. Thierry displayed unfailing gallantry that evening. During dinner he was both eloquent and discreet, attentive to each person at the table. On the way home, Nadine watched him driving, touched by just seeing him there, reassured because he was beside her. She could even see herself, one day, as Madame Thierry Blin.

She could not possibly have imagined that she had just spent the evening with Paul Vermeiren.

Nicolas Gredzinski

God knows, Gredzinski knew a bit about worrying. His anxieties could be sneaking, hesitant or conspicuous, he had experienced them all and could even name them when he felt them first prickling in his entrails. This morning's was of unknown origin and it stopped and questioned his every move. It was accompanied by disturbances which, in this instance, he must have been the only person not to recognize: a dry mouth, a vice over his skull and general tiredness. He identified them by cross-checking: a hangover. Nicolas lacked the inner strength to survive such bleakness; the first drinking binge of his life would be the last. He had never needed any help reaching such a shadowy place, his natural pessimism directed him there anyway: for him, coming back to life every morning was like a piece of bad news he eventually had to accept, but a hangover turned it into a sentence with no chance of an appeal.

The two aspirins he took as soon as he got up refused to take effect; he was going to have to put up with it. On the way to work, he closed his eyes for a moment to locate the nerve centre of this migraine which had stopped him feeling himself since the moment he woke up. He identified an area between the left lobe and the sinciput, perhaps the very seat of guilt, the place where all moral decisions – and, therefore, all punishments – originated. How could he know if this really was a punishment? Had he asked too much of a body ill-prepared for so much liquid corrosive? Doctors would tell him that you should not drink more vodka in one evening than you have drunk in an entire lifetime, but they would also say that we are not all equal in the face of human vices. Some live for nothing else, others die from not having experienced any. Nicolas still did not know which wood he was carved from.

At the time when his neurons usually went into fibrillation at the thought of a coffee, he would have given anything for a bit of sparkling water. Water, cold and bubbly. He intuitively felt that this combination of three elements represented the only means of battling this unbearable chemistry of remorse. As he walked into the atrium of the Parena Group, he stopped briefly at the coffee shop to buy a tin of iced Perrier before taking the lift. With his eyes half closed he said hello to Muriel, the switchboard operator on the fifth floor, and went to take refuge in his office. He drank his can down in one and gave an animal groan; the chill of the water dispelled the horrible feeling that his tongue had swollen and stuck to the roof of his mouth.

Still nowhere near over the worst of it, he opened a couple of letters, leafed through one of the reviews his department subscribed to, picked up the Vila file which he had been trying to finish for the last three days, and closed it again just as quickly. Nothing could take his mind off a dull ache which made him more than usually pessimistic about the future of the planet and his own future in particular. He crossed his arms on his desk, rested his head on them, closed his eyes and saw himself, the previous evening, onto his umpteenth vodka, ready to take on the world; the image struck him as so unbelievable, so excessive that he thought he would never be able to file it alongside his own memories.

*

On that wretched day, as he stood with his tray on the rack at the self-service canteen, he surprised himself by replying, "I don't know" to the question "Basquaise chicken or shepherd's pie?" He tried but failed to allay the suspicions of the other people at his table. None of them tried to find out more, and they each talked about what they had watched on television the night before. Then they moved on to the coffee dispenser, where Gredzinski took a last-chance double espresso before going back up to his office.

The building site he could see from his office – destined for the Group's Telecommunications department – was coming on extraordinarily quickly. Parena was consolidating its position from month to month, gaining ground and driving out others in every sector with a ferocity cited as an example in business schools. Nicolas spent half his life at 7 Allée des Muraux in Boulogne-sur-Seine, a quaint address which disguised an empire on the banks of the Seine. Three buildings: an oval one which housed the Environment department and the administrative offices, another one which contained the Electronics department, and a more modest one for Communications, to whom Nicolas was answerable. On the tree-lined esplanade in the middle of these three glass buildings there was a café, the Nemrod, a mini-market and a newsagent. A huge footbridge ran over the Paris ring-road, providing a link for most of the personnel to get to the RER train station. With Distribution and Waterways, Advertising, Cable, Satellite, Energy, Computing and now

39

Telecommunications, the Group's Paris offices had 3,200 employees, including one small, depressed man who had done nothing to deserve all this. Magda came into his office to ask him for his holiday dates. Caught unprepared, Nicolas said he would have to wait for his manager to get back. Nicolas's holidays depended, as they did every year, on when Bardane took his, and he was a man who liked to decide at the last minute: one of the privileges of being a client manager.

"Can't you ring him?"

"If I disturb him just to talk about holidays, he's going to think I'm an idiot. He's with a client in Avignon."

In Gordes to be more precise, in a friend's magnificent country house: the official opening of the swimming pool. Bardane had left with a day's notice, leaving his assistant with only a fraction of the necessary information on the Vila file. Just a slip of the mind or a deliberate withholding of the facts – Nicolas did not try to understand. For three years he had been playing his part as the interface between Bardane and the team of graphic designers, rereading contracts, checking mock-ups, overseeing projects, giving quotes and so on.

"Come back tomorrow morning, Magda, he'll be back. He's got a management meeting at 4 o'clock."

"Where are you planning to go this summer?"

"If I get a couple of weeks in August, I think I'll accept an invitation from some friends who're taking a house in the Pyrenees."

"Like last year?"

Magda had a good memory, and he commented on it. The minute she had left, Gredzinski closed his eyes tight shut to try to make out the little monsters which had been fluttering in his head since the morning.

They were tiny nebulous things, but very real, very noisy and very determined to take a hold. He was woken by the telephone ringing.

"Monsieur Gredzinski? I've got a Jacques Barataud asking to speak to you."

"Jacques who . . .?"

"Barataud. It's personal."

"Thank you, Muriel. Put him through."

Nicolas recognized Jacot and was annoyed with himself for being caught out like that. How could he have forgotten his name was Jacques Barataud?

"How are you, Gred?"

The question was well meant, the reply impossible. How could you talk about a headache to a man with cancer? Jacot had nothing in particular to say, he was only calling to talk about *it*.

A few months earlier, Jacques Barataud, barrister-at-law in Paris, had had enough natural authority to reassure his clients and unsettle his adversaries. He had plucked Nicolas from the clutches of injustice in a civil responsibility case which was trying him unfairly. The scene had unfurled like a gag in a film, but no one had laughed: Nicolas is riding his bicycle along a dirt track and comes out on to a small road, taking every necessary precaution. A car comes along travelling very fast, overtakes him and, being extra cautious, gives a slight swerve, which frightens a family of cyclists pedalling in the other direction. The eldest son brakes sharply, his little brother knocks into him and falls, head first, into the ditch. The car is already far away by the time the panicking parents have intercepted Nicolas and called the police, their insurance company and their lawyer. This worthy collection of people work their way back along the chain of guilt and, for want of anyone better, all eyes turn to Nicolas Gredzinski himself.

It marked the beginning of a Kafkaesque period which his fragile nerves could have done without. The child had a big bump on his head, but the parents dramatized the event to the point of claiming exorbitant damages. As the scapegoat for the whole thing, Nicolas was caught up in the machine. No one thought to question his "terrible mistake", and he saw the gates of hell opening before him, the gates of prison in this instance. He did not know any lawyers but remembered a school friend he had bumped into by chance many years later: Barataud. He was summoned to the county court, the trial took place a year later, and Barataud succeeded in incriminating the driver and the older brother's overreaction, which had caused the boy to fall. The nightmare came to an end for Nicolas. In that year his anxiety had gained a little more ground every day, to the point of taking priority over everything else, over life itself; a depression which dared not speak its name. Barataud, who had become Jacot, had known just when he was needed; his words had the power to calm a mechanism of anxiety which could be set in motion at any time, especially at night.

"Jacot? Did I wake you? I know it's late but . . . Do you think I'm going to go to prison?"

". . . No, Nicolas. You won't go to prison."

"I can hear it in your voice, you really want to reassure me but you don't believe a word of it."

"It's the voice of a man who's been woken at three in the morning."

"Well, will I or won't I?"

"No. It wouldn't be possible, not in a case like this one."

"And what if the judge is some man whose son was a victim in a car crash? He'd want to take his revenge out on me."

A baffled silence from Barataud.

"You're not saying anything any more . . . You hadn't thought of something like that."

"No, I hadn't thought of something like that. But that doesn't change anything. You won't go to prison. Even if you get the maximum anticipated sentence, you won't go. Do you trust me on this?"

". . . Yes."

"I've got to hang up. I'm in court tomorrow."

"Jacot! One last question: are there different kinds of prison?"

Now, however indebted Nicolas felt, he was terrified at the thought of talking about *it*. He knew neither how to reassure with words nor how to listen intelligently. Behind his silences, you could feel the discomfort, sometimes panic.

"I had some results yesterday. The leucocytes are good, the haemoglobin's good, it's the platelets."

". . . Really?"

"They've been going down since the beginning of the treatment, there's a risk of haemorrhaging, they're going to give me a transfusion."

Silence.

"I was meant to be going to the country for a couple of days to recover from the chemo, but I think I'm going to stay. Are you here this weekend?"

"I don't know yet."

"If you're free, shall we go for a coffee?"

"I'll give you a buzz."

The hangover was lingering, and this surge of cowardice at the end of the day did nothing to help. Instead of making the most of the balmy June evening, Gredzinski left his office with the firm intention of getting to bed before nightfall. Once outside, he took a deep breath to drive out the miasma of air conditioning, and headed for the footbridge to the left of the esplanade. On the terrace of the Nemrod, José, Régine, Arnaud, Cendrine and Marcheschi invited him to join them for an aperitif. This daily drink had become a relaxing ritual: the place had a happy hour – two glasses for the price of one between 6 and 8pm – and the members of this ultra-select little club, to which Nicolas belonged, were no longer doing any recruiting, as if the perfect balance had been established.

"You must have five minutes to spare, haven't you?"

Nicolas felt that he ought to resist and leant towards José's ear.

"I had a bit to drink yesterday and I've been paying for it all day. I'm going home."

"That's the worst thing to do! You need the hair of the dog! Sit down."

Nicolas Gredzinski had never learned to say no; it was one of the numerous perverse effects of his anxiety.

"What did you drink yesterday?"

. . . What had he drunk, the day before, to put him in such a state?

"I think it was vodka."

José turned to the waiter and ordered an iced vodka to reconcile the remedies of old wives' tales with a universal state of drunkenness. The others watched the rush hour of the Group's employees, some of the faces inspiring them to make merciless jibes. Nicolas could not be described as one of the best at this game. Like everyone else, he had his share of nastiness, but his natural shyness – particularly in front of Régine and Cendrine – meant he could not find the killing adjective. Jean-Claude Marcheschi, on the other hand, was not short on repartee, it was almost his job. As a bigwig, Managing Director to be precise, in the Mergers and Acquisitions Department, he juggled with financial markets, and bought and sold all sorts of companies around the globe. The Group was indebted to him for a handsome contribution to its turnover, and therefore a far from negligible share of the salaries of the people sitting at that table. While the waiter put the little ice-cold glass in front of Nicolas, they all listened to Marcheschi having a dig at the financial director of the three cable chains owned by the Group. Smiling at his well-chosen words, Nicolas took the first sips of the colourless, odourless and apparently soulless liquid, that bearer of disillusioned tomorrows.

"Has Magda been to see you for your holiday dates?" Régine asked the assembled company.

"First fortnight in July at Cap d'Agde," said José, "and second fortnight in September in Paris to finish my building work."

With the very first mouthful, Nicolas felt he had been given an uppercut in the chest; he closed his eyes for a moment and held his breath, waiting for the burning sensation.

"I'm going to Quiberon with my family," said Arnaud. "A nice rest, I need it."

And contained within that burning was a sense of imminent pleasure, of deliverance. A purifying fire was driving everything out: his wasted day, his bad conscience, his futile remorse, his dark thoughts. Everything.

"If I've got enough money I'm going to Guadeloupe with my loved one," said Régine.

The blaze died down quickly, leaving just a spark somewhere inside. Everything would be better now. He could feel it in every part of his body. Without even realizing it, he heaved a serene sigh, as if his heart were at last reaching a point of inertia and balance. Of peace.

"For me, it's the sea," said Cendrine, "it doesn't matter where, otherwise I feel like I haven't had a holiday."

The taste was only just beginning to appear. Subtle: pepper, spices, salt and earth. Brute strength.

"I can't decide," said Marcheschi. "I've been invited to go rafting on the Verdon, but I could also go to Seville to see some bullfights."

And so it was that on this lowly earth there was a liquid capable of triggering a blazing fire in a thimble, and of delivering him from the burden he had been carrying since forever. He emptied his glass, hoping to find one last stab of pleasure on his tongue.

"What about you, Nicolas, are you going back to your friends in the Pyrenees?"

He did not even give himself time to think, his life had just stepped on the accelerator, horizons were opening up, and he felt he had the strength to confront them all.

"I'm going to the Tobriand Islands to play cricket with the Papuan Indians."

It had come to him just like that, the most exciting – and, therefore, the most sincere – answer possible.

"Haven't you ever heard of the Trobriand Islands, off the coast of New Guinea? You know, Papua New Guinea? It's a former British colony from early in the twentieth century. The colonizers didn't leave a single trace there except for cricket, the natives turned it into a sort of ritual ceremony."

". . . Cricket?"

"Their cricket isn't anything like the English game any more, the teams are usually made up from two neighbouring tribes, and there can be as many as sixty players instead of eleven. They wear warrior costumes and war-paint, the bats are protected by magic rituals and the balls are made of wood polished with boars' tusks. After each point, the team that's just scored dances and chants: 'My hands are magnetic! The ball sticks fast!' And the umpire is a member of one of the teams, he can play himself and cast spells."

Nicolas was enjoying the sudden stillness around him. Without actually meaning to, he had become the centre of a conversation which could no longer be called one. His whole body was relaxing after so much battling against a pitiless day. This early evening felt to him like a new dawn.

"Have you been there before?"

"No, that's just it."

José asked him whether this was an old dream, a whim or a decision he had made a long time ago.

"All three. At 15,000 francs, it's a gift. A flight from Paris to Sydney, then from Sydney to Port Moresby, the capital of Papua New Guinea, then a little prop plane to Kiriwina, the main island of the Trobriands. Idyllic beaches and virgin forest. There are two villages that play cricket, and you sleep in someone's home. It's no good if you want to use the phone every five minutes but apart from that, it's bliss."

They asked him again where he had got this strange idea from, whether he often made such long journeys, and whether he was planning to go alone; and all their questions turned him into an adventurer. Nicolas Gredzinski was the exact opposite. He would not have been able to place Nairobi on a map, or endure a trek in Nepal, he had no desire to drink tea in a Ukrainian datcha, and he would have been bored in Chicago's Museum of Modern Art, at the Rio carnival or at the religious festivals in Kyoto. In his physiotherapist's waiting room he was much less interested in *National Geographic* than *Paris-Match*. But when *National*

47

Geographic was the only available magazine, he was capable of reading an article about the customs of some indigenous people and of retaining the most colourful details. The thought of going to see the Papuan Indians playing cricket was irresistible to him. He tried, and failed, to think before it was too late of one good reason why he could not go to the Trobriand Islands.

*

Sitting, alone, on a terrace on the Montagne Sainte-Geneviève, he studied the glass of Wyborowa in front of him. Night was falling slowly, the air was warm, all the weariness of the day had been erased. He no longer wanted to go home and just tried to hold on to the moment, to feel it between his fingers before he let it slip away. A burst of serenity, a moment stolen from himself. Taking a sip of vodka, he paid homage to all those who had contributed to the fact that this nectar was now running down his throat. God probably had the biggest hand in it; by creating man, he had created intoxication. Or perhaps man had created that all by himself, which Nicolas found even more pleasing. One fine day, a man had distilled some grains of barley in a still, and thousands of other men had started to dream. Nicolas even remembered the lorry driver who had made the journey all the way from Warsaw to this little side street in the Fifth Arrondissement of Paris, and the waiter who had taken the trouble to put the bottle in a freezer so that it was at its best. This third glass brought him a new feeling of peace, an absence of anxiety, true peace. At the Nemrod he had only felt it as a sweet promise. He drank this vodka extraordinarily slowly, as if meditating. He had all the time in the world, this evening. And the world could fall apart, it no longer frightened him.

Peace.

Only yesterday it was a word he was forbidden. He hardly dared formulate it for fear of putting his demons in a rage. The peace of ancient philosophers, of before the big bang, the peace we taste with our eyes closed. Why wasn't life always like this? If there was one worthy answer to this question, Nicolas wanted to find it.

The previous evening came back to him all of a sudden. What was that madman's name? Brun? Blin? With his thick beard and his ferrety eyes. He must have woken up in a tunnel, equally ashamed of all the nonsense propounded the night before. They must both have been as drunk as each other to have come up with that ridiculous challenge. In the state they had been in, they could just as easily have climbed up the Arc de Triomphe or sung under the window of some happily married ex-girlfriend. Instead of that, they had dreamed of becoming someone else.

Where would they be in three long years' time?

Despite the complete absurdity of the challenge, Nicolas could not behave as if it had never been thrown down. He had to cancel it before it was too late.

*

"He came by an hour ago."

"To play?"

"No, that's what was so odd."

As he answered Nicolas's questions, the attendant watered and smoothed the surface of a court which had been trampled by four men now discussing their match round the drinks machine. Night had fallen at last, the wind had lifted to cool everything down. A mixed double came to the end of their set before finding themselves in complete darkness.

And Blin had disappeared.

"What did you think was odd?"

"He asked me to rescind his membership of the club."

"Sorry?"

"He used the word 'rescind'. He'd only just joined. Normally, people just don't come back and that's the end of it. But he wanted me to give him the form back."

"And did you rescind his membership?"

"It was the first time I'd done it, I even had to call the manager."

"But you must have some way of contacting him, or have his details on computer?"

"His file didn't have time to get onto the system, and even if I did have his details, I couldn't give them to you."

Nicolas apologized and asked him to tell Thierry Blin he had asked after him, should he reappear. He already knew it was pointless. Blin would not reappear.

Back in the centre of Paris, he asked the taxi driver to drop him in the Rue Fontaine. He had liked vodka for less than twenty-four hours but it was already so familiar to him that he needed to have a quick tête-à-tête with it about this disappearance. He looked for somewhere to go and was drawn to the Lynn, a classic bar all in red and black leather with waiters in white uniforms and a wooden bar counter even more impressive than the one the night before.

They say it takes one fool to know another. Nicolas no longer even wanted to know whether he had found something he was looking for in Blin's madness or Blin had in his. One thing was sure, Blin had taken what they had said seriously, down to the last word, as if it was a project that had already been kicking about in his mind for some time, and meeting Nicolas had given him an opportunity to give it some substance at last.

He ordered a glass and downed it in one. From the full height of his serenity, he let himself slide into euphoria. He raised his glass high and addressed Blin as if talking to a dead friend.

We'll probably never see each other again, Blin, but if you can hear me, wherever you may be, please tell yourself that our drink-fuelled words yesterday only warranted being lost in the mists of sleep. No one can become someone else. Don't take any of it seriously, you risk losing yourself in a place you'll never get back from. Believing in this challenge and trying to win it would be utter madness: it's bound to lead to some strange, irreversible situation. Just thinking about it would be going too far. We mustn't wake our inner demons or ridicule them by finding replacements for them. Ours have already been appointed, guarding our souls like fortified towns, watching over us! Do we really have the nerve to turf them out? They'd never forgive us. We can't change anything about who we are, everything is written down, anchored, engraved, and nothing can erase that. Our minds aren't a repentance, a page we rewrite every day. Our hearts can only ever beat as our hearts, they won't try to find new rhythms, they found their melodies long ago. What's the point in changing them, it took years to compose them.

He suddenly felt like having a cigarette, and he asked the waiter for a packet.

"We don't sell them."

"You wouldn't have one you could let me have, would you?"

"I've given up."

"So have I, but . . ."

"I'll go and ask."

Nicolas noticed a packet of blue Dunhills beside a woman who was sitting close to him at the bar. If he was prepared to ditch his good resolutions, then he might as well choose a real cigarette, a strong one which tasted of something, like the ones he had smoked until five years before. The waiter handed him a filterless Craven, which he put to his lips, aware of the risk he was taking; if he smoked it, thousands more might follow, none of them as good. On his worst, anxious mornings, some of them might even taste of death. He spotted a Zippo lighter next to the woman's glass – it was the first time he'd seen a woman using a petrol lighter – and he borrowed it. Before lighting his cigarette, he hesitated a little longer, the time it took to have another vodka.

And what if he wasn't so predictable after all? And what if, after this cigarette, he only smoked another couple, just to make the most of the intoxication of the moment? And what if he, Gredzinski, had the strength to triumph where others had failed? To outplay a script which had been written long before, to dismiss both camps – the inveterate smokers and the reformed smokers – without coming down on either side. He made the flame spring up, lit his Craven, froze for a moment with his chest filled out, then let out a sigh of smoke.

The future would decide what happened next.

It was half past midnight, the place was light and cool, the ventilation system swallowed what little smoke came from his lips, his glass left no mark on the wooden bar, he had no meetings before ten the next day, and there was nothing to stop him having one last drink. With each new drag on the cigarette, a snatch of expensive perfume teased his nostrils; for a moment he was surprised by this curious phenomenon and discreetly sniffed his own fingers, which should have smelled of petrol. Without asking for permission from the woman, he picked up the lighter and smelled every part of it.

"Don't tell me that instead of refilling it with petrol, you fill it with perfume!"

"Miss Dior. Otherwise it's disgusting," she said. "It burns just as well, and it gives a pretty blue flame too."

Her eyes were blue too, you just had to be curious enough to look at them, which he eventually did. In fact, they were practically all you could see, but she did not really play on them. Nicolas would have liked to see that face by the light of day; something told him that that steely gaze was there to contradict the warm harmonies of her olive skin and chestnut hair. In normal circumstances he would already have stammered some social nicety and looked away shyly, caught out and quite incapable of responding to this peculiar girl's innocent charm. But this evening, with his cigarette in the corner of his mouth and his soul at peace, he looked her in the eye and made no effort to furnish the silence with smalltalk, letting the moment run its course without needing to be one step ahead of it.

"Do you think it would work with vodka?" he asked.

She smiled. Intrigued to see what she was drinking, he leant towards her glass.

"What is it?"

"Wine."

". . . Wine?" he repeated, surprised.

"You know, the sour red stuff which changes the way people behave."

"I didn't know you could get it in bars. To be honest with you, I'm a beginner."

"What do you mean by that?"

"I've only been drinking since yesterday."

". . . you must be kidding!"

"I got drunk for the first time last night!"

Despite the irresistible ring of truth, she refused to believe it.

"I swear it's true. This morning I even made acquaintance with the hangover!"

"What was it like?"

"I wanted something bubbly."

"So?"

"I drank some Perrier."

"Any good?"

"I haven't surfaced all day."

"I shouldn't say this to a novice, but the best thing is beer. It's a shame to say it, but it does work."

Nicolas looked at her in confused silence.

"You're so lucky to be starting so late! You've got a liver like a baby's, a stomach ready for anything and a cardiovascular system that's not going to give up on you for ages. If I were you, I'd do a world tour of gut rots, they all have a slightly different effect and don't necessarily take you where you want to go. Something tells me you have an adventuring spirit."

"And your favourite destination is . . .?"

"I only drink wine. Not much of it and only very good ones. They have an excellent wine list here, which is quite rare for a late-night bar."

"I'm Nicolas Gredzinski."

"Loraine."

She was wearing a fine grey pullover, a long black skirt which came down to her ankles, a jumble of bracelets on her right wrist and ankle boots in leather and black canvas. Her prominent cheekbones and the natural depressions under her eyes did not make her look worn but lent her whole face a certain elegance.

Her slightly golden skin was darker on her cheeks and forehead. A Latin skin on Slavic features. A unique face, which Nicolas had just imprinted on his retina for ever.

"So, what do you do in life?" he asked.

And everything stopped dead.

The unexpected moment of grace came to an end at that precise moment.

She asked how much she owed, took out a banknote and put the cigarettes and the lighter away in her bag.

"I never answer any sort of personal questions."

Nicolas, caught unawares, did not know how to backtrack other than to offer her another drink, which she refused with a curt gesture. She picked up her change and left the bar without a backward glance.

Before going home to bed Nicolas drank one last vodka to check whether it knew how to forget failure as well as it celebrated victory.

Thierry Blin

He hesitated between *Bereavement* and *Stocktaking* for a long time. Superstitiously, he avoided the first but could not resolve to use the second and scribbled *Closed due to exceptional circumstances* in marker pen on a piece of cardboard. As he taped it to the window in the shop's front door, he wondered how long he would be allowed to let the exceptional go on before anxious customers contacted the police.

"We liked him very much, officer. I was worried from the very first day I saw his sign. Monsieur Blin had never closed like that before."

He could quite see Mme Combes playing out this little sketch in the hopes of finding a decomposing body behind a sheet of Plexiglas. A belated heroine, proud of her intuitions, this might be the opportunity she dreamed of, to go from self-portraits to still life (oh so still!) in her work. Blin would not give her the pleasure; he needed only one day to do his research and would be back before the evening. He did not choose the shortest route to the city centre, but the only one on which you could see the sky and the Seine flowing by. *Closed due to exceptional circumstances.* What was exceptional was the strange feeling of freedom he had as he put the sign up. He had just succeeded in doing something revolutionary, in capsizing the established order. However banal it might seem, his closure due to *exceptional circumstances* was a hazy cloud amid the transparency of an entire life, a secret which – already

– he could no longer share, a public lie; it took very little to get to the point of no return.

He went to the offices of a daily newspaper and was shown to the archives. He was asked to wait next to a hot-drinks dispenser, between a scratchy sofa and a full ashtray. Intrigued, he watched the comings and goings of the people he assumed were journalists. Thierry could not conceive the very idea of work as anything but a solitary exercise. If heaven and hell gave him the strength to construct the person he wanted to be, he was bound to be more alone than anyone else in the world. Safe and warm in his retreat, barricaded in his manic isolation, carried by the fervour of those who believe the outside world is just an illusion. That man would live incognito among his contemporaries, praying that his subterfuge would go on as long as possible.

"I'd like to see all the articles about private detectives that have appeared in your paper."

He said *private detectives* as if the words themselves were troublemakers, harbingers of chaos; they had the same resonance as *exceptional circumstances*. Blin felt they were somehow compromising, deliciously dangerous. Although he was not duped by his own paranoia, he saw it as a sign of his determination and a promise to take seriously the adventure he had sworn to himself that he would live.

Sitting there with her cup of coffee, the archivist could never have imagined his inner turmoil; she rattled on the keyboard and printed out all the passages in which the words "private detective" had appeared in the last twelve years. Less than an hour later, Thierry Blin was sitting at a table in the library at Beaubourg, surrounded by papers, with a highlighter in his hand. There he found a book cited in one of the articles – a rather fastidious history of the profession, which he got through in twenty minutes – with an exhaustive bibliography, which gave him plenty of other leads. By early afternoon, he already knew a great deal more about it and even revelled in the twist of investigating the work of investigators. A student came to his help, amused by his puppyish expression as he watched the screen scrolling through thousands of Internet sites with various degrees of relevance to the subject. His enquiries were going faster than anticipated, he had already collated an impressive amount of literature, complemented by a how-to guide, indications of related articles and more references than he needed. In a bookshop he ordered a copy of *The Private Detective's Research Today*, considered the most reliable book about the profession, its myths, realities and legislation. He had time to go back to The Blue Frame to hide his file away and, convinced that no one had noticed his absence, rip down the *exceptional circumstances* sign.

*

The clinic was on the outskirts of a far-flung suburb, between a dated high-rise estate and a football ground where half the grass had been scuffed off. At nightfall, he parked his car in a side street beside the building, and went into the entrance lobby just as the street lights were coming on.

"I have a meeting with Professor Koenig."

"And you are. . .?"

"Paul Vermeiren."

There, he had said it. When he had made the appointment, he had succeeded in coming out with the name over the telephone, but the face-to-face test was a much more delicate affair.

"Will you wait a moment, Monsieur Vermeiren?"

Thierry was left alone in the waiting room, feeling uneasy. Hearing the name spoken had made his heart beat as if he had been crossing a border with a suitcase full of cataclysms. Paul Vermeiren was born that day, 28 July at 7.30pm. The receptionist in a suburban clinic had brought him into the world without even realizing it; that would be his birthday from now on. There was no going back for Blin now. He was going to play sorcerer's apprentice with himself, without doing anyone any harm, and who cared if it was forbidden by law.

Professor Koenig asked him into his consulting room, a simple office with an examination bed.

"This is the first time we've met, Monsieur Vermeiren," he said with an impossibly blank expression. "What can I do for you?"

I'm forty years old and I want to prove that there is life after life.

"I'd like to change my face."

An imperceptible blink from the doctor, who thought for a moment.

"Could you explain that a bit for me?"

"It's not easy to say . . . I'm finding it more and more difficult to put up with this face. I'd like to change it. Apparently it's possible."

"You can erase little defects, details that are a bit obsessive, but you're talking about something more radical."

"Don't tell me I'm the first person to ask you this."

"How did you find me?"

"In the phone book."

". . . The phone book?"

The doctor's face lost its peculiar immobility, and not in the way that Thierry would have liked.

"Would you really trust your face to some practitioner recruited from a phone book?"

Thierry said nothing.

Koenig got up from his chair and gestured to Blin to follow him to the door.

"Monsieur Vermeiren, I don't want to know your reasons. You should just know that there are only 300 plastic surgeons in France skilled enough to perform this sort of operation, but that there are 2,500 in practice. You're bound to find someone in amongst them."

He closed the door firmly. Feeling a little unsteady on his feet as if the slight ambient smell of ether had anaesthetized him, Thierry went back to his car. Although he could not know whether Blin would have fared any better, he was sure of one thing: on his first outing into the world, Paul Vermeiren had been pathetic.

*

Despite the perennial threat that legislation will make a ruling once and for all on the subject, anyone can act as a private detective; without any qualifications or training, they can open up an agency and practise the profession with no constraints, apart from having no criminal record and being registered with the police headquarters. In short, all Blin had to do was to replace the word *framer* with *investigator* on his shop front and that was it. The bulk of the information he had gleaned from his review of the press was in agreement; he now knew about the bare bones of the profession, its history, everyday realities, clients, rates of pay and even its excesses.

"What's all that photocopying?"

Nadine had arrived unexpectedly in the hopes of

finding him at The Blue Frame, and caught him in the back of the shop surrounded by paperwork spread all over the floor. For a week now he had been ferreting through, underlining, filing, cutting out, ticking off and then burning everything he no longer needed. A week spent discovering a different world, at the expense of his own world and his work. He was careful to stow his *Guide to the Work of the Private Investigator* in a drawer to hide it from Nadine. This book had the advantage of stripping a fair amount of cliché from the job and describing its day-to-day realities. That very morning he had read an interview with a private eye who described his work in simple precise terms, a tone which inspired confidence and put paid to a good many prejudices.

"I asked for some info about the guy who invented the Cassandra and the Carabin."

"The what?"

Nadine was already onto something else, wandering round the workshop, hoping to find a little something to look at.

"He's someone I knew when I worked at the museum. He's just invented two frames which can be screwed directly into the wall. I'd be happy to explain it to you, but only if you're interested."

"Are you going to use them yourself, these frames?" she asked, looking at an original *Scarface* poster that needed framing by the following day.

"No, I don't think so, but I want to know why *he* invented these frames and not me."

"How do you think you're going to answer a question like that?"

"If you'd seen the guy at the time . . . there was something blinkered about him, awkward, how can he possibly have had such a brilliant idea?"

"Are you going to take me out for supper?"

From now on, lying was going to be a major part of Blin's life. To him, a lie which stood its ground long enough became reality. Received ideas, stolen reputations and historic compromises were all lies which had stood the test of time; no one thought of questioning them any more. One day, perhaps, he too would believe in a guy from the Musée d'Orsay who had invented this Cassandra frame which screwed directly into the wall; in the meantime, he had put paid to Nadine's curiosity. He closed the shop, got into the car and let her drive him to a Chinese restaurant she loved. He sat thoughtfully all through supper, watching her smiling, wielding her chopsticks and changing her mind about her order. She was not usually so talkative. He listened to her as she chatted about her day in great detail. Their paths would soon go their separate ways, he was going to disappear in the eyes of the world, and the world would not even realize it. He did not, under any circumstances, want to make her unhappy, to force her to cope with his absence, to impose his disappearance on her like a dictate, to condemn her to doubt, to let her hope he might come back or to imagine the worst with no one to contradict her thoughts. This woman who had said *I love you* would not suffer from it. He would never make her into a woman who waits. Someone else would soon replace him in Nadine's affections and would take better care of her than he had been able to. He now had to dream up an end to their relationship before disappearing once and for all.

Watching her sipping her tea, he remembered the limits they had set themselves when they moved in together, as if they had lived conjugal lives before, as if they knew by heart what a couple was and how to make it last. Not trying to change the other had been rule number one. Now, he no longer knew what to think of that, but one thing was sure: he was much more captivated by the idea of changing himself.

Later in the evening, they made love without real fervour, motivated by a tacit desire to respect the normal state of coupledom without having to pronounce the word *erosion*, even if there was no better one.

*

Strange feeling of guilt. Hovering round a phone booth for a good fifteen minutes trying to find the courage to ring La Vigilante, one of the oldest private detective agencies and perhaps the most reliable. Asking to speak to Philippe Lehaleur, the investigator who, during the long newspaper interview, had intrigued Blin with his candour and his detachment. As Lehaleur was out, he was asked whether he would like to speak to someone else; Blin said he would rather call back two hours later. Given the article in question, he was probably not the only person who wanted to get hold of him. Blin had to put up with the delay, and sat in a café reading his bible on the modern private detective. Towards the end of the afternoon he succeeded in getting hold of Lehaleur.

"I read an interview with you in the paper."

"Is this to arrange a meeting?"

"Yes."

"What would suit you?"

"Straight away."

"I'm seeing someone in half an hour, that's not going to work."

"I'm very close to your office."

"If you want me to take on some business for you, it's likely to take longer than you think."

"It's simpler than that but also more complicated."

"Would ten minutes do?"

Lehaleur was not really surprised; it was actually a typical way for someone to proceed if they wanted to get to grips with this job. From the start he tried to warn Blin against the romantic, fantastical image that clung to private detectives; he thought of his job as one of the most demanding, perhaps one of the most restricting and often one of the most difficult. He stressed the fact that there were a great many charlatans, a lot of prejudices and a lot of dubious motivations, all things that Blin had read and reread in his press cuttings. Now he was hearing them for the first time from someone whose job consisted of following people in the street, being stuck in a car with a thermos, and taking photos of couples kissing on café terraces. With one eye on his watch, Lehaleur ended the conversation by saying that the only way to get to know the job would be to do a work placement with an agency which would have him. His own did not need anyone, but he would give it some thought.

"I'm forty. Is that too old to start?"

"When I come to think about it, it would probably be an asset. If, that is, like the people you're watching, you can take the risk of losing your private life completely."

*

The house was ailing, empty but still on its feet. Yvette and Georges Blin had set up home there as soon as they had met and had eventually bought it for a song. That was where they were married and that was where they had made room for their only son. That was where Georges had come home one evening complaining of a pain in his left shoulder. The following morning little

Thierry had seen the house full of people. And his mother, who could usually answer all his questions, had not uttered a word.

From then on it was just the two of them, condemned to the place. After all, it was a little suburban house with its corner of garden, its peaceful neighbourhood – so many other kids from Juvisy had to make do with the wastelands next to the high-rise flats. Whoever had planned and built this place had never thought about the well-being of the people who would live there. The house was divided into three identical rooms, three impeccably regular squares, two bedrooms that were too big and, in the middle, a kitchen-cum-sitting-room where there was no room to move and where nobody wanted to sit. Those rooms had known the heady smell of the oil-fired boiler and Yvette's comings and goings with the jerry can in her hand to fill the tank; Thierry used it as a grill and had learned when he was very young to cook popcorn and chestnuts on it. There was red hessian to hide the leprous peeling on the walls, and the unevenness of the lino produced a much more interesting surface for playing marbles than smooth tiling would have done. The bathroom was cold and had absolutely no glimpse of daylight. There was no attic but there was an abandoned cellar – it would have cost too much to convert it. Thierry had never been down there, he imagined he was living over a black hole, a mysterious place filled with all the things stories tell you about cellars. As a teenager he had started feeling uncomfortable within the walls of his own bedroom. He was always eager to be invited to a friend's house, to hang out round a bench in the park until late at night, or to eat in the school canteen when people who lived further away than him went home for lunch. At night he would listen to music on his headphones and project himself to America for the duration of a record. He left home just after his *baccalauréat* to live in a little garret room in a building on the Place Daumesnil in Paris; life could start. He only went back to 8 Rue Jean-Perrin in Juvisy to visit his mother, on Saturdays. She went back to live, and die, where she had been born in the Vendée; because of a family history of the condition, she had lived her whole life in fear of that aneurysm.

Blin parked his car in front of the entrance gate. The street was empty and silent as it always had been, even more so now that there were no longer any dogs. The green shutters on the house were corroded with rust, and couch grass had pushed up through the paving stones. He felt happier waiting outside to meet Keller, a representative of a construction company interested in buying up and joining together five plots, including Blin's. He was an affable man, prepared to play any part to seal the deal; Thierry was careful not to give him any assurances until the last minute. After all, he was not the only one in the running, there was that young couple. Fresh young love, a dream of having an old-fashioned kind of happiness which put their *home* above everything else. With their mortgage already agreed, they could aspire to their own little place which would grow in step with their family and their free time. They were brave and made you want to help them. In spite of everything, Thierry felt happier clinching it with the construction company and coming to a covert arrangement with Keller, lowering the selling price so that he could have some cash under the table, cash he was going to need in the next few months. Besides, he could not imagine a young couple setting up home here as his parents had done. They must at all costs be given an opportunity to build somewhere else, somewhere clean, new, far from the bad vibrations of a past that seeped from every wall. This house would never be a *home*, it had not been that to Georges and Yvette. There was also another reason, though far from the most crucial: Thierry wanted to see it destroyed. The man he was going to become would never be able to find his place in the world with this house still standing, even in his memory.

And so it was that he set out one October morning to witness the show. A bulldozer arrived punctually at 8 o'clock and knocked the house onto its side with one thrust. Hypnotized, Thierry saw the damp-damaged walls collapsing of their own accord, the roof structure cracking, and the tiles scattering like a house of cards; he saw the red walls of his bedroom scrambling with the enamel of the bathroom, the greasy corner of the kitchen opening up to the sky, his parents' bedroom ending up as a carcass of plaster and breeze blocks, a mosaic of little moments from his life entangled together before being reduced to dust. The sink that he used to get to by climbing onto a chair arced through the air before falling down onto the green lino where he had taken his first steps; the wallpaper that his father had hung in the living-room end was ground into the rubble of the front doorstep where the three of them had enjoyed the cool air late on summer evenings; beneath the hessian, which came away like dead skin, wallpaper with big flowers on it appeared and, with it, a series of photographs of Thierry in his cradle, stuck in the family album. The bulldozer's jaws gobbled up and spat back out whole chunks of his childhood until they were razed to the ground.

The engine fell silent at last. Thierry wandered through the debris just for the pleasure of trampling on it, then left the area for ever.

*

Lehaleur was back in touch sooner than he had anticipated and gave him a name over the telephone: Pierre-
Alain Rodier.

"We've worked together a few times. He's coming
towards the end of his career and is looking for someone to see him through the loneliness. He won't pay
you, but he can teach you everything there is to know
about the job. I didn't recommend you but I told him
you would call."

Without holding out too much hope, Blin thought
he would go with the flow until something came along
to stop him. He managed to arrange a meeting with
the man that same week.

Pierre-Alain Rodier had his agency right next to
his apartment in a bourgeois building in the Eighth
Arrondissement. Old carpet, a desk with a computer
on it, encyclopedias, a jumble of files behind a door, a
little frame displaying the house rates, another with a
portrait of Vidocq. Rodier was fifty-eight years old, and
had the build of a contented little man. He was on the
slim side, with hair yellowed by years of smoking, a grey
moustache and tired eyes, but a truly impish smile.
Blin played it straight (he was a framer, he wanted to
change jobs and something drew him towards detective work), and Rodier did the same (he had much less
patience than he once had, he needed the company
and he wanted to pass on what he knew before taking
his final bow). The successful candidate had to be
available day and night, including weekends. He did
not even given Blin an opportunity to discuss the
workings of that last point.

"When can you start?"

"Pretty soon."

"Tomorrow, 7am?"
An expectant silence.
"70 Rue de Rennes. It can be your first tailing job."
"Sorry?"
"There's no other way to learn."

Nicolas Gredzinski

So was this alcoholism, then? He had always been told that someone who drinks suffers a thousand wounds every day, his blood vessels, organs and skin eaten away, sour, prey to gradual decomposition; his whole body gives off an acrid smell; everything leading inevitably to the pitiful, the definitive day when the people gathered around the poor man's grave can be heard saying: *he drank*. To Nicolas, all that was nothing compared to the real tragedy of every alcoholic, the distress in the pit of his heart from the moment he woke up, the regret for having felt happy at last the previous day. When all was said and done, that really was the only thing that he felt was too high a price to pay. Alcohol should be forbidden to the anxious, they are such easy prey: they are weak enough to believe, for the space of an evening, that they have a right to their share of happiness.

There was nothing he could do about it, not a scalding hot shower jetting fiercely onto his forehead, not coffee or sparkling water, not aspirin, not the holy ghost, or the promise that he would never touch it again. He swore that he would not go through the torture of a permanent hangover again. As he passed the coffee shop, he remembered a piece of advice that he should never have taken.

"A beer, please."

He had ordered a glass without thinking, amid the morning bustle when the smell of coffee was spreading through the atrium. He thought better of it and asked for a can of Heineken, which he slipped carefully into his briefcase. He had scarcely set foot in his office before he pressed the ice-cold metal against his forehead. Where the heat of the shower had failed, he could have sworn the vice was releasing its grip already. He drank several mouthfuls, like chilled water after physical exertion.

A second later, he emerged from the rut and started believing in miracles.

"Nicolas, have you got a moment?"

Mergault, from the accounts department, was peeping through the door with his hand on the handle, very impressed to see his colleague gulping back a Heineken.

"Can't you knock? Haven't you ever seen anyone drinking beer before? Don't bother looking at your watch, it's exactly half past nine in the morning."

Defeated, Mergault closed the door again. With no sense of regret, Nicolas drank the last few mouthfuls, alert to the effects of the alcohol on his distress, and nothing in the world could distract him from this feeling of deliverance. He settled deep into his chair, snug and warm, with his eyes closed, stranded halfway between two worlds.

All he could remember was talking to a girl in a bar. If he had not gone and ruined everything he might well have woken up beside her this morning. He would have gone through the whole day touched by the memory of her, impregnated by the smell of her. Fate had never allowed him an experience like that. All the women he had known were part of the furniture and had fallen into his arms for logical reasons; people he had to meet – some planned, others hardly surprising – women who happened to be in the same place as him and had let him know . . . In no circumstances was he the sort of man who walked into a bar for a drink and came out with a woman on his arm. The night before he had missed a unique opportunity to become part of that species, a species he had always admired.

So, what do you do in life?

Why had the girl yesterday got so upset over such an inoffensive question? Nicolas had probably not been sufficiently drunk to avoid all the clichés we feel obliged to come out with in situations like that, but there had been no ulterior motive in his question. He had not even wanted to know what the woman did, there were a thousand things he would rather have known before that.

So, in life, what is it you do?

That was where his headache stemmed from. The regret that he had not been able to help himself being the same man he always was, the regret that he had not had it in him to be the man who walks into a bar for a drink and comes back out with a woman on his arm. He had almost been that man, he already moved like him with his malice and his sense of the here and now, and he spoke his language almost fluently. He tried to reason with himself: approaching a woman in a bar was to set sail for a hazy destination, for the chronicle of a shipwreck foretold and of a feeling of shame in the morning. That moment when the other person is no longer the only other person in the world, but the only one you would like to be on the other side of the world. A brief moment of horror.

Actually, what do I know about it? he asked himself, quite justifiably, as it had never happened to him.

The beer was proving much more effective than anything else: he had the peculiar impression that his brain was returning to its normal size. He was emerging gradually from his husk of tiredness, the day could begin.

"Hello, it's Muriel. You don't know where Monsieur Bardane is, do you? I've got a call for him."

"He was meant to be back this morning."

"I'm not sure what to do. This person's called back several times."

Just when he least expected it, Nicolas felt a distant, featherlight touch of euphoria stirring. He had a sudden urge to do something rather clever.

"Who is it?"

"Monsieur Vernaux, from Vila Pharmaceuticals."

"Put him through to me."

". . . But . . . he called for Monsieur Bardane . . ."

"I've been landed with following up on this file, and I want to avoid getting it all wrong at the last minute because the good man isn't here."

When Vila Pharmaceuticals had merged with the Scott organization, they had asked for tenders from several communications agencies, including Parena, to create a new visual identity for them as well as finding a new name and a new logo. Bardane had had his graphic designers toiling away without giving them clear guidelines, forcing them to improvise.

"Monsieur Vernaux? Nicolas Gredzinksi, I'm standing in for Alain Bardane while he's away. Looking through the file, I think I'm right in saying you weren't happy with the graphics our art department suggested for you."

He was not in the least interested in usurping his boss's position, he was only hoping to salvage something from a mistake. To him, Bardane looked more and more like a waste of space who was about to lose his umpteenth contract.

"You know about that?"

"And I think you're wrong."

A questioning silence.

"The problem is you want something beautiful when we're offering you something effective. The logo we suggested isn't necessarily 'beautiful' but you'll be seeing it for the next hundred years."

"If I understand correctly, you're telling me I have absolutely no taste."

"No, I'd even say you have too much. If you ask one of our competitors for something beautiful, they'll give it to you, they'd give you anything you wanted to have you as a client."

Another silence.

"If you're honest, do you think the packaging for Pepsi is beautiful? Millions of dollars in takings every year. But the packaging for Mariotti coffee is gorgeous, pure Raphael – they went into liquidation last year. I should know, they were one of our clients. He wanted a Renaissance feel, and he got it."

Still no reply.

"I might agree with you on the colour, I'm not that keen on that almond green, too obvious, too deceptive; I'd see it with something more dynamic, a vermilion. For the typeface, we could find something simpler, less modern. What was the name we suggested again?"

"*Dexyl.*"

"Not brilliant. All these interchangeable, pseudo-modern, artificial names, there's nothing to them. Make the most of the merger to merge the names together too – why can't you just call yourselves Vila-Scott? Now, that would give me a feeling of confidence on a box of aspirin."

"I hope you realize you're criticizing the work of your own creative team."

"Would you like us to have one last go at this?"

". . . Look . . . I . . ."

"I'll fax it to you before the end of the morning."

"Just to see, then . . ."

"Will you call me back as soon as you've had a chance to look at it?"

"Of course, Monsieur . . .?"

"Nicolas Gredzinski."

As he hung up he burst out laughing. He had just fallen out with the art department, and Bardane was going to want to skin him for the simple fact that he had spoken to a client and modified a job without his approval. His predicted trajectory within the company would be set back twenty years.

To his considerable surprise, he could not have cared less.

*

Steak haché and *gratin dauphinois*. Nicolas let himself be tempted by a small carafe of red wine. In the six years he had been working for the Group he had never tasted it. As soon as he put the carafe on his tray, he stopped by the cheese to give himself a clear conscience, and took a portion of brie, knowing that no one would notice that but they would all have something to say about the wine.

Cécile found a table where five of them could sit together. He had hardly sat down before he caught sight of Nathalie's sideways glance.

"What are you drinking?"

"Wine."

"Wine . . .?"

"Yes, wine, you know, the sour red stuff which changes the way people behave."

"So you drink wine then?" Hugo asked.

"I didn't know you drank wine," said Cécile.

Nicolas sat there with a fixed smile on his face, having to hold back his rising exasperation.

"It's not that 'I drink wine', I just wanted a change. And you've got to admit that cheese with water's pretty dismal at any time of day."

"It can't be that good," said Cécile, wrinkling her nose.

"What, the brie?"

"The wine."

"If I have wine at lunchtime, it sends me to sleep," said José, "then I can't do anything for the rest of the afternoon."

"I'd happily have some," said Hugo, "if I wasn't worried about getting blotchy skin and breath like a sailor."

Nicolas could not have hoped for all this. What would they have said if they had seen him the day before, under the influence of vodka, facing a woman whose dreams flourished on a good Bordeaux and a Zippo fuelled by Miss Dior? Nicolas suddenly felt a sort of chasm opening up between him and the rest of the table, an insidious but very real rift. His little parcel of land was detaching itself from the continent and drifting slowly away. For the first time in his life, he had been perceived as someone *who drinks*. Something told him it would not be the last.

Nicolas did not follow his colleagues to the coffee shop; he preferred the more peppery smell of Côtes du Rhône to the aroma of coffee. *I only drink wine.* Loraine had said that incredibly unaffectedly, with a combination of gravity and pleasure which seemed to be deeply rooted. Unlike José, Nicolas felt his power to work reappearing at last. There was even more to it

76

than that: a surge of energy shot through with optimism made him want to say hello to people he came across year in, year out without ever really talking to them. He did not have a chance.

"Monsieur Bardane wants to see you urgently!" said Muriel.

"Is he here at last?"

Nicolas made his way to his boss's office to get it over and done with. What had to happen happened, but in a very sorry way; he had to endure the most mediocre dressing down because Bardane had absolutely no talent for intimidation, no skill in using imperatives and no subtlety in his threats. He did not try to have any sort of exchange, settling instead for systematically rejecting anything Nicolas might have said in his own defence. The only surprise was the verdict.

"The mistake is too serious for me to take the risk of covering it up, so you'll have to come with me to the directors' meeting. I've spoken to Broaters about it. It's in his hands."

Nicolas had never been asked to attend a meeting in the presence of one of the Group's director generals, not even the one from his own sector, Christian Broaters. Bardane, whose authority had recently been questioned by the whole art department, had found the perfect opportunity to make an example.

"I'll meet you in fifteen minutes on the eighth floor."

Defeated, Nicolas turned for the door. Bardane waited till his back was turned before delivering his *coup de grâce*.

"Gredzinski . . . have you been drinking?"

Nicolas did not know what to say, left the office, went down to the Nemrod and ordered a vodka; now was the time to see whether he could rely on it for help. Bardane had been innovative in the realms of punishment; from now on Nicolas would set a precedent, the man who had made a professional mistake worth a million francs (that was the budget for the Vila contract). He had not even taken the time to savour or even drink his glass before downing a second one. He could picture himself, starting tomorrow, sitting alone at the zinc bar of a bistro to sew up a day spent flogging all over town trying to find work, reading ads, smiling at Human Resources executives and listening to them saying they were very sorry but they would not be keeping his records on file. Over the next few days, the cocktail hour would get earlier and earlier until Nicolas grasped the fact that the perfect time was immediately after waking up. He was quite capable of that, he had had the proof that very morning.

The director's PA welcomed him in and asked him to wait in a little lobby where a handful of managers were standing waiting. Having very little to lose, he took the liberty of sitting down on the sofa. It would not change anything in what was a predictable verdict: he would not be made redundant but would have to make amends. As far as the team leader Bardane was concerned, *men* fell into two very distinct categories, and Gredzinski was in the second. Nevertheless, Bardane was not familiar with one law that Nicolas knew, having always been an underling: those who are arrogant will one day be servile. In other words, the more you trample on the weak, the more you are inclined to lick the boots of the strong.

Broaters greeted them all with an elegant nod of the head, which meant he could avoid shaking so many hands, and suggested they went through to the conference room. Nicolas headed for the back like the naughty schoolboy that he was, to discover an extraordinarily empty room with no notebooks, bottles of water, marker pens or overhead projector, nothing except a magnificent circular table in pink marble and a mantelpiece, which was also perfectly empty. In amongst so many smart austere suits, he could not help noticing the famous Alissa, a beautiful fifty-year-old from Mauritius who was the boss's assistant and did pretty much everything for him. No one actually claimed that they were lovers, which demonstrated the woman's genuine power. One of Broaters' right-hand men spoke first, but Nicolas did not listen to a word; unlike the others, he had no need to understand what was being said, nor to visualize, anticipate or conceptualize everything that was at stake in the meeting. Like dunces who exempt themselves from listening to lessons, he was being asked to wait for his rap over the knuckles with a ruler before he left the room.

"Krieg will entrust us with their communications only if we can guarantee them the lobbying with the ministry. I have, incidentally, discovered that Dieulefils from Crosne & Henaut is a great friend of the Principal Private Secretary, but I've also heard tell that he is less and less a friend of Crosne."

Feeling a wave of heat rising inside him, Nicolas finally understood what people meant by "seeing double" when they talked about drinkers: the gift of double vision. His eyes could see beyond physical presences, and his senses were sharpened to the point that he could perceive the least sign, grasp every element of the scene playing out before him. Over and above the responsibilities, hierarchies, roles, codes, wordings and implications, he found he was just sitting amongst men and women, little creatures who, like him, were struggling through this life, more often than not barely coping with it despite considerable effort.

Filled with a sudden rush of kindness, he found them touching and endearingly naive, feverishly eager and prepared to be led astray, like children.

"Except, what we really do need is someone like Queysanne."

"He's just been indicted!"

But there must have been hearts beating beneath all those Paul Smith shirts and Lagerfeld jackets. Thrust into this torment in spite of themselves, stressed rather than stimulated by the very idea of competition. The tall man on Broaters' right had a good rural face, the sort of man you would want to buy milk and eggs from; giving orders was a part he had to play. Beside him was a blond woman with a round face, an executive woman; some people talked about her as if she were a shark but Nicolas had seen her in a very different light for the last few minutes; he could picture her praying to God and putting herself in His hands when things were going really badly; a spiritual side which, occasionally, competed with her ambition.

"You wait, it's going to be like British Airways all over again."

And the one who was almost going to sleep, taken on for his perfect mastery of Japanese and his connections in Tokyo, a man who could read Kawabata in the original and watch Ozu films without the subtitles, and who could have given the others the benefit of his Zen education.

"Monsieur Meyer, could you say a word or two about the Lancero file?"

Now, you must be the one called Lugagne, you're entrusted with branding whole countries who want to boost their image in the West. You're the only one who has that weird tomato soup from the drinks machine. No, not the only one, there's Laurent too, the photocopier repairman. Who knows if the two of you haven't got other things in common, if you couldn't become the best of friends and if, at weekends, you wouldn't like getting together with each other's families for a barbecue. No one will ever know.

"A word on the Vila business?" Broaters ventured.

All eyes turned to Nicolas and the sudden silence woke him from his thoughts. Broaters had said the word "business" with a gentle irony to defuse a situation which was becoming far too tricky for his liking. Bardane set off on the offensive and Nicolas listened absently as he acted out his little sketch. The vodka running hot in his veins maintained his contemplative state. He did not see them as the warriors they thought they were, officers in the theatre of operations, exposed like everyone else. He did not see them as men recycling their natural aggression in business life. He no longer saw them as strategists ready to take on latter-day enemies far more frightening than those of old because they were masked. He saw them only as children playing a favourite children's game: war.

". . . I can carry on as if this fax had never been sent," Bardane concluded. "It'll be the second and final time that I save the day on this, and it'll be the last."

Bardane had had the decency not to indicate him directly, but all the managers turned towards Nicolas again, waiting for the poor man to speak at last and publicly admit how much he regretted his initiative. He said the only thing which came into his head: "If it's the final time you save the day, Monsieur Bardane, it's bound to be the last."

The ensuing silence was not of the kind recorded in business school. This was the law of retaliation put into practice by a foot soldier. It was the anathema of the condemned, spoken from the full height of the scaffold. If, just moments earlier, Nicolas might have got off with some sort of vague justification in public, now his boss was going to want to skin him alive.

The youngest participant raised his hand discreetly to speak; he was one of the art directors recently taken on at Broaters' request.

"I was speaking to Vila's Director of Communications just before coming to this meeting: it looks like they're about to go with the vermilion."

Nicolas was no longer listening, relieved that someone else was speaking. The new mock-up for the job was passed to Broaters.

"Combined with that typeface," he said, "there's an immediate feeling to it . . . reassuring and alternative at the same time."

Unbelievably, the gathering seemed in agreement with this "reassuring and alternative".

"Perhaps," he added, "we could entrust the future of the Vila file to Monsieur . . ."

"Gredzinski," said Alissa.

Nicolas acquiesced with a nod, and that was the signal to leave. He was first to go, avoiding Bardane's eye at all costs. In the lift he thought of the millions of soldiers the earth had brought forth since man had invented warfare. On the scale of history, only a handful had gone to the front; the others had waited a whole lifetime for something to happen. Nicolas swore to himself that he would no longer be one of their number.

*

"A woman, sitting just there, yesterday, she was drinking wine, alone."

The barman from the Lynn thought for a moment, cocktail shaker in hand. Bored by Marcheschi's ramblings at the aperitif club, Nicolas had left first, to head for the Rue Fontaine, still needled by his blunder of the previous evening.

"She's at a table, at the back on the right."

The fact that Loraine was in a late-night bar on two consecutive evenings said a good deal more about her way of life than the "personal questions" she was so afraid of. He downed a vodka without tasting it, without giving his taste buds or palate an opportunity to appreciate it. The anxious have never learned to savour. The ethyl alcohol molecule, known as ethanol or C_2H_5OH, had only just come into his life. He used it like some gadget you use as much as possible for fear of it breaking. He eventually found what he was looking for at the bottom of his glass: courage, liquid, transparent courage.

"I don't want to know who you are, I'd just like to have a drink."

Her pale eyes were already agreeing, but Loraine left him dangling for a minute before inviting him to sit down. He promised himself he would stay clear-headed to avoid the misunderstandings of the previous evening.

"Was it tough getting up?"

"I took your advice: I drank some beer and everything else raced past incredibly quickly. I've got this weird feeling I've lived three days instead of one."

"Do you believe everything you're told in bars?"

"I've finally grasped what everyone else has always known: the poison is in the remedy and vice versa. The worst of it is the dark looks from colleagues."

"They're not the only ones who'll give you a bad conscience, there are friends and family as well, not to mention children."

Mustn't jump to the conclusion that she has a family and children.

"You mustn't hold it against them," she went on. "People who love you worry when they see you drinking, only the people you don't matter to find it reassuring."

"Reassuring?"

"The sad people who don't have much of a life, who have no one to love, nothing to think or to give – they have one last little pleasure left in life: other people's vices. They find seeing you drink reassuring, they haven't yet stooped that low."

Without having formulated it so clearly, that was exactly what he thought of Mergault, who had caught him with the can of beer in his hand.

"Another piece of advice, but this is one you should take: whatever you do, be discreet. Not from a feeling of shame, just to deprive them of their pleasure."

Sitting there with Loraine, everything – especially outrageous things – seemed possible to him. He needed this element of fantasy in his life in the same way that he needed the intense energies in a glass of vodka.

The chance diversions and small pleasures of conversation; the serious alongside the anodyne, one anecdote following another; Nicolas let himself be carried into this happy spiral, no longer paying attention to "personal" aspects. Two hours later, during the course of a sentence, he mentioned his friend Cécile who could "draw a cross-section of the Châtelet Métro station, with all its exits" and elevated her to the level of a "genius of industrial design". Loraine pulled up short at the word genius, a word which, in her view, should be handled with care. They both started to circle round the idea of genius and their conversation got its second wind.

"Genius is my chosen specialized subject," she said. "I'm a collector."

"What do you mean?"

"I've got bookcases full of geniuses. I look after them and I'm always on the lookout for the ones I don't know. I sometimes find new ones, but they're few and far between."

"And what is it that you mean when you say 'geniuses' so specifically like that?"

"Nothing personal, my understanding of the word is the dictionary definition. I'm talking about the recognized geniuses, the famous, indisputable ones: Mozart, Shakespeare, da Vinci and the like, the ones who are above all suspicion, the ones you just have to bow down in front of. I read everything I can on the subject. Nothing very arduous: biographies, essays that are accessible to someone like me. I find out about how they got to where they did, particular moments in their lives. I compile anecdotes, which I regurgitate to the people around me."

"Have you been collecting like this for long?"

"Since I was about fifteen or sixteen. Because I'm not an artist or a scientist myself, I'm not afraid of the shadows they cast. What I like most of all is the idea of precociousness, of talent driven to extremes and of an infinite capacity for work. Each of them is a form of revenge for the bad faith all around us, the universal laziness and general destitution. They're like ramparts against self-sufficiency and contempt for others. Each of them forces me to look at myself, to understand my limits and to accept them."

Nicolas was listening to her with his arms crossed and his eyes fixed on her, touched by the very elegant way she talked about herself without saying anything about her life – he had just gathered in passing that she had bookshelves and that there were people "around her" – but speaking from the heart about the things she felt were important.

"Loraine, I will buy you your next drink if you choose one of the jewels of your collection and tell me about it."

"You're mad!" she said, laughing. "That could take a long time."

He ordered a vodka and a glass of Sancerre.

"I've got all night."

They had turned several corners together, but this was one of the most delicious: the moment when each could sense that the other had no desire to be anywhere else.

"You choose from my collection, I don't have any preferences. Shakespeare? Beethoven? Pascal? Michelangelo?"

He had all night, but it would be brief.

Thierry Blin

Nadine was worried about Thierry's insomnia. He gave all sorts of excuses, and these excuses had a much better ring to them than the truth. The truth was far and away the most absurd and least admissible, rather like a bad joke or the ramblings of someone who was still half asleep: I have an appointment tomorrow morning to tail someone.

To do what? Tail someone? That doesn't really happen. Tailing, fine in airport books, clichéd American films and paranoid fantasies, but not in real life. At about 4 o'clock in the morning, Blin came back down to earth, and back down to himself, the self who was a craftsman in a world where you do not follow people in the street. Did that world really exist? Did men and women really ask Rodiers to find out secrets about other men and women? He could not think of anyone he knew who had needed a private detective and had never heard a single first-hand account, not even an anecdote. At 4.20am he felt like the victim of a practical joke he had strayed into all by himself. *Don't worry, I'll be there*, Rodier had said; it was one of the most worrying sentences Thierry had ever heard. He pressed himself against Nadine's back, brushing his lips over the nape of her neck and putting his hand on her hips, and yet no couple in the world had been separated by such a distance. Nadine would have forgiven him for losing his savings at poker, sleeping with her best friend or sneering at her photographs in public, but how could she forgive him for excluding her to this extent from his life and from his dreams which were becoming reality?

"Are you getting up? . . . Already?"

"Instead of going round in circles, I might as well go to the shop, I've got a backlog of work."

"Kiss me."

They kissed, and it was unexpectedly tender. For those few seconds, he almost lay back down next to her and forgot about all this madness.

*

The 7 o'clock Métro. The quiet one, with yawns and half-closed eyes. The sun was barely up when he came out at Saint-Germain; he was ten minutes early. Rodier was already there, in his little blue Volkswagen, parked opposite 70 Rue de Rennes. Blin sat in the passenger seat and they shook hands in silence. The car was clean, quite tidy in the front, a bit more of a mess on the rear seat where there were piles of magazines and half eaten packets of biscuits. Rodier was wearing the same clothes as the day before, beige trousers and a black leather jacket. He was sporting a smile like a priest's, discreet, reassuring.

"There isn't a café outside number 70. We're going to have to wait in the car till he comes out."

"Who?"

Rodier opened his worn leather briefcase and took out a photocopy of a snapshot showing a young man of less than twenty, standing with his back to the sea, smiling at the camera.

"It's the most recent photo his parents had. He's called Thomas and is living in a garret. He's stopped going to lessons and isn't showing any signs of life. His parents are convinced he's become part of a sect, or he's homosexual, which seems to be the same thing as far as they're concerned . . . They want to know who he sees and what he does with his time."

"Are we sure he's up there?"

"No. The surveillance officially starts at 7.30 and will end at 10 o'clock if we can establish for sure that he spent the night somewhere else. We start again tomorrow once it's agreed with the father; never forget that you always have to work out the hours with the client so that they don't waste their money and you don't waste your time. If, on the other hand, we see him come out, we'll follow him, all day if need be, and perhaps some of the night. I get 300 francs an hour for tailing."

Nicolas was not sure whether to pick up his notebook for fear of looking like a student trying to earn good marks. Rodier took out a little square case of CDs.

"I prefer classical music, it helps. I think this is a good time of day for Vivaldi."

The day was getting under way now. Little old men were out walking their dogs, a few metal shutters were being raised, the street lights were going out and the light suddenly changed from red to blue. Blin tried to catch his own eye in the wing-mirror and saw someone who looked like a conspirator with his head hunched between his shoulders. Since he had been sitting in this car, he no longer saw people in the same way: they all had something to hide, starting with that woman passing them now, pulling her shopping trolley long before the shops were open. Had the world been the same ten minutes earlier?

"How do you tail someone?"

"It's simple and very complicated at the same time. It's like everything else, you can only do it with practice and years of experience. When I started with my first tailing jobs, I was terrified of being seen, I couldn't help myself looking like a policeman or a thief. Now, it's lost all its excitement. I go off to work dragging my feet, and the advantage is that I no longer look like anything in particular. I've become invisible or better, transparent, the man in the street, the nobody, same colour as the walls. I'm no one. If the guy I'm following goes into a café, I might have half a glass of beer right next to him and he won't notice a thing. People forget me because I forget what I'm actually doing myself. To get that sort of detachment, you need to have bathed in adrenaline, sweated buckets, failed a thousand times, lost hundreds of people in the Métro and wasted bloody hours waiting in the wrong place at the wrong time."

"The instinctive factor is mentioned a lot in the things I've read about the subject."

"That depends what you understand by 'instinctive factor'; all I can say is that, if I've been following a woman for a few days in a row, I can tell just by the way she walks if she's going to see her lover."

Blin pondered this example with a feeling close to happiness, and was asking endless questions about intuition, anticipation and all the things that fascinated him when Rodier cut him short. "I've spotted a fast-food place not far away. The coffee's probably disgusting, but I want something hot. Shall I get something for you?"

". . . You're not going to leave me here on my own, are you? Let me go."

"I need to stretch my legs a bit, and anyway I won't be a minute."

"What if that's exactly when he comes out?!"

"Try and improvise."

Rodier slammed the door and disappeared round

the corner. *Bastard!* What he needed was a whipping boy to brighten his last few days, it was all becoming clear. *That bastard Rodier!*

Blin was in hiding for the first time in his life.

As he might have expected, he heard the door of number 70 clicking.

The concierge appeared, and looked around. Blin slid down in his seat and tried to look detached. The man took the dustbins in. Rodier reappeared with two cups.

"There's your coffee, they've got separate pots of cream and the sugar's in these little sticks."

"Don't do that to me again!"

"We're not even sure he's in there," he said, looking towards the roof of the building. "His room looks out onto the street but none of them have got the lights on, see for yourself."

With his coffee in his hand, Thierry glued his nose to the windscreen and looked up searchingly. He did not see anything worth noting, but derived a tingle of pleasure from the gesture.

"I've restricted myself to three coffees a day," said Rodier. "I always have water in the boot. I drink a lot. If you do the same, make sure you check that there's somewhere close by where you can pee. It seems stupid, but make a note."

"If he comes out, will we both follow him?"

"Why not? What a luxury! Two tails for the price of one."

"Stop joking about it, and tell me what we'll do if he appears."

"There's nothing to get stressed about with a job like this. Look, if it makes you feel any better, we'll give him a ring at home."

Blin looked at him questioningly.

He took out a mobile, keyed in the number and let it ring while he swilled his cup of coffee. Blin strained his ears.

"Answerphone."

"He would definitely have answered if he was there," Thierry suggested.

"If he's depressed, which his parents are afraid he is, he could have taken tranquillizers or sleeping pills in the middle of the night."

"In that case he could just as easily stay in bed all day."

"Possibly. Either way, we stop altogether at 10 o'clock, as agreed. Between now and then, we've got time to get to know each other with Vivaldi in the background."

The day had slowly made its presence felt. Blin had a thousand questions but preferred to hold them back; no point gathering raw material without any real application. The time spent waiting in silence like this already said so much. His apprehension had given way to terrible curiosity: Blin could not wait to see the boy come through the door. He had lost any detachment from the events. He did not belong anywhere else, under more sensible skies, but well and truly here, in this car, sitting next to a man he did not know, waiting for a man he did not know. It all seemed less and less strange to him and was becoming increasingly real.

"Do you have any Métro tickets on you, Thierry?"

Rodier recommended that he bought some for the days to come, and took the opportunity to open the whole chapter on transport. Half the tailing he did in Paris took place in the Métro. Scooters were practical for following a car in the city but would soon be spotted on the outskirts or in the country; there, a car was more useful. Thierry was too busy trying to remember what he was being taught to notice the sudden intensity in Rodier's eyes as he asked: "Is that him?"

"Where . . .? Who..?"

In a momentary lapse of concentration, Blin had not heard the front door clicking. A figure had appeared on the pavement.

"Is it him or not?" Rodier insisted, as if leaving the decision to Blin.

Panicking, Thierry snatched the photo. Rodier had already got out of the car and was waiting outside. From behind, it could have been him: the colour of his hair, the way it was cut, his build. He had a bag over his shoulder, a scarf round his neck as if it was the middle of winter, jeans, walking boots, the same sort of boy as in the photograph.

"It's him!" said Thierry, as if giving a verdict.

"You have to follow your intuition. Let's go."

Blin, way behind, saw him trotting off towards the young man who was going down the Rue de Rennes, and followed him at a run.

". . . What should *I* do?" Thierry asked, picking up on the urgency.

"Carry on along the same pavement as him. I'm crossing over – stay a bit further back than me."

He did as he was told, with no idea of the distance he should keep or how to behave. Rodier walked with the nonchalance of a tourist interested in the old stone-work while Blin measured every step, sidled along the walls with his arms tight in to his body and his eyes so distracted that they did not come to rest on anything. He tried in vain to catch Rodier's eye, then he locked onto the outline of the boy who turned left into the Boulevard Saint-Germain. As he followed him, strange thoughts came to mind. He imagined the boy in the throes of a family psychodrama, his mother in tears, his father raising his voice: we don't know you any more! He could picture him at night, blind drunk, bellowing his freedom in the face of the world: I'll do what I want with my life! The strangest part of it for Blin was the feeling that he could clearly read the soul of the man he was following through the streets of Paris, without even needing to look him in the eye. The way he walked was enough; the peculiarly dogged way he went from A to B was typical of a disoriented youngster going through life in a haze. Two hours earlier, Blin could not even have known he was alive, let alone anything about his situation; now he might know more about Thomas than the boy did himself. The latter made the most of the last few seconds of a red light to cut quickly across the Boulevard Saint-Germain. The traffic barred the route to the two acolytes, who ended up next to each other, momentarily unaware of each other as they watched their prey going down the Rue des Saints-Pères.

"It looks like he's going to the Medical Faculty," said Rodier. "But his parents told me he was doing business studies in the suburbs . . ."

Thierry was taking his role very seriously. He said nothing in reply but took great strides to catch up with Thomas, settling fifteen paces behind him. Rodier was right, the boy was heading for the massive cast-iron gates of the Medical Faculty. It was, after all, time for lectures and Thomas, with his little bag over his shoulder, looked every inch the future doctor. Thierry had to admit it: the slowness which he had taken for an obvious sign of depression had perhaps just been complete absorption in a traumatology tutorial. He cut short all his speculation about Thomas's life and concentrated on following him, trying to narrow the

94

gap a bit more even though he had to slow down as he went through the entrance to the building where masses of students, twenty years younger than himself, were streaming in. What did they look like, he and Rodier, in all the comings and goings on the concourse? Weirdos? Dirty old men? Not exactly honest, anyway. And they weren't, were they? Thomas headed over towards the cafeteria corner and slipped some coins into a drinks machine. A convenient pause for them.

"Well, is it him or not?" Rodier asked again.

It could not not be him . . .

Unless . . .

Thierry no longer knew which version was the right one. They sat down at a table where two girls were comparing their work and paid no attention to them. Rodier looked at the photo again and Blin did the same: they may well have had the young man right under their noses, quite relaxed, cup of coffee in hand, but they were incapable of saying whether he was the right one. Rodier was growing impatient, his fists were balled tightly and his feet beginning to jig. Thomas or not Thomas? A future manager hounded by his parents or a future doctor keen to jump every hurdle up to the Hippocratic oath? He threw down his paper cup and headed very obviously towards a classroom. For the first time Blin saw Rodier's cheeks flush.

"Thierry, forget what I'm about to do," he said, clearly very calm.

He turned back towards the cavernous hallway and shouted: "THOMMAAAAAS!"

The walls reverberated, Rodier's shout echoed back and dozens of figures turned towards them. Except that of the boy who quietly walked out of sight into a lecture room.

"That way, at least we know for sure," said Rodier with relief.

*

He wanted to go back to 70 Rue de Rennes to ferret round the garret rooms, and asked Blin to stay downstairs for the obvious reason of discretion. However, he did ask him to dial Thomas's number so that he could identify the right door from the ringing. Thierry rang several times in succession. Rodier came back out quite quickly and spoke briefly to the concierge before getting back into the car.

"He can't have spent the night here. No point wasting our time, we're going back to the office."

"I'm really sorry about earlier. For a minute I really thought it was him."

"It's not your fault, I had my doubts and you might have been sure. Now you know a bit more about the 'instinctive factor'."

On their way to the office they talked about one thing and another, and Blin unwound, freed of the pressure that had been building up since the early morning. Something had happened, something unthinkable which he could now think of as his first tailing job, even if it had drawn a blank. He felt he had got rid of his virginity and was ready to have thousands of other experiences. As they walked, he asked how you proceeded with the client when nothing had happened, like that morning.

"In cases like that, you have to make a 'report', invoice for the three hours and agree on a day to start the investigations again. Thomas can easily wait for us till the weekend."

In the agency's main office Blin sat down in the

client's chair and watched Rodier picking up his messages and looking at his faxes as he made some coffee.

"This is the bit I like best," he said, "planning it all out, nice and easy in my office. Everything I loathed twenty years ago. I'd make a brilliant bureaucrat now, happy to give up my desk blotter to get home to my slippers."

"Do you always know what you're going to be doing from one day to the next?"

"More or less. If the Thomas job had been delayed, I would have typed out a report and this afternoon I would have taken care of another job. Some man complaining about paying his ex-wife astronomical alimony. He suspects she's found work she isn't declaring. If I can establish that she's working, he'll have the figures revised accordingly. He might even be able to wriggle out of this alimony – which seems to obsess him – once and for all. To be honest, I'm still not sure about it."

"Why?"

"I've got a feeling this guy hasn't told me half of what I ought to know. We'll go and have a look, anyway."

"In the meantime, what should I do?"

"I'll show you what a report should look like. You can root through old files while I'm typing."

His liking for Rodier was growing by the hour. Blin found considerable charm in his rather mannered phrasing, which gave a slight air of the white-collar crook. He could not understand how Rodier kept his cool in the face of his clients' feverishness. How did he manage to come to terms with the crises in other people's lives, with their anxieties and preoccupations, without sinking into depression or cynicism himself, but maintaining his very Rodier-like good humour?

While Rodier took a telephone call, Blin wandered around the room and looked out of the window; there were some children playing noisily in a little courtyard. It occurred to him that he could call the answerphone at the shop, but there was no hurry. The sleepless night was already forgotten, and something told him that this evening he would be far too tired to have another.

"Change of programme," said Rodier as he hung up. "We've got a little job in the car."

And he grabbed his jacket without another word, already out on the landing, key in hand. Even though he may have been lacking in enthusiasm, his reflexes had not been dulled. Following him down the stairwell, Blin tried to imagine him as he would have been in his early days.

"It's a woman who rang me last Sunday. She lives at Rambouillet with her husband, a sales rep who retired six months ago. She's wondering what he gets up to for two whole afternoons a week in Paris. He's just left the house to talk to the bank about his pension fund, and he won't be back until this evening."

"What are we doing?"

"We're going to go there and wait for him. It's very close."

In less than ten minutes they were there on the Rue de Berne in the Eighth Arrondissement. Rodier slowed down as he drove past the building and looked for a parking space.

"We've got plenty of time," he said. "The retired ones take care of their cars, they never double park."

"And what if he doesn't come?"

"Then his wife's doubts are probably justified. We'd have to arrange to start tailing him from home."

Rodier parked his car about ten yards from the front door of the bank. The game of solitaire would start again but this time in the full light of day during the lunchtime rush; even if their presence seemed less suspicious than it had in the morning, Blin wondered once again what two men sitting in a parked car really looked like. He could come up with only one answer: two detectives hiding.

"If I'm an attentive, conscientious pupil, how long do you think it'll be before I can manage on my own?"

"Now, how can I answer that? It all depends on how emotionally involved you get and how you cope with the stress."

"No idea . . ."

"Let's say that in a year you should be able to assimilate up to sixty or seventy per cent of what you need to know in this line of work. It takes a good deal longer to get to ninety. Personally, I'd say five years."

Blin had never asked such a vague question, and had never been given such a precise answer. He found it hard to imagine that he would be fending for himself in one short year, and yet one thing was emerging: he felt that he was a good pupil and, if he did change his mind along the way, there was one thing that would never be dulled: his furious desire to put his learning into practice.

"In some ways you're lucky to have landed up with me. My hard-bitten fellow detectives have quite a taste for secrecy and only delegate out the harmless little jobs. If you're ready to play the game, I won't keep anything from you and you'll make faster progress than someone else might. It's not to do with talent or having a sixth sense, no one in the world is born to find out strangers' secrets. As with everything else, you just have to pay attention and take a personal interest. I won't ask where you get your particular interest from, it's none of my business."

An elegant way of avoiding exposure to the same kind of question himself.

"How about a sandwich?" he asked.

"You're not going to play the same trick on me twice. I'm going to do the shopping."

"Get me something with ham in it, cured ham if they've got it, and a beer."

Thierry used the opportunity to ring Nadine in case she had tried to get hold of him, which she clearly had. He explained that he had had to go to various suppliers, and asked her not to wait supper for him. Before he hung up, he could not help himself saying, "You know I love you," when a "Bye bye, darling," would have done. The thought of splitting up with her, or rather of pushing her into splitting up with him, made him feel sentimental.

"No one makes good sandwiches any more, that's pretty pathetic for a place with several million inhabitants! All you can find is Teflon bread wrapped in cellophane with soggy ham – pitiful. You know, Thierry, it's also little things like that that are driving me into exile in the country. I'm too old for tailing, I'm too old to eat rubbish and, worse still, I'm too old to be making a fuss because nothing's what it used to be."

Thierry chewed away, looking doubtful: "Don't tell me this job doesn't give you any pleasure any more, not even a little tingle of excitement from time to time?"

Rodier took a moment to think. He wanted to help this apprentice by giving him his own points of reference without unloading his experiences on him.

"Tingles, excitement, thrills, we're not in that sort of territory. It's always nice to know that you weren't wrong, that your intuition brought you to a quicker conclusion. But for those three minutes of gratification there are so many hours of boredom with your bum on the seat of a car!"

The weariness that Rodier was keen to underline seemed unimaginable to Thierry Blin. If that sort of depreciation was lying in wait with all human activities, how many thousands of enquiries did you have to carry out before you began to feel worn?

Suddenly, a number plate caught Thierry's eye: the last two numerals, 78, meant it came from around Rambouillet.

"Our old boy does drive a grey Datsun doesn't he?"

"One point to you."

As if to contradict Rodier, the man parked his car right in front of the driveway, opposite the door to the bank, and slammed his door without locking it.

"Highly strung," said Rodier.

"Is that a disabled sticker on his windscreen?"

"He must think that means he can do whatever he likes. It's not going to stop us finishing our sandwiches."

Perhaps not, but it was no longer possible to chat happily. Automatically, Blin quickly closed his window. Bruno Lemarrecq had arrived in the place where the other two were waiting for him, and it had nothing to do with chance. How could he possibly guess that two men chewing on sandwiches were watching the door to the bank out of the corners of their eyes?

"After our failure this morning, I'm rather pleased to see him," said Rodier.

Blin felt all the indecency associated with the very fact of being there in that car, secretly hoping that Bruno Lemarrecq had something to hide.

"What did he used to sell?"

"Hot-water tanks."

They had time to clean up the crumbs, throw their packaging into a dustbin and regret not having a cup of coffee before Bruno Lemarrecq reappeared and got back into his car.

"It's hard enough following a friend in a car," said Blin, "but if you've got to do it without the driver knowing too . . ."

"By car it's the first five minutes and the last five minutes which are the most difficult. The rest of the time I try to keep another car between theirs and mine. Unless the guy's got very serious reasons to be paranoid, he won't see a thing."

Lemarrecq turned onto a main road and stayed on it for a good half mile; Rodier let a red Toyota overtake them to act as a screen. Blin looked anywhere other than at the Datsun, as if afraid of catching the man's eye in his rear-view mirror, which made Rodier smile. The Toyota forked off to the right and Lemarrecq was directly in front of them once again.

"At the moment, we're heading for Rambouillet."

"And what do we do if he goes home?"

"We follow. He may have his own little ways close to home, it's not unusual. You must have heard of the famous case of 'the husband's adultery on the party wall'."

Blin raised his eyebrows questioningly.

"Until quite recently, a wife's adultery was recognized pretty much everywhere, but a husband's was only punishable if it actually took place in the conjugal home. One case set a precedent, where the man hadn't found anywhere better to have it away with his neighbour than on the wall between their two gardens. The question was, did this constitute adultery?"

Rodier stopped talking and braked sharply when he saw the Datsun stopping at a red light. He tucked his car behind a van double parked about fifty yards further back.

"Even if he doesn't suspect anything, and whatever else happens, the less he sees you, the better. Do it automatically. If the roads are clear like today, there's no point in sticking right to him. Try and find little corners to stop and wait."

The light changed to green and Rodier set off again following the little Datsun, maintaining the fifty-yard distance, and he carried on with his story as if nothing had happened.

"Luckily, the husband was found to be in the wrong."

"Luckily for sexual equality?"

"No, for a good hard worker like me who got masses of women customers as a result of it."

Blin, who was still hypnotized by the rear window of the Datsun, smiled just to please him.

"When you're following a car, look for the blind spot, and put yourself in it as much as you can. If you know where he's going it's sometimes useful to go on ahead."

The Datsun was following the banks of the Seine towards the western suburbs.

"At the moment, he's still heading for home," said Rodier. "If he goes down the Rue Mirabeau, he's trying to get onto the ring road, and we'll be in for a stretch on the motorway. But he told his wife he wouldn't be back till late afternoon . . ."

For fear of disturbing Rodier's concentration, Blin no longer dared open his mouth, even for the most mundane comment. Supple, invisible, even his car did nothing to catch the eye. Lemarrecq put on his indicator and, at the Pont du Garigliano, turned off, away from the ring road.

"This is beginning to get interesting," said Rodier, who was still calm but much more intrigued.

Blin pictured Lemarrecq on the roads of France with his car full of catalogues of hot-water tanks. Cheap hotel rooms, service stations, basic meals reimbursed on expenses, impatient customers, tired colleagues and, occasionally, a bored middle-aged woman at the end of the bar in a two-star hotel. Since he had retired, he missed all that, of course, and his wife could not understand, she had always been sedentary. He was not as old as all that, after all, he could still appeal to someone.

"And what if he's going to some friends to play poker with his savings?" Thierry asked.

"Why not? As far as I'm concerned, that doesn't change a thing. I've been asked to find out what he's doing and I'll report on what he's doing."

The Datsun set off into the maze of roads in a residential part of the Fifteenth Arrondissement; it was no longer possible to hover in his blind spot. Rodier stayed a good hundred yards back, at the risk of having it turn off some way ahead of them.

"If he was depleting their savings or if he had a mistress, could his wife use the information you give her in court?"

"In theory, no. But just think of a judge who's onto his twenty-eighth divorce of the day; he's hungry, he's tired, he wants to make a phone call. If the plaintiff's lawyer submits a photo of the husband kissing some young lady full on the mouth, it's likely to strengthen their case, wouldn't you say?"

The Datsun stopped abruptly, Lemarrecq had found a miraculous parking space.

"Oh shit, shit, shit and shit!" said Rodier.

He forgot that Blin was there and acted as if he were alone. He abandoned his car across the entrance to a garage, leapt to the boot without losing sight of Lemarrecq, grabbed the camera with its telephoto lens already screwed on and hid behind a four-wheel drive to take pictures of the man who was still walking along unsuspecting. Rodier dumped the camera into Thierry's hands.

"Why should we take a picture of a man on his own in a street . . .?"

"To prove that he was in the Rue François-Coppée at ten past one, and that I was there too at the same time. Haven't you ever heard of justifying the expenses?"

Lemarrecq had just turned into another street. Rodier left his trainee there to follow him again. Blin, his heart beating fast, put away the camera, ran round the corner of the street and saw Lemarrecq keying in a security code before disappearing through a front door which Rodier just managed to catch at the last minute before slipping, alone, into the building a moment later.

Thierry wiped away some drops of sweat and caught his breath with a few deep breaths. He closed his eyes for a moment and gave a great sigh, just long enough to dispel the last of the adrenaline still burning through his limbs. He would probably always remember that moment, that thrust on the accelerator that he had just given to his whole life. Was he going to force himself to make wooden frames for much longer when the minute he had just lived had been far more intense than the last five years spent in his workshop? He felt as if he had achieved something, as if he had surpassed himself, even though he had still only been a spectator, even though he had been frightened like a little kid who is not used to being naughty. Was it his fault if he had felt an unfamiliar excitement as he followed some unfortunate man who had every right to make the most of his retirement as he saw fit? It was all absurd. And unhoped-for.

Rodier came back out at last with a notebook in his hand, and headed for the car.

"We're going back to the office."

Unable to contain his impatience, Thierry begged him to tell him what he had just seen.

"He went up to the second floor. I followed him up the stairs and stopped when I was level with his feet. He rang the bell of the door on the right, and someone let him in."

"Go on!"

"Well, after that I could only hear what was going on. A young woman's voice with an oriental accent, Miss Mai Tran, second floor on the right."

"She might be a friend."

"No doubt about that, she greeted him with: 'Oh, sweetheart, I waited all day yesterday!' Only a friend would open a door with so much enthusiasm."

They got back into the car; Thierry slammed his door jubilantly, completely at home in his new persona. He had never felt so much himself.

"Don't go thinking this happens often. In normal circumstances, it would have taken two or three days to get a result like that. And the most amazing thing in this whole business is that Madame Lemarrecq is going to get all the answers for just 600 francs!"

*

Nadine was sleeping, in exactly the same position as when Thierry had left her. The same abandon. He sat on the edge of the bed.

"Are you asleep . . .?"

"Of course I'm asleep," she mumbled, smiling.

She came and snuggled in his arms. Weakly, Blin could not help himself talking to her, right there and then, as she dozed.

"I'm going to take a year's sabbatical."

"A what . . .?"

"If I don't do it now, I'll do it in twenty years' time, but it wouldn't be the same then."

Her silence was full of surprise and concern.

". . . Are you sure? How are you going to manage . . .?"

"I'm going to appoint a manager for the shop. Brigitte will tell me how to go about it."

He had already talked about it with his accountant, and she had thought it an absurd idea. She was going to have to cope without the complicity with Thierry which she valued so much.

"I've found a youngster who wants to start out in the business. Brigitte's done the accounts, I've got some money put aside, don't worry."

"I'm not worried . . . All this is so . . ."

"Go back to sleep, we'll talk about it in the morning."

She turned onto her side and stopped thinking about it so that she could sink back to sleep.

Blin wondered whether Lemarrecq dreamed of the mysteries of the Orient as he slept next to his wife.

And whether young Thomas felt protected by the darkness or terrified of it as the night trickled by.

Rodier, who was waiting for him at 8 o'clock the following morning, had thought it worth mentioning that it might be quite an eventful day.

Nicolas Gredzinski

If only he had slept with her.

   He was left with nothing of the previous night, apart from waves of words breaking inside his skull. Being drunk generated a lot of sound, perhaps a bit of fury, but rarely any memories. Above and beyond the frustration of not having held Loraine's body in his arms, he was annoyed with himself for having suggested they spend the night together. The ethyl alcohol had acted directly on his sense of the ridiculous, and, in just a few minutes, it had breached the rampart he had spent years building as a result of childhood humiliation and teenage awkwardness. He had built it the traditional way, fashioning it with great patience, thanks to women – but mainly against them. His acute awareness of the ridiculous had probably meant he had missed out on some delicious moments but it had also spared him some foreseeable blunders. Everything had fallen apart in one blow because of a simple sentence pointing out where a bed was. However hard he tried to convince himself that Loraine's refusal was a "maybe" with a promise of other tomorrows, he had well and truly fallen into the oldest trap in the world like a young fool. *God, it's awful being young again like that.* That was his first conscious thought when his alarm clock went off, just two hours after he had fallen asleep in a heap, still clothed, and alone. Why had no one chucked him out of that bar? He thought he was protected by various laws – wasn't there something about curbing public drunkenness? But no, they had let him drink, and talk, and drink some more, until he ended up in the small hours with just enough strength to raise his arm to hail a taxi, barely able to give his address, keying in his security code as if he were learning to count and, to finish off, knocking over the lamp in the hall: for God's sake, what the bloody hell was that doing there, anyway, in his way like that! In amongst all the words still swirling round inside his head, just one word, a two-letter one, had been properly registered: Loraine had said *no*. An elegant *no* but one which meant *no*, just *no*. He even wondered whether she had recoiled slightly when, in the heat of conversation, he had leant forward to say something in her ear. If there had been any complicity, he had blown it clean away with that head-on attack (which had the sole virtue of being free of innuendo). What could be more pathetic than a drunk suggesting a bit of fooling around to a beautiful woman? The same man the following morning.

As he fumbled for a clean shirt, he was tempted to go back to bed and to dump the Group in favour of a bit of sleep and oblivion. Not to think about anything any more, not to worry about being brave, to forget about remorse, to stay in the half light, buried under a quilt, to set off to some unknown land and come back healed. And if that weren't enough, to fall into the final sleep and be done with the little animal which had been nibbling at his insides all his life.

There was no question of resorting to beer; coffee and aspirin would be enough, as they were for everyone else, the people who experienced hangovers as the other side of the coin, a fair price to pay when you have enjoyed such unfounded merriment. Why should he break with it? He would just have to celebrate this pain, it reminded him of what he was, a forty-something dreaming beyond himself, who would never be able to summon up the strength to go to work in two short hours. He needed to be alone to understand the nostalgia he felt for the man he had been the evening before. Where did he come from, this guy who talked so prettily to a stranger and drank like a sailor with his eyes wide open and his every movement aggressively purposeful? Where had he gone now, that bastard who had had a good laugh at his expense? This morning Nicolas was paying that other man's bill, and that was the worst of it: he was no more real than the woman who hung around in bars and talked about the Renaissance as if that was where she came from.

Somewhere in the crook of his ear he could still hear Loraine's lecture about the beauty all around them – you just had to know how to look – and beauty had eventually appeared; the colour of the bourbon in the whisky glasses, the little movements made by the lovers around them, the black-and-white photographs of a music-hall performance, the night owls on the bar stools and, especially, Loraine, who at that precise moment eclipsed all the others.

During the tortuous journey that took him from his bed to the office, only ugliness appeared to him. The world really was this dismal thing built by his ancestors and by himself, all of them convinced that they were doing the right thing, each following their own unique logic. Nicolas got out of the lift, preparing to slam the door to his office so that he could be heard from some way away. To be left in peace, that was all he asked. Muriel stopped him halfway and peeled a Post-it note from her switchboard:

"Alissa would like to know if she can have lunch with you today, she's sorry it's such short notice."

110

"Who?"

"Alissa, Monsieur Broaters' secretary."

"What does she want from me?"

"She didn't say."

"Where's she taking me?"

"To the Trois Couronnes."

That was where they discussed the most important issues, where Marcheschi used all his powers of persuasion.

"Tell her that's fine."

"There's also a Monsieur . . . Jeannot, I think . . . who called this morning."

"Jacot?"

"I couldn't really hear his name. To be honest, things didn't seem to be too good."

Jacot picked up straight away at the sound of Nicolas's voice on the answerphone. He had just got back from the clinic, his course of chemotherapy, which was meant to start in a month, had been brought forward to the following week, and that was just the beginning. Nicolas did not understand much, except for the urgency.

"Muriel, cancel the lunch with Alissa," he said, stepping into the lift.

". . . But I've just confirmed it!"

Never mind. He hopped from foot to foot as the lift went down, and rushed across the hallway, then the footbridge to the taxi rank. Once outside Jacot's house, he hesitated for a moment and asked the driver to drop him at the nearest café. He had never come close to illness, real illness; he was one of those people who shook at the slightest rash, and could see themselves ending their days in a sanatorium at the first sneeze.

"What can I get you?"

The question begged several more. Was Nicolas so

naive as to think that he just had to swallow anything strong to produce miracles? Knowing how to talk to women, confronting the irritating, comforting the sick? Was he blessed with a transcendental power which could be unleashed with just a drop of alcohol?

"What's pretty stiff that I could drink at this time of day?"

"You could have a calva coffee or a brandy."

"Brandy."

"A large one or a regular?"

"Large."

Why was Jacot calling on him instead of someone close to him at such a crucial time? You don't go talking about your cancer to the first person you meet, you don't send up a cry for help to someone who doesn't inspire complete confidence. *The sick have a sixth sense for finding a kindly ear. Why me, for God's sake!*

The coffee awakened his taste buds and introduced them to the taste of brandy, which he did not know. He found the shape of the glass pleasing and he swirled it in the palm of his hand as he had seen others do, not taking his eyes of the amber swell.

Jacot welcomed him into a terrible mess, apologized for it without really feeling apologetic, and asked him whether he would like something to drink, hoping he would say no. Nicolas looked the place over, a bachelor's retreat with piles of files that Jacot no longer consulted.

"Up till now I was responding well to the treatments."

Nicolas waited in silence.

"They're going to give me some platelet transfusions."

"What does the doctor say?"

"He says that my psychological state is going to have a big effect."

"And why shouldn't he be right?"

"Because when you've got what I've got, you *know*."

What Nicolas had been afraid of did not happen, but the absolute reverse.

The diffuse heat of the brandy came to appease him at the most unexpected moment. Relieved of his apprehensions, he managed to devote himself completely to the other man's words. The message was getting through to him clearly, intact. He not only heard every word, but also the rhythm of the sentences, the tone and, particularly, the punctuation, the commas, breaks and full stops, not to mention the pauses, silences and sighs, which said a great deal more than the rest. No desire at all to flee.

At last he could listen to someone. Right to the end. That was all that was being asked of him.

*

Nicolas was back at the Group at the stroke of midday, consumed by what had just happened to him. He now had an answer to the question *why me?* Someone close to Jacot would not have done.

Jacot had chosen Nicolas for his announcement that he would no longer be doing battle. From now on he would offer absolutely no resistance to death if it decided to come looking for him, even if turned up earlier than expected. For the first time, Jacot had talked about it as if it were obvious, and he had summoned someone urgently to announce his official surrender. Nicolas had not tried to contradict him at any stage, for fear of being condemned to a lesson on hope which would only have underlined the depth of the crisis. He was now the depository for Jacot's resignation, for his distress, which suddenly had come to rival

113

his own good old anxiety and put it in perspective. Exhausted and losing the effects of the alcohol, he thought he deserved two hours of complete solitude in his office.

"Alissa had already left when I tried to cancel, and I can't get hold of her on her mobile."

"What shall we do?" he asked, stifling a yawn.

"She must be waiting you at the restaurant, she booked a table for 1 o'clock. If you leave straight away you may not even keep her waiting."

He went back across the hall towards the esplanade, haunted by the look in Jacot's eyes. For the last few hours, Nicolas Gredzinski had no longer been immortal. He suddenly wondered whether his perennial anxiety was an irrepressible fear of death or, conversely, a twisted way of forgetting about it.

"A table with Madame . . . I don't know her name . . . Christian Broaters' assistant."

"If you'd like to follow me."

She was there, looking fresh, with an explosive smile on her face, almond eyes, her hair almost shaved. Long, slender, with a coppery tan: a matchstick, incendiary.

"I'm so glad you were able to find the time."

"I like off-the-cuff invitations. It makes a change from the canteen."

"I never have time to go there, too many outside meetings. Let's order straight away, I've only got an hour."

She hailed a waiter and ordered a grilled steak with no sauce; Nicolas just had time to spot a fresh cod fillet with ceps.

"What would you like to drink?"

"Red wine, even with the fish," he said as if it were self-evident.

114

He was supposed to choose the wine but she did it spontaneously, which suited him: he knew nothing about wine, and he was going to find out how much he was valued by management.

"Talbot '82."

She handed the wine list back to the sommelier, then, seamlessly, launched into a diatribe on the lack of communication in the communication sector; Nicolas smiled to keep her happy and let her voice melt into the slight hubbub around them without paying attention to the content, a vague preamble which promised something more pointed to follow. The sommelier reappeared with the precious bottle in his hand, carried out the usual ceremony and poured a couple of drops into Alissa's glass. She managed to ignore him completely but still brought the glass up to her lips. Here again Nicolas watched her with a certain detachment; the last time he had tasted the wine in front of a woman, she had been the one to point out it was corked.

"It's good," she said, momentarily interrupting what she was saying about the problems in the art department.

He brought his glass to his lips, took a sip of Château Talbot '82 and held it in his mouth for a moment before swallowing.

"Tell me, Nicolas – may I call you Nicolas?"

". . . Sorry?"

"I asked whether I could call you Nicolas."

"Did you say this wine was good?"

"Is there a problem . . .?" she asked anxiously, tasting it again.

He took another mouthful, then another. He tried to hold them for a moment but he let them glide down his throat and finished the glass. He knew nothing about wine, about how it evolved in the mouth. He would not have known the body from the nose, he would have classed a fruity one as all tannin and an everyday bottle as vintage. And yet he had no doubt about how exceptional this moment was. He closed his eyes and opened them to find his glass full again, as if by a miracle.

"A plate of spaghetti with basil on a summer's evening after a swim is good. A warm towel on your cheeks after shaving is good. A winning passing shot at break point is good. But with the wine that you've chosen, we're not in that category, we're into wonderful. It's like a fairy story with a castle, a princess and a dragon: all that's inside this glass. The worst of it is I don't even know if I'm really enjoying it. In fact, if I had to describe what I'm feeling at this precise moment, after drinking this wine, it would be something like sadness."

She look at him in perplexed silence.

"It makes you want to cry like a bride at the high point of her wedding. Too much happiness brings tears to the eyes. But I'm also sad because it's taken me forty years to experience this, sad because no wine of this calibre has ever come my way, sad when I think of the people who drink this sort of thing every day without appreciating what it is they have. And, finally, sad because from now on I'll live in the knowledge that it exists and I'll have to live with it, well without it, actually."

She was still speechless.

"To get back to what you were saying about the art department, if there are any problems, money won't resolve anything. Take on someone who knows how to talk to a printer, who knows how a rotary press works, that would save you a lot for a start. You've got people

116

who know how to do things, find the ones who know how to get things done."

He regretted this last sentence almost before he had spoken it. Alissa did not need to hear more. "Don't you think there was something awful about that meeting? A feeling of settling accounts. I like Bardane, but he sometimes turns something really minor into a matter of principle. Matters of honour, in the old-fashioned way."

The wine was already flowing in Nicolas's veins. He felt confident, free to take liberties. "Bardane chose to be arrogant, a choice only someone mediocre would make. Trying to establish authority over underlings is a sign of servility. I don't think he's incompetent. If only he could be a bit more sure of himself, then he'd know how to lead his team."

"How would you feel about replacing him?"

This time it was Nicolas who looked up in questioning silence, but Alissa did not answer.

"It's not me that you want, it's him that you don't want any longer."

"The position needs energy."

"Is this Broaters' idea?"

"Yes."

"The problem is I'm not ambitious."

"You like the Talbot '82."

"What I really like is peace of mind, which is actually very new to me."

Alissa stood up, she was in a hurry and there was nothing to keep her at the table any more. Nicolas promised to ring her before the end of the week to give her his answer. He ordered a plate of cheese with the sole aim of finishing the half-full bottle. There was no question of leaving a single drop. He was experiencing the most delicate intoxication and was drinking, alone, not needing anything; this feeling of impunity was

117

something he had always needed. No Mergault in the vicinity, no colleagues in the canteen ready to make stupid remarks, he no longer felt guilty. Loraine's words came back to him: "Whatever you do, be discreet. Not from a feeling of shame, just to deprive them of their pleasure." That simple sentence, under the alchemy of the precious molecule, acquired an unexpected dimension. Abstruse ideas came to him and a whole mental structure began to emerge. Feeling inspired, he left the restaurant, went back to the Group, took a can of Coke and a can of Heineken from the café and made a detour via José's office because he had access to the tools in the technical workshop. He borrowed a fine metal chisel and some sandpaper, promising to bring them back before the end of the day.

Half an hour later, hidden safely in his office, Nicolas attacked the can of Coke (which he had emptied out into a basin) with surgical precision. First he pierced the bottom with the point of the chisel and cut off the base, then he cut off the top, being careful to cut the metal as cleanly as possible. To finish the job, he split the cylinder vertically and opened it out like a shell. Despite a few snags at the edges, he managed not to chip the tin. The moment of truth had come, he felt slightly perturbed – it was such a long time since he had made anything with his hands! And this contraption must have been the greatest thing he'd ever seen. Holding the cylinder open, he slid the full can of Heineken in, and something miraculous happened: the red packaging of the Coke wrapped itself automatically around the green of the Heineken. It just took a little pressure of the hand to close the shell and make the full tin disappear completely. There it was, Nicolas Gredzinski had just invented decoy beer. To celebrate the fact, he pulled the seal off the can of Coke, which rewarded him with the crisp bitterness of hops.

Muriel came into his office. "You're lucky you can drink real Coke, Monsieur Gredzinski. I'm condemned to Diet Coke, otherwise it goes straight to my hips."

There was still the rest of the world to conquer.

*

"A pastis, a large one, with lots of ice."

In the summer, that was allowed. Nicolas was not the only one drinking it, José was on his second glass. Marcheschi and Arnaud were sticking to their daily beer, Régine and Cendrine to their kir.

"What are you up to this weekend?" asked Régine.

"Are you thinking about the weekend already?"

"All the time, it's how I hold out for the rest of the week."

"On Saturday I'm going to the country with the children," said Arnaud.

"What about you, Nicolas?"

"Given how odd this week has been, I'm not making any plans."

"And you, Cendrine?"

"I'm going to the fair at the Place du Trône with my sweetheart."

"I'd love to come with you," said Régine.

Nicolas listened to them as he let a warm sap rise through his arteries and invade his cerebral cortex. His state of intoxication needed to be aroused gently, voluptuously.

"This weekend, rest," said José. "I'm going to rent five videos, ones which will give me a complete change of scene, and punctuate them with little siestas right through to Sunday evening. When I need to catch up on sleep, it works well."

Sleep? What was the point of sleeping, Nicolas wondered. Did Loraine ever sleep? The night before, she had left as the bar closed, without suggesting anything further. Nicolas could not see straight and was stumbling over most of his words; what more could anyone envisage with a man in that state? He reached for the mobile number that she herself had slipped into his jacket pocket just before she put him in the back of a taxi.

"And you, Monsieur Marcheschi, what about this weekend?"

He was the only one they spoke to with a degree of respect, never using his first name; without really meaning to, he had created this distance. The thought that one of the Marcheschis of this world could come across Loraine, drink without reeling and end the night in her arms infuriated Nicolas. Everything about Marcheschi exasperated him. In him he could see an unstoppable mechanism; he did not make a meal of everything, nothing dampened his good humour, his purpose and initiative acted like a suit of armour, shielding him from doubt and all life's petty disappointments. Nicolas could not get away from the thought that Marcheschi spent time with the Nemrod "club" with the sole purpose of having a guaranteed audience, conquering without glory, enjoying being admired for nothing.

"Well, this weekend, I'm going to make the most of my ceiling . . ."

He left his sentence dangling in the air, with a smile on his lips, waiting for one of them to probe further. Cendrine did the honours. Nicolas mentally dismissed her as an idiot.

"What's so special about your ceiling?"

"In order to explain, I'll have to tell you what I did last weekend. Have I already told you about my little place in the Eure? Well, picture this, last Saturday at eight in the morning, all on my own, I tackled some beams which had been abandoned for thirty years. Various different problems: insects, grease, rot – you've no idea the insults wood is subjected to. For months an architect friend had been telling me to deal with them as soon as possible if I didn't want the roof to come crashing down on my head. But, you know what it's like, the weeks go by and I kept putting the job off to the next weekend, then the next, and the whole thing started to overwhelm me. I no longer dared even to suggest a weekend in the country to my conquests for fear of ending up as a news item! So, last Saturday I took the bull by the horns and tackled the job, on my own, remember, to get it done once and for all. You should have seen the get-up! Khaki overalls splattered with paint, a bandana round my head, another scarf over my nose and mouth, like a bank robber. Armed with a brush, a rasp and sand paper, I went up the stepladder and what followed is tragic. A beam is a living thing, full of mystery; sometimes it gives in but it can put up resistance too. I started this hellish rasping with the patience of a saint, and the first hour was probably the hardest. With the very first brushstroke, the dust falls straight into your eyes, and there's nothing you can do about it. Nothing! You try all sorts of solutions, but even goggles specially designed for that sort of thing get covered really quickly, so you have to clean them every two minutes, not to mention the sweat running over the bridge of your nose. When I got to the end of the first half it was already midday. Three yards in four hours ... You think the world is a terrible place, and you can't stand DIY, but you carry on. Gradually, the whole thing becomes a challenge, a challenge you set yourself, and that's how you have to see it if you're going to find the strength. By mid-afternoon, your arms are giving up, the smell's seeping into your nose as the dust gets through the mask, and you're sneezing every ten seconds, regular as clockwork. The work's coming on, slowly, but you don't notice it. Your neck's about to explode from being twisted into the most stupid, the most absurd position the body ever had to tolerate. Your shoulders are reduced to a rod of pain, and all this pain joins forces to get you to give up. Your will wavers, and you're about ready to make a bonfire of the whole bloody house to give the neighbours something to watch for miles around. When night fell, I went to sleep right there, on the ground, fully clothed, drunk on the pain, a broken man, groaning and feeling about as alone as I'd ever been. The next morning, the nightmare starts again, undimmed, but this time you're no longer carried by the ignorance of innocence, you know you're going to suffer for it right from the start, but you go back to it, because downing tools now – and it would be literally *downing* tools – would mean all the work so far was for nothing. When the spectre of giving up surfaces again, when all the elements are lined up against you to get you to give in, when your eyes are burning, when your mouth's fetid, when your determination's shrunk to a little puddle at your feet, the miracle happens at last: you've just finished the last bit of the last beam. But there's no question of screaming triumphantly at this stage, the torture's far from over. You have to face the rack again and varnish everything that you've rasped and sanded. And there are all sorts of new pleasures waiting for you now:

122

asphyxia, headaches, burning eyes, tears, and still the same God-awful position, bent double, breaking your back so that you feel you'll never stand upright again. To cut a long story short, it gets to 2 o'clock on Monday morning and now, at last, it's all finished. I was overcome by hysterical laughter and I just lay on the floor for a good hour, letting my body relax. I got into the car to come back to Paris. The next morning I was in the office, fresh and clean, suffering like a martyr but that didn't stop me securing the Solemax contract before the end of the day, and having an aperitif with you in this very spot."

Silence. Admiration. Stifled exclamations, a tentative ripple of applause, outspoken commentaries. On the strength of this, everyone had another drink. How could they not congratulate Marcheschi? What could you add to that? He would leave, convinced he was a hero, and there was something exasperating about that. Nicolas took a good swig of pastis, put down his glass and waited a little longer for the conversation to fade before speaking.

"In 1508 Michelangelo Buonarroti took on a commission from the Pope: to paint the twelve apostles on the ceiling of the Sistine Chapel. He would be given five assistants and 3,000 ducats (the price of a house in Florence) for the work. He discovers that the scaffolding's ineffective and is damaging the ceiling, so he designs a new, much cleverer one which puts purchase on the walls. He paints four apostles but isn't satisfied, he wants to make something really exceptional of this place, and suggests to the Pope that he should tell the story of Genesis over the whole vault of the ceiling; more than 500 square yards of frescoes and 300 characters, each anatomically authentic, moving authentically and with a proper role to play. Michelangelo is down to just one assistant to prepare the filler and mix the colours. And the work starts in a terribly hard winter. It's perishing cold and the chapel's impossible to heat. He paints by day and at night he does the sketches for the following day. On the rare occasions when he sleeps, he sleeps fully clothed and doesn't even take off his shoes because of the cramps and the swelling in his feet; when he does manage to get them off, the skin peals away with the leather. He takes his provisions and his chamber pot up on the scaffolding so he doesn't have to come back down and works up to seventeen hours at a time, perched more than twenty yards up, standing, arching backwards with his neck twisted back and paint dripping onto his face; he has to close his eyes with every brushstroke, as he has learned to do when sculpting, to avoid the shards from the chisel. He's afraid he'll go blind from straining his eyes, and he can't focus beyond the painting he's working on; when he's handed something, he has to hold it up above him to identify it. He refuses to speak to anyone to avoid questions about his work, and forbids access to the chapel, even to the Pope. People in the street think he's a madman with his rags, his face daubed with paint and his teetering step. This torture goes on for four long years. On the day of its inauguration he's not even there, too busy choosing blocks of marble for the tomb of Julius II (which he used to sculpt his Moses). The Sistine Chapel makes a living legend of him; his peers, his detractors, the whole world bows before his work, which, to this day, remains one of the most beautiful creations by the human hand. And yet Michelangelo was so excessively humble that he didn't think of himself as a painter but as a sculptor. He was still only thirty-seven years old, he was to go on to build churches, construct domes, design

124

flights of steps, paint hundreds of walls, sculpt tonnes of marble . . . In an age when life expectancy was forty, he died at eighty-nine, with his chisel in his hand."

After a moment's silence, Marcheschi, with his eyes on his watch, stood up and took his leave.

*

Nicolas had to acknowledge the fact: Loraine liked him. God knows where she was and God knows what she was doing when he rang to suggest they meet for a drink at the Lynn. On the telephone he had not been able to help himself listening, in vain, for clues, noises, something in the background; was she at work, at home, in the street? He did not know how to interpret her quiet, almost meditative voice; at first he pictured a library, perhaps a church, then a child's bedroom or a bathroom not far from where her husband was reading the paper. On the whole, he was happier thinking she was in a library researching her beloved geniuses. This beauty's mysteries made him take a fresh look at his own daily existence; he only had to have Loraine beside him for his work to be reduced to a vague digression, a compulsory scuffle which was neither particularly captivating nor especially tedious. Things had changed overnight: his work for the Group could no longer claim the lion's share of his life. Alissa's proposal did not tempt him: however much energy he spent trying to work his way up the hierarchy, it would never earn him enough money to compensate for so much lost time. It was better to accept the idea that he would not make a career in anything, that he would experience no form of fulfilment from nine until six, and that this sacrifice in the name of the Group was his guarantee that he could keep the best of himself to be expressed where and when it suited him. With Loraine, for example.

"Well, Nicolas, three evenings in a row, aren't things getting a bit suspicious here between the two of us?"

Suddenly, without actually knowing what strange impulse he was obeying, he put his hand on hers as if it were the most natural thing in the world. She did not move hers, but said: "How did you know I was left-handed?"

He smiled tenderly and the same feelings of happiness he had had the day before came back to him, intact, as if nothing had interrupted them.

"If we end up meeting a fourth time, I shall need to be given a reason," she said.

"Give me a bit of time."

"People who like vodka have their own interpretation of time, just like they have their own interpretation of the world. We need to settle the question straight away: sing your praises for me."

Nicolas looked confused.

"When people first meet, they love talking about their faults, hoping they'll be absolved in advance. The listener, who's already completely seduced, finds these confessions so charming, so romantic! As a general rule, things start going wrong very soon afterwards. We're not going to fall into that trap; tell me what you like about yourself, the things you know you're good at, make a list of all those little things that set you apart from other people."

It seemed a pleasant enough exercise to him, but a risky one. Although it was neither a failing or a good quality, anxiety was his main characteristic, the key to his whole personality. She was making him go more slowly, more softly, more gently than anyone else. He would have been the first to know if the world belonged to the people who got up early and got on with things, first and foremost he was one of those who dared. From time to time he was tempted to carve out his own little place without feeling sure that he had any right to. There, in front of Loraine, he could not not mention this infirmity which stopped him seeing his own good points but which also shielded him from a number of excesses.

"I'd find it difficult talking about my good qualities but I do know some bad qualities that I don't have. I'm not aggressive, and I'm proud of that."

His anxiety had always forced him to recognize his limits and to avoid any sort of power struggle. All that time wasted on preparing for the worst had made him very self-effacing. Not without spark, or timid, just apart. You had to have no doubts to be on the offensive or even just threatening; Nicolas was full of doubts. He would never forget the day he had arrived bang on feed time with some friends who were proudly introducing their twins to the world. One of them was a grumpy baby, frantic to suckle; afraid of unleashing his screams, the mother fed him first. The other was shy, restrained, waiting his turn in silence. Nicolas saw it as a universal metaphor: the pains in the arse always came first.

"I don't need scapegoats in everyday life."

To be more precise, he did not try to make others pay for his failings, he already had plenty to get on with with the little sharp-toothed animal sheltering in his stomach.

"And I'm not cynical either. I feel sorry for people who laugh at the darkness around us."

Without actually courting finer feelings (his anxiety precluded that too), he could not bear apocalyptic gloom or out-and-out decadence. They were only there to make his life more difficult, and Nicolas was good enough at that himself.

"I think I can say that I always try not to judge my contemporaries."

He sometimes envied them but he did not judge them, that was a luxury he could not allow himself.

"In a crisis, I can very easily take things in hand and sort the situation out."

This phenomenon was difficult to explain, a perverse effect of his anxiety. Paradoxically, Nicolas was unexpectedly calm at times of widespread stress, his mastery of his own anxiety became an asset in certain complex situations. If someone fainted in the Métro, he proceeded calmly, keeping a hold on the general panic so that the person could come to gently. Put another way, if some form of anxiety came to rival his own, he was able to gauge its significance and appease it.

"I'm afraid I'm going to have to stop there," he said with a mischievous smile.

Everything about him that was good or bad derived from this unspecified fear. The rest was just talk. As far as possible, he had been honest with his answers and he now wondered whether this honesty would pay. He saw a little something in Loraine's eyes which might mean things would go on from there, and he ordered another drink.

Thierry Blin

"Try to find the client's real motives, even if he doesn't know them himself," said Rodier. "Example: a senior manager, good-looking man, very elegant, asks me to follow a woman who's just left him without explaining why. He suspects she's met someone, he wants to know who. I follow the girl all over the place but don't find anything, I'm going round in circles, the bill's getting up towards 20,000 francs with absolutely no result. I try to tell the man that his ex is living alone and only seeing girlfriends, he refuses to believe it. I keep on kicking about until it gets to 35,000 and I give him another report, which doesn't say any more than the previous one: in all likelihood, the girl hasn't 'met someone'. The client's annoyed with me about this, he thinks I'm swindling him, the girl must have fallen in love with someone else, he's convinced; but I really do have to stop an enquiry which is going nowhere. To be absolutely sure, he goes and asks the girl, who just confirms what I've said: she hasn't met anyone. She was just bored with him, a man who never had any doubts about anything, let alone his own charms. By coming to me he was actually subconsciously asking: 'How can a woman leave me, me, a senior manager with a flat stomach? I'm irresistible.' To him the only possible answer was: 'For someone richer, better-looking and more prominent.' "

"What happened to them?"

"He came by to tell me what happened after

that – they often do, don't be surprised if it happens when you're working on your own. The girl – touched because he was still thinking about her – went back to him, they lived together for another three months, and he was the one who left her in the end."

Rodier ordered another *paupiette* and poured every last drop of the cream sauce onto his plate. There was something almost fatalistic about this, a guilty greediness.

"Are you having anything else, Thierry?"

"Fruit salad's on the menu today. That's what I'll have."

"At your age it didn't matter – food, I mean. It caught up with me round about fifty. I would never have guessed it would become the biggest worry of my life."

"If I ate as much as you do, I'd be three times my weight."

"It's the only physical advantage I had at birth: I've always burned up everything. In the long run it can prove dangerous. I never put on any weight, I never had to watch anything, now I have to keep an eye on my cholesterol level and my diabetes.

"With *paupiettes*?!"

"Don't look at my plate, I get enough of that from my wife."

In three months Thierry had learned to let him speak about his longings, his aches and pains, his lottery hopes, his fly-fishing and his cholesterol. As the weeks passed, they had created an exchange which did more for both of them than they could have hoped. Rodier was coming down the home straight with a co-pilot he found he could lean on, and every day the ever-attentive Blin absorbed a key idea, a formula or a new message which would have taken him years to decipher on his own. When their commitments permitted, they had lunch at Chez Patrick, a little restaurant in the Eighteenth Arrondissement which had no particular cachet but was used by other investigators, most of them former police detectives who, for whatever reason, had felt obliged to leave the force. Only the day before, Rodier had rather unwillingly invited one of them to join them so that he could introduce his new recruit to him, setting him up in the profession with due form and ceremony. Thierry was especially friendly and played the part of the novice to win over the man who, grateful for a break from his loneliness, started telling old veteran's anecdotes to impress him; Rodier could have done without the last of these. Twenty years earlier, he and four colleagues had cornered a blackmailer as he took delivery of a trunk full of money – the price of his silence – at the left luggage desk at the Gare de l'Est. Without thinking, Thierry asked a question which was perfectly legitimate but struck the other two as ridiculous.

"Why didn't the victim contact the police?"

"Why do you think?"

". . . Because he *couldn't* contact the police?"

The grounds for the blackmail were real and serious, the man would have risked being taken to court if he had gone to the authorities. To get rid of the blackmailer he had had to take on a whole squad of private detectives, who had accepted the mission without any scruples. *We were young*, said Rodier, to exonerate himself. Thierry had not had the nerve to mention the conscience clause: was it right to save one criminal from another criminal's clutches? The question unsettled him for the rest of the day until late into the night. In the early hours of the morning, he had not found an answer but promised himself he would avoid that sort of case if it were offered to him, more for his peace of mind than on moral grounds.

Today they were the only representatives of the profession at Chez Patrick, and they were having lunch at their usual little table set slightly apart from the others.

"A fruit salad, a crème brûlée and two coffees," Rodier ordered.

"How does he come across to you, this Damien Lefaure?"

"A crook."

Only recently, Rodier had let Blin attend his first meetings with new clients; very few of them had anything to say about it. Blin would put himself in a corner with his arms crossed, and would listen without ever interrupting, hiding his nerves as best he could behind a pro's smile, pretending to be the sort who can listen to anything because he has heard it all before. But he had never heard anything like it, it was even the very first time he had been confronted with bizarre human circumstances where helpless confusion existed side by side with anger, greed with candour and generosity of spirit with revenge. Three days earlier they had received Maître Vano QC, a business lawyer who regularly called on Rodier's services to check the reliability of various individuals who were preparing to work with his clients. Maître Vano's caution was often rewarded, as it had been that time: the man by the name of Damien Lefaure was no newcomer to fraud.

In forty-eight hours Rodier and Blin had learned a great deal about the character. The day after his sixteenth birthday Lefaure had achieved the status of "emancipated minor" to set up his first company, Synenum, which went into liquidation five years later because of insufficient assets. He appeared in several more-or-less fictitious video and sponsorship companies, and in three modelling agencies which had never secured for any girl a single contract in the world of fashion. His tax debts had risen to two million francs and, in order to continue operating, he had himself declared a "legally incompetent adult". Because he was now a ward of court, only his wife's name appeared on official papers. On top of that, he had been under tight administrative scrutiny – not to mention the scrutiny of Rodier's agency – for some time. Blin and Rodier knew all his account numbers, how many shares he had and what they were worth, the names of all of his companies and the addresses of his managers and administrators; they even suspected he had interests in an Internet prostitution network, but that was still only a rumour and would not appear in the report that Rodier had to submit to Maître Vano QC the following day.

"This man went from being an 'emancipated minor' to being a 'legally incompetent adult' as if he'd never actually been a normal adult," said Blin.

"Well, at the end of the day, maybe that's what a crook is," said Rodier.

"In my framing workshop, I was more the type to be diddled by my customers. Even the tax inspector was suspicious; I was too honest, I must have been hiding something. There were days when I would have liked to have had the guts of someone like Lefaure."

"You must be joking, he's just a common thief."

"Is that what you're going to put in your report, then, Rodier? Lefaure is a common thief?"

Despite their complicity, the disciple always spoke with a note of respect and could not call him by his first name. Rodier did not understand this standing on ceremony.

"I'm not going to put anything in this report, you're the one who's going to do it."

"Me?"

"You're going to have to start doing them one day, aren't you?"

Rodier asked for the bill and refused for the umpteenth time to split it with Thierry.

"So, this report," Rodier asked. "On my desk in three hours?"

"Not before 7 o'clock, I've got something to do first."

Rodier did not ask what. He was only interested in other people's business if he was paid to be.

*

Doctor Joust's clinic did not have much in common with the previous ones. It was in a residential area a few hundred yards from the Porte Maillot, and could hardly be seen behind a surrounding wall which was covered in ivy.

Joust was prepared to take on the job of giving Blin a face without any need for the story he had felt constrained to supply him with. He had played the part of a neurotic, convinced of his own ugliness, he even went so far as to compare his rejection of his face with an urge to burn down a house in which he had been unhappy. The only way to get rid of, symbolically, this tortured past, was to watch the house collapse in flames. Halfway through one of his sentences, he realized that he was not lying, and he broke out in a cold sweat.

"I must say, Monsieur Vermeiren, I have to tell you there's a degree of dysmorphobia in all this. You're not seeing yourself as you really are."

Joust could not know how far he was from the

truth. All Blin had to do now was accept an estimate of 65,000 francs, and the performance would be over. For a further 25,000 francs, the surgeon was even prepared to change his voice. Thierry wondered which of them was the more insane.

"Can that be done?" he asked.

"A little collagen injection in the vocal cords to fill them out alters the vibrations of the mucous surface; it changes the register of the voice quite a lot. I'm just suggesting it in case you no longer feel like hearing the voice of this man from the past . . ."

Blin heard the note of irony without really knowing how he felt about it. In order to get on with the process, Joust suggested that he should arrange a series of appointments so that he could meet his anaesthetist, draw up a preliminary account, and define as clearly as possible the various alterations to his face.

"For a significant change, you not only have to work on the soft tissue but also on the bone in order to add or take away prominent areas. It's what's called a mask-lift. Then, you have to restore the muscle- and skin-tone of the face in the frontal, facial and cervical areas. We could start with a cervico-facial lift and a frontal lift if you want a real change of look."

Blin heard only the last words: *change of look*. The rest flitted away instantly.

"When we restore the muscle tone in the outside corner of the eye, we could add a slight oriental touch. Shall I show you?"

He drew the outline of Blin's eyes on a white sheet of paper, then a few arrows to indicate where he would operate; something appeared out of this vague sketch, a new look which was indefinable, perhaps a little softer and probably more harmonious, already real.

135

"We'll remove the excess fatty deposits which make the eyelids look hooded, and we'll get rid of the bags under the eyes. We'll also take the opportunity to smooth out that little bump on the nose, wouldn't you say?"

"Yes."

"Personally, I can't see anything else that needs doing to the nose. It's a fine, narrow nose, there's no need to improve it apart from that little filing job. On the other hand, your chin's a bit weak. I would suggest bringing it out a bit by adding some bulk to it, a little silicon implant. I could do the same with your cheekbones – have a look at this."

He showed him slides of his previous operations. *Before* and, more particularly, *after*. The most disturbing thing about these faces was neither the erasing of wrinkles nor the smoothness of the skin, but the gleam in the depths of the eyes, which said a great deal about the serenity the patients had found. Listening to Dr Joust, everything that had until then seemed unthinkable to Blin became a formality. It was as if you could just walk into his clinic one fine day with your everyday face on and come back out a few hours later with the one you had dreamed up for yourself.

"The incisions round the eyes and the chin will follow the natural lines of your face. I'll hide the other scars in the hairline. They'll be red at first then virtually invisible. Your barber will be the only person in the world who might see them . . ."

No problem: Thierry would learn how to use the clippers to keep one eighth of an inch of hair on his head. At the same time he would get rid of this bloody beard. Soon he would have nothing left to hide.

*

"You're not there yet," said Rodier, leafing quickly through the pages.

Blin had found him at the Monseigneur, a hostess bar near the Champs-Élysées which still had a whiff of the 1970s as well as the various perfumes of women waiting; coloured lights rotated above the red sofas and the mouldings on the walls. Without trying to work out what they were doing there, Thierry waited for Rodier's reaction after reading his very first investigation report.

"You use subjective words like 'eccentric' and 'upwardly mobile' – that's your personal opinion, no one gives a damn about it. Too many conditionals as well, it makes it sound like we did bugger all. 'M Damien Lefaure should currently be under official observation.' No! Didn't you hear what my informer at the tax office said? They've got the guy in their sights *already*, the Tax Office, the Contributions Agency and the National Insurance people, and they have had for five years. That deserves the present tense, doesn't it? On the other hand, you should have put inverted commas round 'appears' in the sentence: 'Furthermore, M. Lefaure appears in the records of a company called Pixacom', because he doesn't appear officially. And also, when you say: 'M. Lefaure has declared his own incompetence', you have to be a bit more precise for whoever's going to read it – you have to dot the *i*s and cross the *t*s: '. . . which means that he is under the supervision of his wife, Mme Françoise Lefaure'. You could even drive the nail home by adding: 'he is therefore not capable of managing his assets', because that answers the question you were asked in the first place. You're not expected to develop a style, you just have to say what you've found out, and that's it."

"Where have I developed a style?"

"In the sentence: 'During a telephone conversation, we were aware of an eloquent silence from the agency's personnel when we asked for Pixacom.' What on earth is this 'eloquent silence'? What exactly was it saying, this silence?"

Thierry said nothing.

"We were aware of 'some embarrassment', that's enough. You can tell the people at the agency weren't expecting this sort of cross-checking, so *basta*."

Rodier had a kindly way of giving Thierry a rocket, with a half smile and a tone of voice at the lower end of mocking. The verdict was incontrovertible: on the right tracks, but could do better.

"What can I get you, gentlemen?" asked the barmaid.

She did not have the assurance of a manager, the speed of a waitress or the looks of a hostess. She gave people drinks without any style, stood waiting with her arms crossed, coming and going behind the bar, not really sure what to do. A red angora sweater, black stretch trousers and low-heeled brown court shoes, which she wore as if she had gone to some trouble. Thierry could see her wandering aimlessly through life for years before ending up there, a cheap dogsbody, slightly awkward and offhand. Without taking his eyes off her, Rodier spoke to Thierry with an inane grin. "Have whatever you want, it's on the house."

The words "on the house" afforded Rodier a brief but very real flush of pleasure. They were the most unthinkable words to the woman behind the bar. Nothing was ever offered on this house. It was more than a rule: it was an outright ban. Everything had a price, even smiles, because they were rare and were included in the bill.

"Catherine isn't here," she said.

138

"I know, she said she'd meet me at nine. In the meantime, give us a couple of glasses of champagne," Rodier said firmly.

Two girls who had not heard this exchange got up off their sofa and came over towards them. The one who was making for Rodier was keen for everyone to notice her red fishnet stockings and her black skirt, which was split right up to her hip. Blin had no desire to smile or talk to the other girl. She was neither pretty nor ugly, and stood thrusting her breasts forward; although she was not thirsty, she would order a drink; she wanted to make Thierry feel like touching her, but her own harsh expression let her down. The only thing she wanted was to get back home, and she was quite incapable of disguising the fact.

"Ladies," said Rodier, "we're not customers – it's the other way around: the bar has called on my services. So I'm not going to buy you a drink and you're not going to hold it against me. We're here for purely professional reasons."

The girls got down from the stools but not acrimoniously, not even making them feel guilty for getting them over there for nothing.

"Are you going to tell me what we're doing here?" asked Thierry.

"The boss needs a favour from me. And she can do me one, too. We can probably come to some sort of arrangement."

Up on the display the two bottles of whisky, the cognac, gin and vodka had not been touched for years. On the other hand, there was a huge ice bucket containing four bottles of champagne, one of which had been opened. Wanting to witness a ritual which he still did not quite understand, Thierry was disappointed not to see a single real customer come through the door.

"Who could fall into this sort of trap, apart from a tourist who's blind drunk? If I had to find a definition for the biggest turn-off in the world, this would be it."

"A man your age doesn't belong in Monseigneur. But when you get to mine, when the bill doesn't matter at all and you need complete discretion, it does the trick. I had some pretty memorable evenings here, a long time ago. But I don't recover the way I used to, and my Monique is the only person in the world I can sleep with."

A tall slim woman of about fifty with blond hair and far too much make-up came into the bar with the confidence of a manageress. She said a general hello, went behind the bar, put her coat away in a cupboard and came and put her arms round Rodier. He introduced Blin, and she kissed him with the same enthusiasm, then sat down on a stool between them. She had managed to keep an air of surprise in her eyes and a more sincere smile than all the other women there. Her black thigh boots identified her as the sort of capable woman whose natural authority no one, and particularly not Thierry, would challenge.

"What are you going to get me to drink, boys?"

"Nothing, you're getting the drinks tonight."

Amused to see the roles reversed, she ordered herself a glass of champagne.

"How do you manage to have a tan all year round in a place like this?" Rodier asked.

"It costs me a fortune, but it's worth it," she said, unbuttoning her blouse to show the contrast between her burnished skin and the white lace of her bra.

Thierry, electrified by this spontaneous gesture, understood that he now needed *this* in his life.

"Can we talk now, my Pierrot?" the woman asked.

"He works with me, you can talk."

140

"I need an ex-directory number. That's not difficult for you."

"Three thousand."

"Three thousand? Well, you'll be able to buy me a drink with that!"

Even though she was the manageress, Catherine never forgot to pose seductively: it was like a second persona which she assumed late in the afternoon and kept until dawn. Thierry would have been curious to see when this woman's sincerity and spontaneity were fully expressed.

"For this number of yours, you'll need to give me an advance of 1,500 and lend me that girl over there, in the blue dress. You can give the remaining 1,500 to her."

"Yvette?"

"I'll send her back in two hours."

Without asking for any explanation, Catherine left them to go and negotiate with the girl in question.

"Am I allowed to know what's going on?" asked Blin.

"I've got a job that's been dragging on for a long time. Believe me, I'd give a lot to get you to go instead of me. I'm even going to have a little whisky to give me the courage."

Even though Rodier had a habit of grumbling every time more work appeared on the horizon, it was rare for him to have to egg himself on like this.

"You'll have to tell me more about it. It's not so much out of curiosity, I just want to learn."

"In my line of work, you often find a problem with money is actually hiding a question of morals. This time it's the other way round: a little question of sex is hiding a major financial problem. A company director wants to be able to prove that his wife goes to a swingers' club. He couldn't care less where she spends her Sunday and Tuesday evenings, he just wants her to be at fault in the divorce proceedings so that he can keep the thirty per cent share in a company they set up together."

Blin eyed him silently.

Rodier said nothing.

"If you want to have a good time with Yvette, spare me the tall story!"

"You can't go into that sort of place alone, everyone knows that. When Yvette and I get through the door, she'll go and sit down at the bar, and I'll go and ferret round the place to find this woman. With any luck, I'll be able to get a picture of her as she's coming out."

Thierry sat listening to him with his arms crossed, about to explode laughing.

"It's like something from one of those American series where men spend their whole lives in dinner jackets and women sleep with their chauffeurs. To round off my training, you're going to tell me why you really need this girl – if it's not too personal."

"I haven't got that much imagination, everything I've said is true; at least, that's how it was presented to me. This sort of thing probably doesn't happen in the life of a framer, that's why you want to change. But it does in mine, and that's why I want to change too. And it's now or never, if this gives you second thoughts, to address moral issues and the whole caboodle. I've accepted this job, others would have turned it down, but I do turn down plenty which line the pockets of the competition. Of the seven deadly sins, there are three or four which I've made a living from up till now, and they'll do the same for you if you persevere."

Blin had not anticipated this call to order, and he sat rooted to the spot.

"This might also be an opportunity for you to back-track, to go home like a good boy, go back to your old work, which won't give you any problems with your conscience and won't disturb your peace of mind. There's still time. We still have a choice."

Yvette joined them just at the right moment, with her coat over her shoulder.

"Shall we go?" she asked.

Rodier put his jacket back on, shook Blin's hand without another thought for what he had said, and offered his arm to Yvette as they went out.

Thierry stayed alone at the bar for a minute.

There's still time.

He automatically ordered a whisky. He was told straight away that this was no longer on the house, and he shrugged. At the same time, Catherine glanced quickly over at the girls' table; Thierry had returned to the status of an everyday customer and was the only sucker there this early in the evening.

We still have a choice.

For a moment he thought of Nadine, who was waiting for him in their bed, waiting patiently, worried by the fact that he was so free in what he did and when he did it. She did not suspect anything very bad and was only worried that he might be depressed. She never raised the question, but Thierry knew that look in her eye.

"Is someone going to give me a glass of champagne?"

A girl had come to try her luck; she had curly blond hair and was wearing a black top and a red skirt. Thierry tried to imagine the story of her life: she was in love with someone who was out of work and hated himself for letting her do this sort of work, but they had to live. Since he had been following people in the street, he had fun dishing out lives as the fancy took him, as if he had the authority.

There's still time.

Come on then, have the champagne! A tiny little flute with two ice cubes in it which she just about brushed with her lips. He wondered what the next stage would be in this tiresome process, which was meant to get him drunk and ruin him while giving the girl enough to feed her for a month.

"What's your name?"

He hesitated between Thierry and Paul. No longer really the one, but still far from being the other. She could not care less about his name; Thierry had no desire to know hers. Rodier was right, all he had to do was get down from this stool, go home, and get back to Nadine and, in the morning, his little shop.

There's still time.

"Are you married?"

No reply.

"You don't have to answer."

He did not.

"Do you want another drink?"

"I'm going to have a bottle, that'll make the boss happy. But I want something in return: kisses on the neck, two or three, right now."

"You or me?"

"Both of us."

"You're a one-off."

She must have thought he needed comforting, and took hold of his shoulders to subject him to a flurry of kisses intercut with other little niceties on his neck. He rubbed his nose in the opening in her blouse so that he was filled with the smell of her perfume. He felt nothing familiar in this strange embrace, nothing sensual, just a hint of complicity with this girl who lived in such a different world.

"Well, well, my love birds," said Catherine. "I'm going to have to call the police or the fire brigade."

144

The kisser started laughing. She had fulfilled her task. Blin stroked her shoulder, paid and left.

*

"You're getting home later every night."

"Weren't you asleep?"

He collapsed into bed, fully clothed.

"Are you drunk?"

Regretting that he was not, he said no to make her think he was.

"Don't muck about with me, you stink of alcohol."

". . . So?"

The way he orchestrated their break-up with a slow process of disintegration was far more diabolical than the way Rodier's client was trying to get rid of his wife.

"We're going to have to talk."

"It can wait till tomorrow, can't it?"

He felt her moving closer and tensing as she smelled him.

He thought he could make out a couple of tears.

In the morning she would find curly blond hair on the pillow. Traces of lipstick on his collar.

The rest was a foregone conclusion.

Nicolas Gredzinski

Naked and with his eyes half closed, Nicolas found a white bathroom and took a shower to wash off – albeit unwillingly – the smell of sex that emanated from his whole body. Still streaming with water, he went and snuggled up to the beautiful woman as she slept. In this state of abandon, revealed only to Nicolas, Loraine's mystery remained intact.

As they had come out of the Lynn, they had tried to find an adjective to describe their state: they were grey. A magnificent night-sky grey, more wolf than dog, with a hint of blue. They were walking along the Seine and had seen, as if by magic, a monstrous vessel drifting towards them – the Hotel Nikko, they would discover in the morning – and had boarded it with all the arrogance of pirates, ready to take on the whole building at the least resistance. Nicolas enquired about what was in the mini-bar before even asking for a room; they went up the stairs, amused at the thought of waking anyone who thought they were safely settled at this time of night.

"Champagne?" he asked, on his knees with his head in the fridge.

"Champagne!"

What happened next was a whole new encounter. *The second time I met Loraine.* He had never in his life manoeuvred so swiftly to undress a woman; he wanted her naked as soon as possible, and the strangest thing was that with every garment that came off he felt more and more naked himself. If she was going to condemn him to knowing nothing about her life, then her body had to be revealed immediately; she did nothing to stop him. In fact she helped him with her laughter and a few gestures which facilitated the striptease and made it a hundred times more exciting. They stayed like that for a while, her completely naked, kneeling on the floor, and him in his suit and tie, slumped on a sofa. As they drank, they launched into a very frank conversation about how self-contained the middle classes were and, against all expectations, this only heightened the erotic charge of the situation. He took this time as a gift from Loraine, who was very conscious of giving so little in other areas; she agreed to show the visible part of herself completely. This gift increased her usual charm tenfold, created a new kind of complicity, swept aside Nicolas's prevarications and reconciled him to the ghosts of all the women he had not managed to undress. Hypnotized by her bare skin and her secret folds, he tried to catch every smell that came from her, a mixture of Dior and natural sweat, of make-up and intimate exhalations. It was that same smell – corrupted by his own smell, compromised by their embraces – that he found again under the sheets when he came out of the shower. If Loraine was still asleep, then she must have decided to be, so it would have been pointless and tactless to wake her and point out that the sun was up. He found the strength to break away from her, got himself dressed without taking his eyes off her little brown leather handbag, and was tempted to slip his hand inside it to unearth a few facts – was Loraine married? What the hell did she do before going and hanging out in bars? Was Loraine called Loraine? – all things that had become less urgent now that they had made love.

Nicolas was happily picturing himself sliding gently through the day with a smile on his lips and a light heart, waiting for the night and all it promised; it would not be too soon to see whether they could be so imaginative without drinking. Now he could get back into the Group, quite ready to dismiss all the tiresome people who could not resist reminding him that life is a challenge.

"Monsieur Bardane wants to see you straight away!" said Muriel.

This information seemed to be urgent. Nicolas paid absolutely no attention, picked up his mail and the usual newspapers, and sat down at his desk to review the papers. He did not need anything, not beer, or aspirin or deliverance. His good mood was enough. An hour later, Bardane knocked on his door. "You think you've scored some points with the DG, don't you?"

No need to reply, even less need to listen. Nicolas tried not smile at the sight of his decoy beer standing at an angle on his desk, right under Bardane's nose. The prototype existed – it now needed a name.

"I can spot people with ambition, I played this game long before you did."

A Canticle?

That sounds nice, Canticle. It's got the "can" in there and there's also the tease of "tickle". It would almost work. But what exactly is a canticle? It's something they sing in church, isn't it? Have to steer clear of religious connotations.

"You have a problem with authority, Nicolas."

A Tubiline?

It's catchy, but it's not going to work in many languages. Decoy beer has an international career ahead of it. I need a name that's going to work well worldwide.

"Anyone who wants out can go and try their chances somewhere else."

Ah, I've got it!
Trickpack!
It's perfect! It sounds like something that's always existed. It's got something gadgety about it. Doesn't everyone have a Trickpack?

"Please don't force me to ask for your resignation."

Bardane left under Nicolas's absent gaze. The decoy beer had been christened! He needed to register its birth right away. Before leaving the building, he rang Alissa.

"I'm calling back, as promised, about your proposal. That's fine."

*

National Institute of Patent Rights, 26b Rue de Saint-Pétersbourg. Nicolas went into the tall grey building with great solemnity, and wandered through the corridors for a while before going to reception, where he was handed a form for registering a patent, with information on how to proceed. He sat himself down in a large circular room like a beehive with a desk in each cell, a few tables for reading and filling in the forms, and things to read on the walls to while away the waiting. Before stepping through the Institute's doors, he had stopped at the nearest café, just long enough to laugh at the absurdity of what he was doing and to dissolve the last of his inhibitions in a glass of brandy. This time the ethanol was no longer helping him to overcome his anxiety or giving him his own free will, it was providing him with the means to see his fanciful idea through to the end, to give it some substance, institutionalize it.

He read through a first leaflet, *Patents: Protecting Your Invention*, where the very notion of invention

149

was explained: you cannot register an idea but its application. Then he read *How to Register a Request for a Patent,* which listed every step he had to take, and he soon decided it was too complicated for him to tackle alone; he was told that he would be able to get some help from the offices of the Inventors' Association.

He was tempted to back down. *Inventors' Association!* Him, a little cog in the huge machine, a worker ant in the community, a brick in the great pyramid, an insignificant part of the whole, how was he going to find the courage to step through the door of the Inventors' Association? As he walked down the corridor he heard the jeers of all the men of science and progress who had contributed to the well-being of the human race.

A young employee greeted him and gave him some practical advice to nudge him in the right direction.

"Which category would your invention fall into: mechanical, chemical, electrical, electronic or information technology?"

By elimination, Nicolas replied: the first. The young man did not ask for any more details and explained exactly how he should put together his file: fill in the patent request form, write a precise description of his invention, and have it looked over by one of the Institute's engineers. A meeting was arranged for the following day, to give Nicolas time to struggle with a written description of his invention. He was greeted twenty-four hours later by Mme Zabel, who read his text.

DESCRIPTION

The present invention puts forward a sliding sheath to cover metal cans of soda, fruit juice or beer, which

150

could be used to display texts, images or inlaid designs. It slips over any standard size can of drink, so as to hide the brand.

The device consists principally of a cylinder with an interior diameter slightly larger than the exterior diameter of a standard can of drink, and exactly the same height as the main cylinder so that it can slide over the latter.

Depending on the specific design, it may also include:

– Above the standard cylinder, a chamfered section below a vertical rim a quarter of an inch deep, mimicking – with a slightly larger diameter – the chamfering and the rim of cans. In this case, the object of this invention would adhere to the can by adjusting the dimensions and the amount of give in the materials used.

– Along the lower edge, a chamfered area mimicking – with a slightly larger diameter – the chamfering at the base of a can, as well as a flat or concave base.

– Along the upper edge, a chamfered section below a vertical rim a quarter of an inch deep, mimicking – with a slightly larger diameter – the chamfering and the rim of cans, and along the lower edge, a system for keeping it attached to the can of drink in the chamfered lower half.

– It will generally constitute a cylinder which corresponds to the entire height of a can, or some part of that height, with or without a base, in such a way that it can slide over the can and cover it.

To Nicolas's amazement, Mme Zabel asked him to make very few alterations; this was enough to make him feel almost like an inventor. On his request form, he had made a mistake, though: in the "Name of Invention" box he had put "Trickpack".

151

"That might eventually be the name of a registered trademark. What we need here is an objective name."

For want of anything better, he opted for "drinks can cover", for fear of suggesting "decoy beer". She checked through the form very seriously, which was irrefutable proof that it was acceptable. She clattered on her computer keyboard for a moment to bring up the patents that might be similar to Nicolas's, and found only two.

"You could stop by at the information department for more details, but it doesn't look as if there's much of a problem."

She gave him a few contacts to put him in touch with manufacturers who might be interested in the patent. At the information department, Nicolas consulted two registers, both of which described inventions intended to help with opening and using cans, no comparison with his "drinks can cover". He stopped at the Registration office, paid his 250-franc fee and left the Institute. He felt, at last, like an inventor.

*

"Apparently, the network went down over half of the fifth floor of the central tower."

"Didn't hear about it," said José. "Did it affect you, Monsieur Marcheschi?"

"Did it affect me! Do you really want to know?"

No one saw fit to say they did not. Nicolas could see he was ready to launch into an illustration of his incomparable merits.

"The power cut happened between ten past and half past three precisely. You must know there's a law you can do nothing about, you can call it Murphy's law or Sod's law, the law of butter-side down. Anyway, everyone knows this law, which means the worst possible outcome has an inevitability we can do nothing about. If you can believe it, since February I've been poised on the brink of finalizing negotiations with a company in Milan called Cartamaggiore. The man I've been dealing with is the formidable Franco Morelli, who I knew at Harvard Business School. He favours me because we studied together – *esprit de corps,* at least there are some good things in life! – but if there's the tiniest hitch, he could always turn to Ragendorf in Frankfurt and they would make him an offer at least equivalent to mine. Franco won't give up on any part of the negotiations. He's like me, only worse."

Polite laughter, just to give him time to draw breath.

"We need an initial document to settle the principal terms, I invite him to the Plaza so that I can put together this letter of intent, he submits it to his board of directors and gets their backing. Over a period of two months I have a lot of trouble getting the complementary technical information out of the Italians, but things are coming along, until today . . . when I need to go back over a few points in this famous document. It's ten past three, I switch on my computer, open the file and underline the points I'm interested in. I want to make this text as easy as possible to read, so God knows what gets into me but I change the font. All I have to do now is click on *Enter.* I have no idea why but I click on . . . *Delete.*"

"No!"

"You didn't?"

Nicolas could not believe his ears. Was Marcheschi's story actually about failure?

"It seems absurd, but it's the truth: the whole text disappeared! Some of you will think, quite rightly, that

153

this wasn't just a slip of the finger but the perfect deliberate mistake, I wanted to frighten myself, to see these negotiations somehow threatened, I don't know. I won't deny the subconscious element in what I did, but I won't go any further with psychological analysis: the damage was done."

"You could always have used *Undo* and the text would have reappeared," said Arnaud. "You must have known that."

"Of course I knew, but that was when Murphy's law came into play. When I was about to click on *Undo*, it was ten past three and the whole network went off in my sector. In case you weren't aware of this, my dear Arnaud, when the computer comes back on, it's too late to click on *Undo*."

"Didn't you have any copies?"

"Yes, that's just it, now this really illustrates Murphy's law: I had a copy. Dripping with sweat, I go through all my drawers and find it, I rush to the first computer I can find, put the diskette in and I see the words: *Illegible disk. Do you want to initialize?*"

"That's really tough," said Régine.

"Like you say."

"So?"

"So, I couldn't see myself calling Morelli back to say, 'By the way, if we should suppress the preferential subscription rights, what did we agree on the maximum number of shares reserved?' He'd think I was completely incompetent and be on to Ragendorf within the hour."

"Is there more?"

Nicolas would have given anything for there not to have been. He would have seen Marcheschi as a human being, human and fallible enough to recover a bit of respect for him. Instead of this, Marcheschi pronounced a long drawn out *yes* to reignite their interest.

"If I had the teeniest chance of getting out of this, I had to try it. I open a new file and go back over all the points of the negotiation one by one. In an emergency like that the thing we call our memory suddenly becomes a fierce precision tool whose strength has never before been appreciated. Today, for the first time in my life, I really had a conversation with my memory. I spoke to it, out loud, asked it questions, gently, like a child, trying to earn its trust. *If the sector is valued at 10 per cent of the Group's market capitalization, with less than 2 per cent after complementary audit evaluations, the capital increase is 32 per cent and for outside investors: X is at 13 per cent, Y at 12 per cent and Z at 7.5 per cent.* My subconscious may have initiated this catastrophe, but it was that same subconscious that went to dig out the information from where it was hiding. *Franco had asked for . . . 22 per cent, when in this country the legal maximum is 15 per cent. Taking paragraph 5 as a condition to the contract, we have a two-thirds majority and an extra seat.* I experienced this peculiar phenomenon which felt like wandering round an old hangar filled with millions of files and trying to find the right ones with a pocket torch. I had to do it, otherwise the world would fall apart; or mine would, anyway. I don't know whether I should thank God, Freud or the fact that I've always eaten a lot of fish, but the end product of this whole saga went off to Milan by e-mail just over two hours ago now. Franco rang me back to tell me his boss agreed on every point. And here I am, loyal as ever, just about to have my second pastis with all of you."

For Nicolas the worst bit was probably that last little touch. Every time Marcheschi treated them to one of his pompous and elaborate descriptions of his own exploits, why did he feel the need to end it with: *And here I am, loyal as ever, just about to have my second pastis with all of you.* Having saved the world, he honoured them with his presence, simple mortals that they were, dazzled by his combination of brilliance and modesty.

Nicolas could not let him get away with it.

"For many years Alexander Solzhenitsyn wrote thousands of pages when he was living in fear of being arrested. To save on paper and to hide his texts from the KGB, he wrote in little green notebooks – he wasn't allowed white paper – and managed to fit about sixty lines of minute writing on every page. He was forty-two years old and suffering from lung cancer when he was sent to the Gulag. During his eight years of detention he no longer had any paper but he carried on writing . . . without actually writing. 'No man knows his own abilities nor those of his memory,' he would say later. To teach himself how to memorize things, he wrote poems in series of twenty verses, which he learned by heart, day after day. He used rosary beads (which the guards let him keep) to help himself do it, making each bead represent a certain number of verses. He remembered 12,000 verses like that, and spent ten days a month running through all of them to turn his memory into an absolutely unique tool. It was with that tool and his courage, his talent and his powers of resistance that he finally managed to 'write' prose, to hold it in his head for the duration of his detention and to reproduce it word for word years later. Alexander Solzhenitsyn experienced the three greatest scourges of the twentieth century: war, labour camps and cancer. When he was over eighty, his impenetrable handwriting still hadn't changed."

Instead of shaking his hand, Marcheschi gave him a little nod as he left the table. The day was far from over

156

and Nicolas still felt like drinking till his insides burned, but not here, not now. He knew exactly where and with whom.

Why should he be deprived of seeing Loraine and her blue eyes? Because of a headache in the morning? Or because of feeling a bit tired round about 11 o'clock? He was forty years old, he was young, he was old, he had experience and had a lot still to learn, everything was starting for real, it was still too soon to deprive himself of anything. What was the point of this sensible attitude, which made him want to fall into line from the moment he got up? What was the point of living if the moments of pure pleasure did not take priority over everything else? On Judgment Day, God would forgive him everything except for failing to make the most of this strange gift He had given mankind. Before dawn, Nicolas would make love with Loraine, and never mind if life seemed terrifying when he woke up. I mean, who could guarantee that tomorrow the sun would rise anyway?

"Hello, Loraine? Am I disturbing you?"

"Not at all, I really want to have a drink with a certain gentleman who'll do everything I ask of him."

"The Lynn in twenty minutes?"

"What about going back to that hotel? If we feel like touching each other at all, we'll have to be ultra precise in describing what it is we want."

Her request did not need any reply. How could he not agree with the proposed programme? He tried to guess what she was doing at that precise moment; his imagination made him hear various different things in succession: a child crying, the public address system in a station, another woman whispering, a man sighing. Nicolas had become the victim of strange symptoms, unconsciously imitating his lover so that he too now had a taste for secrecy; a naive way of trying to prove to himself that they were made to get along. The previous evening, as he lay with his cheek on the pillow in a state of utter abandon, he had enjoyed speculating about Loraine's identity. The game had popped up of its own accord as he held her in his arms.

"You don't have hands like a surgeon."

"You don't wear the right perfume to be a housewife and mother."

"You haven't got the shoulders of a swimming instructor."

"You don't dress like a teacher."

"You're not as hairy as the Mediterraneans."

"You don't make love like a northener."

"You're not Sherlock Holmes!"

"You're not Mata Hari."

For want of anything better, he settled for creating a character which he could alter to suit his mood. Sometimes he would see her as a housewife, leading a string of children whom she would abandon at about six in the evening, leaving them with an obliging husband so that she could go and quench her thirst for solitude and wine. Sometimes she would be a man-eater, Paris crammed with her lovers, and occasionally people walking along the Seine would see the body of one of these unfortunates floating by. Sometimes she would be his own neighbour from his apartment block, who had been endlessly imaginative to hide the fact from him. With a girl like her, anything was possible.

Less than an hour later, as they sprawled on the bed in front of CNN news, she had snuggled into the crook of his shoulder riveted by the deployment of troops in some far-off country. Before nightfall Nicolas had been able to see Loraine's body in natural light. A little more rounded than the one he had made out the day before, which was not a bad thing. Her buttocks and legs only slightly filled out, her hips nicely curved, breasts which swayed the moment she moved. Shapes which had the raw appeal of African idols and which excited instinctive desires. All things he had not been able to appreciate the night before, overrun by drink and in the clutches of the inevitable turmoil of the first time. Fully clothed, Loraine was a city type who knew how to behave and what to do. Naked, she was robust as a woman of the land. When Nicolas held her to him, he dicovered earthly powers he had always been missing.

She switched the television off and drew the curtains. It was time for their bodies really to get to know each other, to become more familiar. Later in the night, they ordered lots of tramezzinis and a bottle of wine.

"I've had a Château Talbot."

"Which year?"

" '82."

"Bastard! It's a masterpiece!"

Between two mouthfuls, between two sips of Chablis, between two images on the screen with the sound turned off, between two bursts of laughter, they made love. Much later, she slid under the sheet, found Nicolas's hand, put it over her left breast, and closed her eyes. Her breathing became deeper and deeper, slower and slower; he felt her drifting away.

He savoured one last mouthful of wine, in silence, happy. He now knew what he was looking for when he was drunk: it was not the *detachment* of the third glass but the here and now of the first, staying there as long as possible. He did not need that big-night-out sort of drunkenness, the one that unleashes passions and flirts with the absolute, is timeless and stands outside life itself. His intoxication had its head in the clouds but its

159

feet on the ground. He did not long to lose all his faculties like most alcoholics, he wanted exactly the opposite, to get right up close to the moment and to appropriate it, like this evening, in that bed, next to the sleeping body of the woman who made his heart beat. He allowed himself to live in the present without asking whether it might be a trap or whether he would have to pay for it later. At last the evidence was there for him to see, and he started to dream of a tomorrow where all that really mattered would be there when he woke up. If he could just capture that evidence, to keep snatches of it, he might manage to keep his everyday confusion at bay. If only he could hang on to the message of its sweet euphoria through until morning . . .

If only.

An extraordinary idea came to him, an idea that was just too simple. Without even thinking twice, without taking his left hand off Loraine's breast, he grabbed from the bedside table the headed paper and the biro with the hotel's name on it. He wrote what came into his head, put the pad back down, pressed himself up against Loraine, buried his face in her neck and went to sleep.

When he woke up she was no longer there. He was not surprised by this and tried to find her smell on the pillow. Suddenly he looked up, fumbled over by the bedside table to get the pad, and made out what he had written the night before:

Take what Loraine offers you without trying to find out more about her.

Remember to clean your shoes at least once a month.

In the B file, use Cécile's idea on the IBM project, turn it

160

around a bit and let the marketing people think they got it right before anyone else.

If you spend too long listening to the storm brewing without actually breaking, you'll waste your life waiting for some disaster which will never happen.

What a perfect feeling: he had found a friend.

Thierry Blin

He had never been so frightened as he was that morning. The moment he woke up he had to battle with his own overpowering fear by persuading himself he was a good man, a man who saw his dreams as reality and his longings as orders. On the way to the clinic he almost managed to convince himself. His fears regained the upper hand, however, when the nurse asked him to put on the strange white nightshirt which tied up at the back like a straitjacket.

At precisely 8 o'clock, he went into the clinic's admissions office and was treated to a Vermeiren in every sentence. He was then shown to his room, where he anxiously answered all the questions asked by a woman dressed in white, who made sure he took a pill to help him relax. Psychiatry has inventoried the different kinds of sick mind which lose touch with themselves, and it has given them complicated names – his condition must have had one of its own. If he had known this wretched word, he might have tried to find a cure – he just needed to be in a different department. Rodier had given him one last chance to change everything on the spot, perhaps Joust would too? The latter came in, drawled a few words out of habit and started tracing lines on his patient's face in silence. The tranquillizer was beginning to take effect; even if he had still wanted to, Blin could no longer change his mind. All of a sudden his shoulders dropped and his whole body started to float. A rapt smile spread across

162

his lips when he saw someone approaching with a stretcher. In the operating theatre, he looked in Joust's eye one last time; it already did not matter any more, as if Blin's consciousness were slowly leaving his body to slip into Vermeiren's. The anaesthetist injected a whitish fluid into his vein, making his arm feel warm, and he asked him to count to five. It was the last face he saw before losing his own.

*

He had not invented this pain, it really was there but it was not making him suffer, it was keeping itself busy, without waking him. He was every piece of his body at the same time, his veins, his blood, his heart, which was beating slowly; he was his muscles and his own sleeping strength.

*

Someone put a damp compress over his lips; something a woman would do, he thought. He could sense her moving about the room from small signs: the clink of a glass, the squeak of her shoes on the parquet, her clearing her throat. He desperately wanted to open his eyes but his eyelids remained sealed, which was terrifying. If he had still had the strength, he would have given in to panic, but the bandaging round his jaw meant he could not cry out. Another dose of painkillers and tranquillizers soothed him.

Not being able to speak again for the rest of his life would not have mattered to him all that much. The power of speech? He didn't give a damn. After all, he was only an *eye*, that had become his job and in that job the less you talked the better it was. Spotting, grasping, discerning, catching. The rest was just photos you could show in silence because they needed no commentary, a report you typed out trying to find exactly the right word. No need to speak. Discretion guaranteed.

Towards the end of the afternoon, he heard different footsteps, more assertive.

"It's me," said Joust. "Don't try to speak. I've come to see if everything's all right with your eyesight. Don't worry if your eyelids are a bit stuck together, that's normal."

Thierry felt the doctor's fingers opening his eyes. A hazy beam of light sharpened the pain. Having set his mind at rest, Joust put the bandage back in position.

"Everything's fine. Have a good night. I'll be here at 9 o'clock in the morning."

Before leaving the room, Joust asked the nurse whether she was on duty for the night.

"No, it's Inès, sir."

The thought of being watched over by an Inès comforted Thierry, who fell asleep for several hours.

*

The night had been heavy with dreams, but none of them stayed with him, not even one image; perhaps a tired, distant memory punctuated by sips of water and waves of anxiety cut dead by the sleeping draught. He had heard the faraway sound of a radio from a neighbouring room, a halo of music which made his internal journey feel somehow like a treasure hunt. Still not sure that he had found the treasure, he had dug and delved; his exhausted limbs were proof of that.

Joust took his bandages off in one swift move, and checked that his incisions had not let him down. Blin managed to open his eyes a little; the layout of the room came back to him as a series of impressions, and his eyes came to rest on a little red bottle.

"I've put a drain into the forehead to drain off the blood. It's already stopped flowing."

He had not felt anything round his forehead, apart from a belt of discomfort, which he had put down to the bandaging.

"You could say a few words if you'd like to."

He declined with a shake of his head.

"I suppose you'd like to see yourself? I could hold a mirror up for you, but you'll see nothing but wounds. Everything went very well, but you may find it quite a shock. Well?"

He shook his head again. He was not all that impatient to see his face in the raw. Vermeiren was not completely finished, and he was afraid that Blin might be shocked by him. Before slipping back into his mummified state, he tried to read Inès's expression. Perhaps – somewhere between the strips of flesh, the cuts, staples and trickles of blood – she could already see Vermeiren's unfinished face.

Thierry had spent the last few days before the operation feeling cocooned. The world was hazy, the sounds of the city and the people around him muffled. In fact he had watched himself doing things as if he were already no longer Blin, but had Vermeiren walking beside him, ready to take over. Paul Vermeiren had legally existed for more than a week now, with an identity card and a birth certificate. Claiming professional interest while he went through files with Rodier, Blin had extracted precious information about how false papers were made and how to get hold of them. Rodier had given the names and areas of expertise of a few specialists who were known for their reliability. Of these, those who were most in demand created false identities using real cards stolen from issuing offices. In return for a crippling sum, they could provide a whole set of false papers which were undetectable because they were real. Thierry Blin had been prepared to pay. His first act as a citizen was to open a bank account in the name of Paul Vermeiren and to put 150,000 francs into it – the under-the-table payment on the sale of the house in Juvisy. He had been carefully emptying out two-thirds of his old bank account, taking cash payments week by week for a year, which gave him 400,000 francs. Part of this money had been used to pay for Joust, his false papers, the deposit on his new home and the lease on his future agency. He had not been able to sell off anything from Blin's life for fear of awakening suspicions, not even the drawings and lithographs that had been lying forgotten at the back of his shop for years. He could have got a good price for them from a specialist secondhand shop which did not care where things came from, but the formidable Brigitte, his accountant, would soon have noticed had they gone. Since she had been working for the new manager at the shop, she had tried to see Thierry again by claiming there was some issue with taxes. She missed him, she just did not have the courage to admit it to him.

"Tell me, Mademoiselle, this boy's not giving you too much trouble, is he?"

"He's a good worker, he understands everything I tell him, he keeps the books up to date – a perfect client. He's just deadly boring."

"A few more months and I'll be back."

One thing he had always liked about her was her doll-like figure; she knew this and was trying to play on it, now more than ever. Her long hair, her high cheekbones and peachy pink cheeks, her shiny satin dresses

. . . He would never have imagined the real reason she wanted to see him: having heard that Nadine had left him, Brigitte had come to try her own chances with him. Instead of which, he simply signed the papers she handed him, without even looking at her.

On the morning he went into the clinic he had left the apartment in Convention leaving some valuable pieces of jewellery in a drawer, a cooling cup of coffee on the corner of a table, a book open on a coffee table, and a window still ajar. Nothing to make anyone think he had been planning to leave.

What happened next followed a script he had rewritten endlessly until he had perfected it. The concierge, amazed to see the mail piling up, called Nadine, who came and opened the apartment with the key Thierry had given her. She then went to the police station to register his disappearance. She filled in the form, gave the most accurate description possible, without forgetting distinguishing features (the V-shaped scar to the right of his groin which intrigued her and disgusted her at the same time), and gave them a recent photograph, probably the big black-and-white one that she had taken for her collection of portraits. The Missing Persons Bureau took over from there, calling the hospitals, the mortuary, the missing man's doctor and dentist, going to his apartment and questioning some of his friends, perhaps also some customers from The Blue Frame. Vermeiren knew the figures: of the 3,000 people who went missing in the Paris area every year, five per cent of cases were never solved. He had played all the cards to make sure he was one of those 150 people and fell into the "pointless to search" category until the end of time.

*

Paul Vermeiren could have come out twenty-four hours after the operation but, worried about ending up alone with himself when he did not really know who he was, felt happier spending an extra night at the clinic. Joust was satisfied with what he had seen of his patient's face and suggested an appointment the very next day – Day 3 according to his calculations – to take the stitches out of his eyelids, and another one, Day 7, for those under his eyes. They would then see each other only once more, on Day 15, to take the staples out of his mouth, chin and cheekbones. As well as the bandages which completely covered his face, Joust advised him to wear a tightly fitting hood between now and then to avoid any problems around the forehead. Looking like something from a horror film, he went back through the admissions department and asked for a taxi.

"To take you where?"

"4 Allée des Favorites at Cholong-sur-Cèze."

He clarified this for the nurse, who could not have cared less: "That's where I live."

*

"You'll be happy here."

These simple words from the estate agent, who was too prosaic to be dishonest, had made his mind up. Why pass up on the opportunity to be happy somewhere, and why should it not be in a simple house way out in the suburbs in what seemed like a patch of countryside: a little place surrounded by trees, beyond the village and timeless. Three of the windows overlooked a tiny road no one ever used, the others looked out over the garden, which had no clear boundaries. A weeping willow, two pine trees, a magnificent maple

168

and a cherry tree. Paul felt like an ageing country squire still clinging to his land to console himself for all the other privileges he had lost. The house was sound and just the right size for him: a sitting room with a fireplace which took up one whole wall, a bedroom which looked out over the garden, and a kitchen which smelled of wood and ash.

Thierry Blin had actually always been the city type. He had wanted to be at the heart of things, in the place from which all the arteries flowed, and even if the beating of that heart had sometimes been too insistent, he could not have contemplated living anywhere else. The world had been beneath his windows; he had felt he was in the bull's eye. He had always been afraid of missing something and thought he had enough energy to face up to the big city. Since humans themselves had become his bread and butter, he had wanted the exact opposite; after days and nights of tailing people, of nervous tension and complications, he needed to set his head straight, far from the madness of others.

Paradox: since his exile, he had never felt so close to Paris. If he could see that City of Light from the top of the bell-tower at Cholong, what was the point of having it at his feet? How can you get a feel for a city when you are caught up in all its torments? Babylon is only Babylon when you see it from afar.

Lying on a chaise longue with his nose in the air, a tartan rug over his knees and a book in his hand, he was waiting out his convalescence in peace. He went back to the kitchen to check on his cauliflower cheese and to open his mail, which had the name Vermeiren all over it. Paul Vermeiren existed as far as society was concerned. The mechanism had set in motion of its own accord. You just had to respect a few rules, to ask nothing of anyone, and never complain. Then, the odd extra citizen went completely unnoticed.

"Is that a Flemish name?" the Telecom employee asked him when he came to install the line.

"It's Dutch originally, but quite a long way back."

All he had left on his face were a few plasters at the corners of his temples. He no longer found it difficult looking himself in the face. The brown contacts gave his eyes a full, deep gaze which sat well with his hair and the texture of his skin – these were the eyes he should always have had, and their slightly elongated shape made his whole face smile, giving it a malicious twinkle. Paul was more proud of his chin than anything else; it gave him a legitimacy, an assurance he had always lacked, a boost to his virility, an unexpected completeness which meant he would never again need the camouflage of a beard. He took pleasure in shaving and massaging his utterly hairless cheeks. Every three days, he ran the clippers over his head, a technique he had mastered straight away. In some places the scars itched terribly, reminding him there was a seam there – but not enough of one to make him feel like a monster. He saw his face asserting itself every day in the mirror. Sometimes, Blin would catch him unawares somewhere beneath the features in a fleeting expression. But this Blin was smoothed, anamorphic and so far away now. Even the glint in his eye had almost disappeared, like a tiny ember going out behind a veil of ashes.

Paul Vermeiren found time for everything and was enthusiastic about everything: cooking, walks, reading under a tartan rug, evenings by the fireside, nights spent watching films, interminable lie-ins, hot baths at any time of day or night. His convalescence even gave him the time to test some long-held dreams and to

170

clear up a few mysteries. He had always wondered how something could stay up in the air, revolving on its own axis, describing a curve, making a complete revolution and coming back to the hand. Perhaps he was not too old to achieve miracles. Every day he learned how to throw a boomerang, on his own with a book open at his feet. He saw this movement as a combination of science, elegance and humility in the face of nature; as a way of paying homage to the mysteries of physics, which fascinated even our primitive forebears. Like a true aborigine, Paul took time checking the feel of the wind, taming it, and circling trees with his deft parabolas. During the hours of apprenticeship when his boomerang disappeared in the undergrowth, he would scour great expanses of meadow with all the patience of a water diviner. The locals would say hello and watch, amused, as he threw – a fad? the latest craze from Paris? – not realizing for a moment that this man was recreating a ritual gesture which pre-dated tractors and cows and perhaps even green grass.

*

"I'll see you again on Day 60, and that will probably be the last time," Joust told him on the morning of Day 30. Clearly proud of his creation, the good doctor asked whether he could take photographs to impress future customers. Vermeiren refused with some regret. Back in his car, he drove beneath the windows of the apartment in Convention, curious to see whether it had already been let, then he stopped for a moment outside the café where he and Nadine used to meet. That was where they had spoken to each other for the last time on Day –5, when they had been apart for four months.

171

"How are you?"

"Fine."

"That blue dress is new."

"I saw Anne wearing it, and I wanted the same one. She sends her love."

No, she doesn't send me her love, she thinks I should get some therapy. She's your best friend, you can't really blame her, she's annoyed with me.

"Don't let her forget she's still got my cotton overall, I really liked that one."

That's a detail you'll remember at the police station. A man who's asking to have his cotton overall back isn't thinking of staging a disappearance.

"What are we going to do about this health insurance business?"

"If I could stay on yours for a few more months, just until I go back to work."

". . . You're going back to work?"

"I've had enough of doing bugger all."

"Are you getting bored, then?"

You're surprised, aren't you? I made it look as if I found my nightly outings fascinating. I may even have gone a bit far. You tried to understand, to talk to me about a mid-life crisis, about the way I wanted to put myself in danger. What happened next made it look as if you were right.

"I might go back to The Blue Frame."

"If you have trouble with the rent, I could always let you have some money for now."

"No, it's fine, I've got enough to see me through."

You know perfectly well that I've borrowed money from friends, and they're sure they'll never see it again. They talked to you about it, which was the whole point of the exercise.

"Don't be embarrassed with me, will you? If you're in debt. . . ."

"Debt, what debt?"

172

"Apparently you're still playing . . ."

Pretty good going, I would say!

"Look, just drop this, Nadine . . . Tell me what you're up to. How's your new apartment?"

"It's on the Rue de Prony, really close to work. It's changed my life so much, I can't believe it."

You still haven't met anyone, but it won't be long, I can tell, you want to captivate someone again.

"Are you in a hurry, Nadine? Do you want a cup of coffee?"

"I have to get home."

When they come to find you to tell you I've disappeared, don't forget anything, the smell of alcohol and sweet perfumes, the ties I used to put in my pocket for when I was going out, my bank account drained in less than a year and – especially – the credit card receipts showing the address of a brothel which I made sure I left lying about on my bedside table. Say things like: "He must have got involved with some shady characters who made life difficult for him." You won't need to lie, you'll be very convincing.

"I'm having a little house-warming party a week on Friday. Would you like to come along?"

"Friday the 17th? I'm not doing anything, I'll make a note. I'll make some zakouski."

I'll have a face full of bandaging, but I'll be thinking of you all. And you in particular.

Nicolas Gredzinski

Nicolas woke up that morning with the appetite of a truly happy man, not a feeling he recognized. Loraine had left the hotel long before he woke, thereby depriving him of the spectacle of her breakfast in bed – when she was still only just awake she craved fresh fruit, buttered toast, tea and everything – a ceremony he had taken a liking to without touching anything on the tray himself; distracting her with a few caresses while she tasted the jam with a finger was enough for him. To wake up feeling hungry in your belly, you really had to like life, he thought. With his face buried in Loraine's pillow, he succumbed to a few thrusts of his pelvis, making the most of a morning erection.

They had been seeing each other on average three evenings a week for more than a year. Most of the time they ended the evening in this same hotel and, out of habit, they asked for Room 318, which had provided a haven for their first moments together. Nicolas made sure he was available whenever Loraine was, with no set days. When he tried to make sense of some clues, they would contradict each other the next time; she obeyed some logic known only to her which made her everyday life unfathomable. With time, he had grown used to it, even though during the course of each day he would have given everything to know what she was doing at that exact moment.

Still, he did have to recognize the fact that mornings were far easier than before. Waking up alone no longer really mattered since that famous night when Loraine had disappeared even before the sun was up. In her usual capable way, she had managed to find a solution to a problem which had been dividing couples for generations.

"I have to get up at about five tomorrow."

"I'll ask reception for a wake-up call."

"No you won't, you'll never get back to sleep."

She was right. The moment Nicolas became aware that the world existed, there was no longer any way of denying it, it had to be endured. That was the story of his life. The subsequent negotiations ("but it really doesn't matter, I promise/it seems a pity, are you sure/it honestly doesn't bother me/you could have another two hours' sleep after I've left," etc) had come to an abrupt end when Loraine had an inspired idea and picked up her mobile.

"If I programme the alarm to go off at five and put the phone under my pillow on vibrate mode . . ."

He could not understand her machinations and went off to sleep, telling her she was mad. Two hours later, while he was swimming through a lake populated with fabulous creatures, Loraine felt slight vibrations near her left ear and woke up. She kissed her sleeping lover on the temples and tiptoed out while it was still dark. Nicolas could go on dreaming of all kinds of paradise lost. There was no doubt about it, this was a giant leap for mankind.

Even without her imagination, he was in love with the element of freedom in her, which manifested itself in the most unexpected ways. A funny little meaningless sentence which did him the world of good, a disconcerting gesture which was actually far more calculated that it appeared, some brainwave which was shrugged off as absurd for fear of being taken too seriously.

Loraine was not the only person to restore his confidence in himself. "The man in the night", his feverish alter ego who sent him messages, now watched over him. Nicolas had initially hated this incandescent *Other* who drank and then landed him with the hangover, who burned the midnight oil without a thought for the mess in the morning. With time, he had learned to listen to him and to make a friend of him. How did he have all this knowledge that Nicolas missed from day to day? How did he manage to orchestrate improvisation and a sense of rhythm while putting everything in perspective? Where did he get his skill for walking the tightrope of living for the moment? How was he the only philosopher in the world who understood everything? Nicolas owed it to himself to be in touch with his Mr Hyde as often as possible, to follow his teaching and benefit from his experience. Like someone rushing to open a letter box, before he even got out of bed he would reach for the little black book in which the *Other* – serene and happy as he watched Loraine sleeping – had scribbled a few decisive lines in the night. There was a bit of everything on those pages: orders, self-evident facts which needed to be repeated, everyday decisions which found their solutions there, but also a few lyrical flights of fancy, written down quite shamelessly because they were sincere.

Before having his shower, he opened the notebook. As usual, he remembered nothing.

People who give you funny looks when you're drinking whisky have no greater ambition in life than to place the word "whisky" on the Scrabble board.

Go back to the dentist. I really mean it.

176

We all say: "I don't care what happens after I've gone," but we're all very keen to know what does happen!

He left the hotel and went on foot to the towers of the Parena empire, stopping at the coffee shop to buy two croissants and a cold beer. He had his breakfast in his office, and felt that his life was utterly coherent. He loved Loraine, but he also liked the thought that people he knew would warn him against this she-devil of a woman. He liked the taste of beer in the morning, he liked hiding it in his Trickpack, and he liked imagining the looks on his colleagues' faces if they found out that his Coke was 6% vol. He liked his most recent discoveries, he already liked the progress he still had to make on the path to inner peace, and – over and above everything else – he liked the opportunity he had been given to become the man he deserved to be. The night, like the others before it, had been short and Nicolas waited discreetly for the little whiplash he would get from the fizz of the hop, a true pleasure every morning which he had taken to as naturally as a cup of tea or a clean shirt. The bubbles were already going to his head, and dancing round in little clusters.

The time had come to devote all his energy to work. His appointment to head up the art department did not really need any consideration; he felt no pressure from his new responsibilities, and played things by ear, trying to give solidarity preference over every kind of authority. He made the mistake of thinking that trust is a good basis on which to operate, and took into account the majority views. Bardane had had a knack for promising the impossible to the client and then allowing himself the luxury of twisting a few ears if no one came up with a miraculous solution. Nicolas had wasted too much time to fall into the same rut. He always asked what the person in charge of production thought, as well as consulting the artistic department, which was made up of three women and two men, all graphic designers and all more or less the same age. He had fun testing the much vaunted concept of "synergy". He had never been a leader, and for as far back as he could remember he had always avoided the idea of competition: he had never distinguished himself at tennis, had never come to blows over a parking space and had generally never looked for any form of promotion. Only someone with as little grasp of psychology as Bardane could suspect Gredzinski of being ruthlessly ambitious.

"I've had some news of your ex-boss," José said in the canteen.

Bardane had left the Group, having come to an arrangement which meant he could keep his head held high while looking for a new job (where he would not make the mistake of trying to humiliate someone to make an example of them). Hearing his name half-way through lunch like that, six months after he had left, had a feeling of commemoration about it. Nicolas could have done without it.

"Molin, who works in my department, is his son's godfather. Did you know that Bardane has two children with his present wife, one with his ex and a fourth one who's adopted?"

For reasons which he had no need to air, Nicolas felt happier changing the subject; José found his embarrassment amusing, and pursued the point.

"He still hasn't found work. Mind you, it's hardly surprising, in communications, when you're over fifty . . . Amber made him an offer of 200,000 francs, as production manager, but he turned it down, of course. The problem is he's proud. Apparently he spends his time arguing with his wife, when she'd be prepared to take any sort of work. In the meantime they're selling the house in Montfort."

José did not succeed in upsetting Nicolas (there were too many people far more deserving of pity than Bardane in this miserable world), but Nicolas cut the conversation short and went back up to his office where there was a message waiting for him from a Mme Lemarié, asking him to call back urgently.

"Who's this, Muriel?"

"She said it was personal."

Nicolas did not like strangers who left personal messages, any more than he liked recorded delivery letters or any sort of summons. Potential danger, cause for concern, the sort of thing that could put his whole life on the back-burner until the business was cleared up. He looked at the clock as he picked up the telephone.

"Madame Lemarié? Nicolas Gredzinski."

"It's very nice to hear from you. I look after your account at the Crédit Agricole. You used to deal with Monsieur N'Guyen, but he's been made manager of our Lyon branch."

Nicolas had absolutely no memories of M. N'Guyen or of any other bank employee since he had opened his account twenty-two years earlier. He asked *nothing* of a bank. He did not know how to make the most of it nor to evade the traps it set. He had never asked for a loan and had absolutely never been subjected to a lecture because of an overdraft. To him the bank was just the link between his salary and his spending; the debit and credit columns should never be anything to worry about. Never.

"I imagine the 435,000 francs which have just been credited to your account won't be staying there."

How could he answer the question? He had not yet

179

had time to accept the idea that an aluminium cylinder might change his life.

"If you were thinking of investing the money, I could suggest some of our products which are performing very favourably on the market. You would need to drop by at the bank to discuss them. Would you have the time next week?"

"No."

"The week after that?"

Nicolas felt just enough resentment towards Mme Lemarié to allow himself the luxury of disconcerting her in a way he would not have thought possible a few months earlier.

"I'm going to have some fun first. I'll spend forty or fifty thousand on all sorts of nonsense. I won't have any regrets about wasting it, life's too short."

There was silence on the other end of the line.

"Don't you think life's short?"

"Yes, I do . . ."

"I'm also going to take this opportunity to make some gifts to people who aren't as lucky as me."

"Be careful with the Inland Revenue."

"This 435,000 is just a down payment, I've got an accountant friend who's going to manage the whole thing for me, don't you worry. Thanks for your call."

The idea she had just unwittingly suggested to him was not all that stupid. Nicolas put his jacket back on, left his office and told Muriel that he was out at a meeting all afternoon. Half an hour later he was trawling through the Galeries Lafayette with his hands in his pockets, eager to give in to temptation.

The first person on whom he should bestow his generosity was Mme Zabel, the plump little woman with the half-moon glasses who had handled his registration at the National Institute of Patent Rights. The

180

advice she had given him, putting him in touch with manufacturers who might be interested in his Trickpack, had borne fruit. A manufacturer of gadgets who had room for yet another absurd object (the world had him to thank for a constant stream of brightly coloured plastic things for kitchens and bathrooms) had asked him to sign a contract which had duly been checked through by a legal advisor recommended by the same Mme Zabel. The rest – the manufacturing and marketing – had gone ahead without him. No one had even needed his opinion on the possible uses for the Trickpack; his industrialist from the world of knick-knacks had found unimaginable ones, not least on the American market, where there was a law forbidding anyone from displaying the label of any alcohol in public. It was not unusual to see people in the street bringing brown paper bags up to their mouths; these were people who would welcome the Trickpack with open arms.

A limited company called Altux had just launched nine different versions of the Trickpack, four of them for invented drinks which played on the logos of well-known fizzy drinks. The others, contrary to all expectations, were well and truly real: five widely available brands (which, to cap it all, included a beer!) had agreed to put their logos on Trickpacks to send out a message which was heavily ironic. The Trickpack was sold in gadget shops and gift departments, and had already earned its creator a cheque for 435,000 francs.

For the first time in his life Nicolas could enjoy himself with no spending limit. He thought of giving himself some extravagant present which he really did not need, but which would have symbolic value. Twenty or thirty thousands francs spent in one go, without thinking about it, would mean he could always treasure the memory of a moment of madness. He started dreaming about a suit like the ones in Mafioso films, pinstripes which can change a man into a thug, the sort of thing that might inspire respect in the likes of a Marcheschi. He tried one on, then another; by the third his heart was already no longer in it. He only had to see the suit jacket on his shoulders to be able to imagine it in his wardrobe, eaten by moth. The need to be invisible, which had been with him since his childhood, had become the only suit he wore; tailored from the very fabric of anonymity, it fitted him like a glove. He tried to look elsewhere for something that would make him happy: the 100 albums that he would like to listen to even if only once, the 1,000 books he had promised himself he would read one day, the films which would tell him about the world around him. But there was nothing he really longed for, the sense of urgency was somewhere else: every day, every night, here and now. Where had he found his share of excitement before? Nowhere – there was no before.

He had to face the facts: since he had taken up his quarters at the hotel (where nothing belonged to him except for the fundamentals, his time, his life and his body), material things had lost all their appeal; he now preferred admiring different scenery. The scenery at the Galeries Lafayette was no longer entertaining, and the urge to treat himself was fading away. If only he had inherited some passion from his childhood. He remembered envying other children their fads for model aeroplanes, miniatures, stamps or fishing; sometimes he had pretended to be interested in them, just to conform, but boredom had very quickly got the upper hand. He was one of those rare children who could sit motionless on a sofa for hours. People saw it as a sort of precocious wisdom, when it was in fact just withdrawal. Who could have guessed? Children have absolutely nothing to worry about, that is what their parents like to think.

He had only the top floor left: bedding. The idea of going and having a look did not strike him as all that absurd. Why not a bed, after all? Some day he was bound to need a huge bed, a bed that was so soft it was indecent, to make up for all the sleepless nights spent with Loraine. A bed that was so exceptional that she would not be able to resist it and would end up sprawling on it. The best bed in the world. A bed that would reconcile its medicinal effects with its hedonistic implications. He found the idea amusing for a moment, just long enough to realize that Loraine already had – but God knew where – a bed of her very own.

*

The bar must have been carved of ancient oak. The patina of the wood beneath his fingers and its warm mellow colour made him feel like drinking something in the same register. There was a whole colour chart up on the wall, rows and rows, so many unfamiliar bottles which deserved to become familiar. Nicolas did not have enough of his life left to try them all, classify them and study them like an encyclopedist, writing the great book of intoxication, a book that the academies would hail as a classic, while he waited to be given a chair at the Sorbonne.

"What can I get you?"

"Something strong. What would you advise? What would you drink?"

"I hardly ever drink when I'm working, and never in the afternoon."

"What's that reddish bottle with the white label?"

"Southern Comfort, a rather syrupy bourbon. Personally, I find it too sweet, it gets to the liver pretty quickly. If you like bourbon, I can offer you one of the best, I've still got a case that complies with American standards, from when it was legal here."

Nicolas looked at his watch: ten past three. Time went so quickly, life did too.

"Watch out, though, it's quoted as 50.5% vol."

"Let me have a taste."

He had eventually found his present. The idea had come to him on the escalator, in amongst all those people. He felt like having this drink, the one the barman was now about to give him, and had gone straight to the men's accessories department where he had been shown three different flasks. He chose the medium-sized one which was slightly curved to fit comfortably in a breast pocket, covered with black leather and with the stopper attached to the neck. The capacity seemed about right to him, just enough to give you a dose of courage if you were lost in the woods, or to help you hang on if you were stuck in a lift – a couple of alibis to justify the gift. Now, he had happiness within his grasp in his inside pocket, and unhappiness too; all that for just 140 francs. Mme Lemarié had nothing to be too horrified about.

"It takes the roof off your mouth, this stuff of yours, but you get used to it."

He said this to reassure the barman when he was, in fact, on fire. His chest was about to explode, he could not breathe, and then he managed a sigh. And it was that sigh which released everything else: his breathing calmed down, his shoulders dropped, his heart settled back into its rhythm, a private smile sketched itself on his face and his imagination began to stray. Only the really important things became

184

important again, everything else was forgotten: the dross, the complications, the prevaricating, the pointless anxieties, the assorted misunderstandings, the time wasted when he should have been getting on with living.

"Can you fill this up for me?" he asked, brandishing his flask.

"A christening?"

"You could say."

"What would you like to run on?"

"On four-star. Vodka. You wouldn't have that bourbon's Polish cousin?"

"The advantage with flasks is that the action itself is discreet, but it's your breath that gives you away. Those quick swigs of vodka can be detected. I've got an eau-de-vie which might help you get past the worst of it without anyone knowing. Would you like to try it?"

"No, I'd rather it was a surprise."

The day was really getting started, everything that had gone before had just been lethargy, now what really mattered was becoming clear and, with it, a certainty: he really was the ungrateful wretch he had always feared! How could he have forgotten Mme Zabel! He put the flask in his pocket, downed another Wild Turkey in one and went back to the department store to rectify the situation.

Fire!

*

"The pleasure's all mine, Madame Zabel. We should always know what we owe and who we owe it to. What would have happened if my appointment had been with the person in that office there?"

"My colleague would have given you the same information I did, and she would be the one holding a magnificent Hermès scarf today, and she would probably say she can't accept it, which is what I'm going to have to do."

"This isn't corruption, Madame Zabel, it's gratitude! And, anyway, this ochre yellow is exactly your colour. You can't refuse it."

Mme Zabel looked at him in helpless silence.

Despite the 50.5% vol. fuelling the spontaneous combustion of his generosity, Nicolas could sense a hint of anxiety behind his benefactor's amused smile. If she thought he was drunk, that would ruin his good mood and his very sincere gratitude towards her. But he actually was well and truly drunk, a little too much for his liking.

"Please, Madame Zabel . . . accept it . . ."

"Don't look at me like that with those dark eyes, Monsieur Gredzinski, you'll make me give in."

"And about time!"

His diction was out of danger, his breath above suspicion.

"While I'm here, Madame Zabel, I wanted to talk to you about an idea which could be turned into a proper project, if you felt it was worth it. I should tell you that, for some time, I've been waking up in the arms of the most beautiful woman."

She raised a questioning eyebrow.

"But, you see, we don't always wake at the same time because the beauty in question slips away at dawn, shrouded in mystery, while I recover from a feverish and generously oiled night. You see, she does everything she can to avoid waking me and, despite the fact that I'd like to hold her in my arms one last time before she leaves, I'm grateful to her for it. I should tell you that ever since I was tiny, I've woken up in a flash, I just have to open my eyes and bang! that's it,

186

I'm wide awake, wound up like a spring, it's terrible. I'm not one of those lucky people, like you perhaps, who can go straight back to sleep."

"I have been known to."

"You should recognize how lucky you are. People like me don't ever half sleep, have a little interlude dozing or take a quick nap. For worriers like me it's as if a blast of reality hits you the minute you regain consciousness, and then the countdown starts, you only have two or three minutes left before all the symptoms wake up too. The first intelligible thought is inevitably pessimistic and gets worse by the second; you suddenly remember you live on this lowly earth, this place built by other people but which you've never tried to change, that the day is going to be as bad as you feared and you're going to have to grin and bear it until the evening. You feel almost guilty for lying in Morpheus's arms and, damn him, he won't open those arms again until you've crossed your daily vale of tears. So picture the universal problem of unsynchronized mornings; she needs to be ready for her 6 o'clock start, he's recovering after working late into the night. There are endless scenarios involving millions of people who share a bed with someone but can't get up at the same time as them. How do you avoid hearing the other person's alarm clock? How do you stay asleep yourself? It's as simple as that! Someone in this noble establishment must have thought about it. Don't tell me I'm the first! Because if I am, I'd like to suggest a very light wrist watch with a vibrating function which pulses with just enough pressure to wake the one without disturbing the other. I've thought of everything. Would you like some more details?"

*

His promotion within the Group had changed nothing in the aperitif club's routine. They had all congratulated him effusively; Marcheschi told him it was his duty to offer them champagne, and had made a point of treating them to a second bottle. Soon it had become accepted fact, and no one mentioned it any more. The get-togethers went on into the onset of autumn; a table next to the pinball machine had taken over from the terrace, and the pastis had given way to wine. Only the time and the main topic of conversation – which José called the "set meal" – did not change. The Group was a soap opera bristling with characters, with an episode broadcast every day; there was probably no one who knew how it would end. The only theme that might challenge it was Marcheschi himself, his life and his life's work.

"I must tell you about someone very dear to me," he said, "the formidable Rémi Schach. He's a mysterious investor who's put the wind up the Stock Exchange. Does anyone know him?"

They could all see it was a loaded question and said nothing.

"I wouldn't expect you to, I wasn't allowed to divulge his existence before today. Three months ago I was given instructions to launch a takeover bid for the Autoniels channel which, as well as the Group, also interested Dietrich in Cologne and . . ."

Nicolas had already stopped listening; at least Marcheschi's escapades had the advantage of making Loraine appear at the table, invisible and always smiling, sometimes naked, silent but there. He remained silent as well and kept himself happy letting his imagination recreate her from top to toe: from the impeccable bridge of her nose; the faint shadows under her eyes, which added an indefinable nuance to their blue;

to her hair, which fell in curls over her ears. Fine tuned down to the least detail, she would cross her arms as if to imitate him, and the two of them would stay like that for minutes at a time, devouring each other with their eyes. There was nothing that could draw Nicolas from his daydreaming then, apart from Marcheschi himself with his booming voice.

". . . and if the Parena Group won the day, it's all thanks to the providential Rémi Schach, the ghost partner, who is none other than an anagram of . . .?"

"Marcheschi!" said Régine to pip the others to the post.

"Are you allowed to do that?"

"In the world of finance pseudonyms are actually encouraged."

Once again Marcheschi had proved to the others that he was both there at the table and also moving in different spheres from theirs, that there was something extraordinary about his life, and that his job was not – as all of theirs were – a tedious daily inevitability.

"What's it like having a double identity?" asked José.

"It's triple! When I'm bored with making money for the Group, I log on to the Internet to play a game called Unreal Tournament. Last week, I had the honour of being included in the list of the thousand best scorers in the world, under my *nom de guerre*, Slaughter."

Nicolas was puzzled. He wondered what this story of multiple identities meant to him; Loraine reappeared to refresh his memory and to smile back at him. Marcheschi must have sensed that the irritating Gredzinski was about to speak, so he started to stare at him as if throwing down a challenge.

Nicolas picked it up.

"In Paris in 1658, a polemicist by the name of Louis de Montalte crossed swords with the Jesuits while correcting the frequent re-editions of his text, the *Provinciales*, which was considered the century's biggest success by the bookshops. At exactly the same time, the young Amos Dettonville invented what we now call 'integral calculus'. Meanwhile, one Salomon de Tultie, a philosopher, was making notes for a colossal portrait on the human condition and how it relates to God: *Les Pensées*. The three are one and the same person, whom we know better under the name Blaise Pascal. His three pseudonyms are all anagrams of what was a key phrase to him: *Lom ton Dieu est la*.* To him, a text, an idea or a principle belonged to everyone, he wouldn't have contemplated claiming paternity with his name. He felt happier disappearing behind fictitious identities. That's the sort of man he was, Pascal."

He stopped talking.

Far away on the esplanade, an apparition of Loraine – proud of what he had said – was waving to him to join her as soon as possible.

*

When they did not sleep at the hotel, she would disappear as they came out of the Lynn without Nicolas knowing which direction she went. She did not even utter a banal *I must get home*, which would not have revealed anything but would still have created an awkwardness. Then he just had to wait until they were back in room 318, where he did whatever came to mind, letting his imagination run wild – no one could have envisaged so much freedom in such a small space. They taught each other manoeuvres that the other did

---

* Man, your God is here (*Lom* being a foreshortening of *L'homme*, man).

not know or dared not use, they rolled bottles over the floor to pass them to each other, played games to see who could throw cards the closest to the wall, dreamed up novel fantasies for themselves, deciphered haikus, licked each other's skin streaming with every alcohol in the world, called up a thousand genies, or slept, for hours and hours, peacefully, intertwined, in the very depths of oblivion.

"Pass me the crisps."

"You're regressing to your childhood, my poor girl."

"I wasn't allowed them when I was little."

There again he did not know how to interpret such a trivial response. Had she been very poor as a child or was she the daughter of an inflexible dietician?

It was half past one in the morning, she still had on matching apricot-coloured bra and knickers, and they were nibbling on a few bits and pieces, having not had any supper.

"Do you want to know exactly when I really fell in love with you?"

He raised his eyebrows to encourage her.

"It was in this room, on the third or fourth night."

"I must have made you come like you never had before."

"Not at all. We were watching TV. It was 3 o'clock in the morning, and we were watching ice-skating championships live from the States."

"Don't remember it at all."

"At one point, one of the girls slipped and landed in the most ridiculous position. The poor thing got up as if nothing had happened and carried right on to the end, like they all do. At that precise moment, viewers fall into three categories. The first, which must be the biggest, are those who can't wait to see it in slow motion. They've seen this girl crashing down and there's something incredibly exciting about it which makes them want to see the terrible moment again. They're usually waiting to see the dismal scores and the close-up of the girl, who can't believe it's happened; they're often rewarded with a few tears."

The covers had rolled onto the floor, the room was steeped in shadows and their clothes were strewn around the colossal bed on which the sheets were still fresh. Loraine was lying on her stomach, motionless, with her arms down by her sides to soothe a slight backache that had not let up all day. Nicolas was in grey boxer shorts, sitting on the bed with one hand on a cold glass and the other on his girlfriend's calves.

"The second category would be the people who generally feel sorry for the poor girl. They give a little cry both times they see the fall. *Oh, poor thing . . . !* They watch her compassionately, but perhaps there's something secret hidden beneath the compassion, something too shameful to mention . . . but delicious; they won't ever know about it themselves."

He leant over for a moment to kiss Loraine's ankle and to nibble her toes without interrupting what she was saying.

"Then there's a third category, who are extremely rare, and you're one of them. When they played it back in slow motion, I saw you look away sharply. You absolutely didn't want to see it again. Too painful. I don't know what you were thinking about, perhaps about the real tragedy for the girl, the months or years of arduous training, then that tiny terrible moment in front of millions of pairs of eyes. You didn't want to add yours to them. A moment later, I was in love."

He smiled vaguely, shrugged his shoulders to show he was embarrassed, and looked away again. The anecdote did not pinpoint anything in particular for him, he had never thought of himself as being in a particular category when watching skating champion-ships; at best he saw himself as one of those who took a keen interest in the way the girls' little skirts rippled as they moved, but he did not remember the fall in ques-tion. And yet Loraine was right on this point: without being any better or worse than the next person, Nicolas avoided the spectacle of other people's distress.

"They're ridiculously small, these packets of crisps," she said.

"Like the shots of vodka, it's all on the same scale."

"Come and give me a hug."

"I love that little apricot-coloured set, I think it's very . . ."

Another frenetic whirl of activity veered rapidly towards cannibalism.

Loraine had said *in love*.

He had in his arms a woman who was *in love* with him.

He tried to understand the words, what they were hiding, their implications. He found delicious syn-onyms for them and took another swig of vodka. Still lying on her stomach, Loraine grabbed the remote control, switched on the television, cut the sound and found something worth watching: ducks flying in a V formation over a large lake. Nicolas tried to remember the last woman who had admitted to him that she was in love; he had to go back a long way. Such a difficult time in his life that he chose to cut short the remin-iscing and bite Loraine's thigh to provoke renewed hostilities. Making love with her was one of the few things in the world which was natural, self-evident. The spontaneity of their bodies, the way they belonged to each other, appropriated each other, needed no thought or comment. He had not dreamed of a single gesture which he had not gone on to realize, he had not once regretted a situation that he must have been the only person on earth to have imagined, or attempted one manoeuvre that she had blocked. Their fantasy had no choice but to follow them. Some nights, like that night, it ran on ahead of them and kept them awake until dawn.

He picked up his little black notebook to write:

Beware of other people's wisdom. Nothing has any meaning. Everything contradicts itself, even eternal truths. No one can know where you're going because you don't even know yourself. The complicated paths you take may seem unclear – they are, but make sure no one turns you away from them.

Paul Vermeiren

As he had done every morning for a year, Paul Vermeiren glanced at his agency's brass plaque as he walked under the porch of 8b Rue Notre-Dame-de-Bonne-Nouvelle. The day he had come to look at the premises, the name had imposed itself: *Agence Bonne Nouvelle,* the Good News Agency. It had not been a mistake. The gentle irony lurking in the address inspired confidence: a good many clients had been susceptible to it. He walked across the paved court-yard, went up staircase A and entered the second floor apartment without having to unlock it. The layout of the rooms was ideal: a small hall which acted as a wait-ing room and led to two independent offices, his and that of his associate, Julien Grillet. A third room, which had a kitchenette and a shower leading off it, served as a pied-à-terre for Paul when the demands of an enquiry meant he could not get back to the country, which happened on average twice a week. He put his leather jacket over the arm of a chair and headed towards the kitchen, where Julien was making some coffee.

"So, how was Saint-Malo?"

"Didn't have time to see," said Paul.

"And the work?"

"It went well, a bit tedious towards the end."

While he listened to the messages on the answering machine, Julien told him about his weekend of total inertia. Paul went to finish his cup of coffee in his office, eager to get to work: writing a report on his mission in Saint-Malo – the client had insisted on having it that very evening. The time had come to go back over his notes, to decipher some which were now illegible and to transform them into something clear. He switched on his computer, opened a new document in the *Reports* folder and gave it the same name as the client: *Leterrier.*

The man had contacted him two weeks earlier regarding his wife, who was a manager in a large company of estate agents. She had been complaining for three months that she had to keep going over to their Saint-Malo branch to sort out appalling problems with the management. One weekend in three she would ask her husband to bear with her and be patient. Instead of which, the husband was sending Paul Vermeiren on the job.

Confidential
Not to be divulged to any third party.

SURVEILLANCE REPORT

Purpose: Surveillance of Mme Elizabeth LETERRIER (indicated by colour photograph) on Friday, 6 May from the Immotan Agency, 4 Place Gasnier-Duparc, 35400 Saint-Malo.

0700 hrs: Mission begins (depart Paris, arriving in Saint-Malo at 1015 hrs).

1130 hrs: Set up surveillance equipment for 4 Place Gasnier-Duparc in Saint-Malo.

1425 hrs: Mme Leterrier arrives in her car, which she parks in the company car park. She goes into the Immotan building. She is wearing a grey jacket and has a black handbag.

1650 hrs: Mme Leterrier comes out of Immotan alone. In the car park she opens the boot of her car and takes out a brown suitcase. Then she goes on foot to the Lucky café, on the Place Jean-Moulin, and sits at a table on the terrace (see photograph No. 1).

1705 hrs: A grey Safrane, registration 84 LK 35, parks a few yards from Mme Leterrier's table. A man of about fifty gets out, joins Mme Leterrier and sits down at her table. He wears a grey suit and sunglasses. He is fairly heavily built, about five foot ten or eleven and has short brown hair.

1710 hrs: Mme Leterrier has a cup of coffee with this man, and he drinks a pastis. He puts his hand over Mme Leterrier's hand several times.

1725 hrs: They both get into the Safrane and drive a short distance before stopping in the Rue des Cordiers. They buy some things from a greengrocer and in an 8 till 8 mini-market.

1740 hrs: They leave in the vehicle.

1750 hrs: They drive to a block of flats called "Mandragore", 52 Boulevard Henri-Dunant at Saint-Servan-sur-Mer, and park in the car park. They walk past a garden and go up an external staircase, which leads to an apartment on the first floor of the second building (see photograph No. 2). Mme Leterrier is carrying her brown suitcase. The name Bernard NANTY is written on the letter box which corresponds to the apartment.
NB: There are four windows from that apartment which look out over the Rue de la Pie. Surveillance continues in that street.

1810 hrs: Mme Leterrier's figure appears in one of these windows. She is wearing a dressing-gown and has a towel twisted round her head. She draws the curtain.

2140 hrs: No light from the apartment can now be seen from the Rue de la Pie.

2145 hrs: End of surveillance and installation of the "witnesses" (pebbles) under the Safrane's wheels.

2200 hrs: End of mission.

197

To stretch his legs a bit, Paul went to make some tea and offered Julien a cup.

"It'll kill my appetite. Why don't we go and have some lunch instead?"

Surprised, Paul glanced at his watch: it was already 1 o'clock.

"Haven't got time. Bring me back a sandwich, tuna and salad, and some sparkling water."

"Oh, a Monsieur Martinez rang, you can get hold of him at his shop this afternoon."

"Thanks."

"What is this shop?"

"It's a sweetshop. He wants to check whether he's been swindled by a manufacturer."

Paul would deal with him after doing this report, which he had to finish before his meeting at 4 o'clock.

Confidential
Not to be divulged to any third party.

SURVEILLANCE REPORT

Purpose: Surveillance of Mme LETERRIER on Saturday, 7 May, from the Rue de la Pie side of the Mandragore apartment building, Saint-Servan.

0700 hrs: Mission begins.

0730 hrs: Surveillance equipment set up on the Rue de la Pie side of the Mandragore building. The curtains are still drawn in the apartment. The Safrane is parked in the same place as the previous evening. The "witnesses" are still under the vehicle's wheels, indicating that it has not been moved.
NB: Information established from the concierge: the man in his fifties seen the previous day with Mme Leterrier is indeed M. Bernard NANTY, the official tenant of the apartment under surveillance.

1000 hrs: The blind over the apartment's bay window is opened.

198

M. Nanty stands looking out of the window drinking a cup of coffee. He is stripped to the waist.
Mme Leterrier's figure can be seen In a navy blue dressing gown.

1045 hrs: M. Nanty and Mme Leterrier come out of the apartment and get into the Safrane. She is wearing jeans and a pink jacket, and is holding a sports bag. He is wearing jeans, a black T-shirt and sandals.

1050 hrs: They leave the apartment block.

1110 hrs: The Safrane stops beside the beach known as L'Andemer on the Saint-Briac road. Mme Leterrier gets out of the car and comes round to the driver's side of the car where M. Nanty is still sitting in the driver's seat with the window open. They speak for a moment (see photograph No. 3), seem to hesitate about something, then Mme Leterrier gets back into the car and they drive off again.

1120 hrs: The car stops beside an almost deserted beach just over a mile from the woods known as the Bois Bizet. They sit down on a large blanket on the sand. Mme Leterrier is wearing a black one-piece swimsuit. They kiss each other on the mouth several times.

1150 hrs: Mme Leterrier and M. Nanty go for a swim.

1205 hrs: They are sitting on the blanket. Mme Leterrier's head is resting on M. Nanty's shoulder. They are looking out to sea.

1220 hrs: They get dressed and leave in the Safrane.

1245 hrs: They park the Safrane in the Rue de Chartres in Saint-Malo.

1300 hrs: They go into a men's clothes shop. M. Nanty tries on several shirts with Mme Leterrier watching. They do not buy anything, and leave.

1325 hrs: They go into the Crêperie Mitaine on the Rue des Grands-Degrés, and sit down at a table for lunch (see photograph No. 4).

1450 hrs: They come out, go back to the car and leave.

1510 hrs:	The car drives up to the Mandragore building, and Mme Leterrier and M. Nanty go up to the latter's apartment. They draw the curtains at the windows overlooking the Rue de la Pie.
1615 hrs:	Mme Leterrier leaves the first floor apartment alone. She unlocks a shed, takes out a bicycle and rides off.
1635 hrs:	Mme Leterrier locks her bicycle to a post on the Rue de Chartres. She goes into a chemist and comes back out with a paper bag in her hand. Then she goes back to the men's clothes shop and buys one of the shirts previously tried on by M. Nanty.
1650 hrs:	She leaves on her bicycle.
1655 hrs:	She stops in a street full of shops close to the Place Vauban, and buys some vegetables and a joint of meat.
1710 hrs:	She leaves on her bicycle.
1725 hrs:	She goes back to the Mandragore building, puts the bicycle away and goes back to M. Nanty's apartment.
1830 hrs:	Mme Leterrier appears from time to time in the windows overlooking the Rue de la Pie, particularly in the room on the extreme left-hand side, which is clearly the kitchen.
1915 hrs:	M. Nanty comes out of the apartment to go to the communal cellars and comes back up with a case of wine.
2110 hrs:	M. Nanty closes the shutters of the three main rooms and puts on the lights.
2230 hrs:	End of surveillance. All the lights are out.
2300 hrs:	End of mission.

He re-read the report and corrected a couple of words, imagining Rodier leaning over his right shoulder. Paul often thought of him now that he was fending for himself, and felt guilty for not getting in touch with him, asking for news of him or telling him his own news. He hated the idea of appearing ungrateful to someone who had spared nothing when he was training him for this madman's profession, saving him from countless pitfalls, all things that Paul could now fully evaluate and appreciate. Rodier could not understand what extraordinary reason Thierry might have had for refusing the offer of taking over his agency and its client base. Practically gift wrapped. He had been prepared to do as much as possible to make the handover smooth, negotiating the lease, warning regular clients, finding an associate, and much more.

"Do you really want to start from scratch?"

"Yes."

"I don't understand, but it's your decision."

"Thanks, boss."

". . . Will you let me know how you're getting on?"

"Of course."

That was the last time they had spoken. A week later he became Paul Vermeiren; his remorse at having to let his former mentor down was still eating at him today.

Paul blew between the letters on his keyboard to get rid of the crumbs. If he carried on at this rate, he could finish his report before the 4 o'clock meeting and have a coffee in the little place opposite.

SURVEILLANCE REPORT

Purpose: Surveillance of Mme Leterrier on Sunday, 8 May, starting on the Rue de la Pie side of the Mandragore apartment block, Saint-Servan.

0700 hrs: Start of mission.

0730 hrs: Surveillance equipment set up on the Rue de la Pie side of the Mandragore building. The shutters are still closed.

1130 hrs: Mme Leterrier opens the shutters to the main room. From the Rue de la Pie, M. Nanty can be seen to put his arms round Mme Leterrier from behind her. He slides his hand under her nightdress at breast height. He kisses Mme Leterrier's neck for about a minute.

1510 hrs: A delivery boy from RAPID'ZA delivers a pizza to M. Nanty's apartment.

1715 hrs: They come out of the apartment and get into the Safrane. Mme Leterrier is carrying her suitcase.

1740 hrs: M. Nanty drops Mme Leterrier by her car at the Immotan Agency's car park. She puts her suitcase in the boot. They hug each other for several minutes and then part. The cars set off in opposite directions.

1750 hrs: End of surveillance.

2200 hrs: End of mission.

Invoicing   Friday, 6 May: 0700–2200 hrs = 15 hours
Saturday, 7 May: 0700–2300 hrs = 16 hours
Sunday, 8 May: 0700–2200 hrs = 15 hours

Total number of hours : 46 hours @ 300 francs, making a total of 13,800 francs (net)
EXPENSES (hotel, meals, car hire, fuel, various) = 3,225 francs (net)
Four photographs = 1,600 francs (net)
NET TOTAL = 18,625 francs
VAT @ 19.6% = 3,650.50 francs
TOTAL INC VAT = 22,275.50 francs

Back on that Friday evening, the lights in Nanty's apartment had hardly had time to go out before Paul had rung Jacques Leterrier to tell him he felt that what he had seen was enough. But the husband had insisted that Paul describe hour by hour the weekend that his wife spent with her lover, supported by photographs. With cases like this, men and women alike, they always want to see their rival's face. Most of the time they find them unbelievably ugly.

Paul Vermeiren read his report through once more before printing it out. He anticipated his client's reaction to each sentence. Leterrier was prepared to stomach quite a lot: the urgency of the first few moments, the little love nest that they hardly set foot out of, the towel in her hair, even the nice supper which she prepared lovingly, demonstrating an appalling everydayness. One detail was going to hurt much more than all the rest: the shirt. The shirt that Mme Leterrier went and bought secretly to surprise her lover. The sort of present a woman gives *her man*. Paul could still remember the look on her face as she came out of the shop, how much she wanted to please him. On her way back, alone on her bike, she had sung to herself, happy, with her face in the wind and a gift-wrapped package in her basket.

Paul concentrated on this episode and the way in which to describe it in his report. All things considered, the shirt might not need mentioning; there was certainly no risk of it changing any aspect of Leterrier's decisions. He cut out the escapade on the bike as if it had never existed. It was one tiny little event in the private life of two complete strangers, and he had the power to erase it, to give it back to the couple who had lived it.

Then his eye came to rest briefly on:

1205 hrs: They are sitting on the blanket. Mme Leterrier's head is resting on M. Nanty's shoulder. They are looking out to sea.

Paul remembered this image that he had not wanted to photograph. The lovers had sat silent and motionless for a long time, gazing at the waves on the incoming tide. It was not the silence of an old couple, but a perfect moment of harmony, something that went far beyond affection, sex and sin, expressed something inexpressible, an inner happiness that was so peaceful and so shared that it needed nothing. The account Paul gave of it in one sentence interpreted none of all that, but kept something of the exceptional nature of that moment. He printed the text out as it stood, and put it in an envelope. It was ten to four, too late to stop off at the café. He made the most of the little break to ring back M. Martinez and arrange a meeting. Someone rang the bell; Paul opened the door to a young woman of about thirty whom he had never seen before, and he showed her into his office.

"I have a chain of three sandwich bars which do a lot of home deliveries. I've had cheques from two clients which were tampered with after they were presented. The first one, for 345 francs, was changed to 62,345 with an automatic machine – do you know the sort of thing I mean?"

"Yes, I do."

"Right. The second one was altered by hand. The police made some enquiries, and we now know that the cheques were endorsed by two individuals who opened accounts in false names and withdrew virtually all the money in cash. I want to know whether the cheques were stolen from one of my letter boxes or whether I should suspect someone who works with me. That would be the worst possible scenario."

Paul made a few notes but he looked the woman right in the eye. Rodier had warned him to be wary of new faces.

"When you start your own agency, don't automatically believe everything your first clients tell you. You'll be so pleased to see any! Watch out for a natural tendency to empathize just because it's you they've come to."

Rodier was referring particularly to jobs involving people's feelings. Adultery cases were by far the most irrational and required the most delicate handling. In one of his very first jobs, had the husband not asked Paul to follow, not his wife, but her lover?

"I want to know what he does with his day, who he sees."

"Can I ask you why?"

"I want you to prove to me that he's a prick."

Paul waited, perplexed.

"A real prick, who does the things pricks do and has the habits pricks have. With the proof to back it up, Angèle will stop seeing this prick."

Not long after that, Paul met the female equivalent of this: a woman of forty who had been married fifteen years, asking him to follow her husband's mistress.

"I want to know if she has any other lovers."

"Why?"

"Because he can't stand sluts."

The clients had many more reasons to be wary than the investigator. They were so on edge they were prepared to listen to the first person likely to get to the truth . . . and for someone who is suffering, there is only one truth.

*

Watching Julien Grillet was somehow both fascinating and terrifying. Unlike Paul – who was a "tail" by trade, a grass-roots man – Grillet had been an "investigator" for twenty years and forced himself to respect office hours with the regularity of a metronome, never getting up out of his chair. First thing in the morning, his fax would be spewing out lists of names generated by a variety of payment organizations, property companies or even landlords suffering at the hands of bad debtors, all calling on him to find new addresses for these dishonest individuals. He dealt with an average of fifteen cases a day, and solved three quarters of them. Starting with the last known address, he would ring the administrative organizations that might be able to give him information. He knew the various organizations and what they did, not just the access codes, formalities and key words, but also the customs and psychology of every kind of minor official, and how to bend the rules. He played on the permeability between different departments, and gained access to information that official powers would have trouble getting hold of because of the weighty procedures. Paul liked hearing him passing himself off as someone from the tax office asking a favour of a colleague or, better still, a policeman. His natural affection for forgers and liars meant he felt considerable admiration when he listened to Julien fooling the whole country. Once he had got hold of the address, Grillet checked it on Minitel,* found the telephone number of a close neighbour and passed himself off, amongst other things, as a representative from some office who needed to know what to do with an overpayment for Monsieur X. Ten times out of ten, the neighbour in question was delighted to confirm that Monsieur X did indeed live there. When there was a risk of someone else with the same name living in the building, Grillet would get hold of Monsieur X himself to avoid any mistakes – to be sure he did the job thoroughly.

A tail like Paul often needed an investigator for an address or a name, or for research into someone's solvency or inheritance. In the early days of their collaboration, Paul had asked Julien whether he missed

* A public-access information system similar to the Internet, which has been available in France for many years.

the grass-roots work. Julien had known, ever since his childhood, that the less he was seen the better it was for him. *If I was tailing someone, I'd be the only person they'd see in the street.* On the other hand, he could get anything he wanted on the telephone: it was a gift. As a teenager, he had been the one who managed to persuade the girls to come to parties; once there, not one of them would come to talk to him. What Julien liked more than anything else was passing himself off as a Telecom employee, a lance sergeant, a paymaster, a cousin from the provinces or Father Christmas himself, what mattered was that people believed him. For the space of a phone call, he felt as if he almost was all those characters.

Paul Vermeiren and Julien Grillet had been a team for nearly a year, and the Agence Bonne Nouvelle was running smoothly. Neither of them wanted to know more about the other.

*

At the end of the day Paul found time to go to the sports hall to battle against impending flabbiness and an expanding waistline. After which it took no more than twenty minutes to get back to his little corner of the countryside that once more had been spared the sound and fury. He settled himself under the pergola to sip a little glass of port in the dwindling light and sit in silence thinking about the day that was just finishing and the one that lay ahead. He never lost sight of the fact that the bottom half of the hourglass was filling day by day: from now on every grain of sand had its own significance.

As he got ready in front of the mirror, he had a quick look at his scars, which were growing steadily whiter.

His features had become fixed forever and had replaced the mask that Joust had drawn.

That evening he felt like wearing a tie; he wanted to please the woman who would be waiting for him in a café in Montparnasse at about 10 o'clock. Eva liked good manners and thoughtfulness, especially in the early days of a relationship. If theirs was to die that night, it would not be a tragedy or a source of regret for either of them. Eva knew how to cut up raw fish herself to make sushi, and almost always wore black lace. She thought Paul was a caricature of a private eye, and that he was taking her for a ride on the rare occasions when he told her about his day. He took her to dinner in a quiet place, where they had fun imagining the children they would never have. She asked whether he would like to go back to her apartment, where they could make the most of the terrace and make love under the sky. Before getting there, Paul made a detour in the car to identify a building in the Twelfth Arrondissement where he would start his tailing job at 10 o'clock the following morning. When Eva asked him why he had made the detour, he told her that she had made him lose his sense of direction.

Nicolas Gredzinski

"Of all your beloved geniuses, who are your favourites?"

"Stupid question, my friend. It proves you haven't understood anything about genius!"

"Let's put it another way: which one do you feel particular affection for, a little inexplicable weakness?"

"Are you applying for the position?"

"Answer the question."

"I like Rimbaud because he had weak knees, and I think that goes well with genius. I've also got a soft spot for Freud because he committed suicide by cigar with a furious dedication which his doctors found disconcerting. Michelangelo is also one of my favourites because he was mad enough to make fakes."

"Fakes . . .?"

"Once, because he needed the money, he made a fake ancient sculpture which he buried in his garden and which, once it was discovered, was worth ten times as much as a Michelangelo! If anyone put an estimate on it nowadays, it would definitely be the most expensive fake in the world."

"What do you like best, of all his work?"

"I've only ever seen reproductions."

"What would you like to see *for real?*"

"The Sistine Chapel, the *Pietà* and probably his *Moses*."

"All three of those are in Rome, aren't they?"

"Yes."

A trip to Rome: now he had found something to

give her. After all, surely she was the instigator of the Trickpack, not to mention the individual alarm watch? Loraine was on the right scale to inspire a Renaissance artist or a picaresque novelist; Nicolas did not feel worthy of his muse.

She preferred the charm of a railway carriage to an aeroplane; going by train struck him as a more everyday option, and the possibility of experiencing new sensations was attractive. So they conformed to the fantasy of the sleeper train as they sipped their white wine, served by a conductor who momentarily found himself back in the days when the tips were so generous that they made his salary look ridiculous.

Nicolas's salary seemed even more so, compared to what the Trickpack was bringing in. Other brands of fizzy drink had got caught up in the game but also, and he had to see it to believe it, a brand of wine and a champagne. You could hide your beer or your sparkling water in a golden sleeve embossed with the coat of arms of Paul Garance et Fils champagne. It had been the most widely sold Trickpack over the last few months, snobbery in the extreme for 40 francs. The whole range was producing very good results; the patent had been bought for Italy, Germany and all the Scandinavian countries. Hugues, Nicolas's accountant and now his business associate, was looking towards Asia, particularly Japan, where the Trickpack's success seemed a foregone conclusion. Nicolas was rich, the few people who knew about it kept telling him so, but he refused to believe it. He just about had a feeling that something was piling up somewhere in a safety-deposit box. It seemed absurd to go on working for the Group, but the thought that his everyday life could come to an abrupt halt frightened him: he kept putting off the decision from one day to the next.

210

Nicolas felt guilty for having so much money. Pleasing the people around him was a way of healing his guilt. He started with his team, the art department and its administrative counterpart. Nicolas discovered by chance the common denominator of all these individuals: football. They had all revealed themselves as fans when he had told them that the Parena Group was taking on a small club which was about to be promoted to the first division. A whole identity had to be created – shirts, logos, transport – and the graphic designers had buckled down to the job. It was when he saw their enthusiasm that he had the idea of giving each of them two seats for a final at the massive Stade de France. He gave Muriel the biggest bottle of a perfume she said she couldn't ever buy for herself. The whole floor was entitled to his generosity too, as well as the aperitif club and many others. He had to lie about the origins of the gifts, claiming he had a friend who was on good terms with the French Football Federation, another at Guerlain, and a whole host of others pretty much all over the place, when he had, in fact, paid out of his own pocket. In his largesse, he had taken special care of Jacot by taking him to sample the cuisine of the greatest restaurants in Paris in an attempt to put a bit of weight back on him. One evening, at the Grand Véfour, he asked him: "Do you really have to be in Paris to rest?"

"No, I could just as easily be in the country but I've always found it depressing."

"Why not by the sea?"

"At this time of year?"

"With a few wahines."

Jacot looked up inquisitively.

"Kauai. Do you know where that is?"

"No."

"In the Hawaiian islands."

Jacot had come back still just as thin, but tanned, relaxed, feeling as if he had stolen this dream month from the enemy – a victory. If money could buy a little comfort and combat worry, then there was no better investment. And, who knows, with all this playing Father Christmas, Nicolas might find that money could buy him some confidence, discretion, enthusiasm and – most paradoxically – some sincerity.

Loraine had concerns about exploiting his generosity, a trait peculiar to those born without a fortune, who work their entire lives. During their escapades Nicolas realized that Loraine got up in the morning, day after day, to earn a living. He tried to picture what sort of work she might do, but could come up with no interesting answers. He almost asked her the question directly, but the protective shadow of his inner demons held him back just in time. In the notes that he left on the bedside table the *Other* was very firm: *Don't push your luck with this girl!*

In a double compartment on the Palatino train Loraine lay on the bottom bunk watching the darkness flitting past at her feet. At daybreak Nicolas opened his eyes and found her in the same position with a book in her hand and a cup of coffee on a tray.

". . . Where are we?"

"We've just passed Pisa."

"Could I have some coffee too?"

"I'll ask for some more from Monsieur Mésange."

"Who?"

"The conductor."

"Are you friends already?"

"Neither of us was asleep. He told me about his life on the trains – it was fascinating. When we left Turin, I came back into our compartment. I checked that you were OK, and I started reading."

212

She opened the door and waved along the corridor; the conductor arrived two minutes later with a breakfast tray, which he handed to Nicolas, then he exchanged a few niceties with Loraine before leaving the compartment.

"I'd like to have your gift for making friends," he said.

"Isn't there a hint of irony in that?"

"Not at all. I have to really know someone to feel comfortable with them."

"I just go by the first impression."

"I never do! I can radically change my mind about someone between the first and the second time I meet them."

"The first impression is more reliable than the second," she said, "for one very precise reason: it's the product of much longer experience."

One of the thousand reasons he wanted to wake up with Loraine every day: hearing her embark on a theoretical conversation at 7 o'clock in the morning. He adored her convoluted lines of reasoning, especially when she was lying on her front.

"Every time you meet someone for the first time, you judge them according to criteria that have matured over forty years of experience. Consciously and subconsciously your mind analyses all the signs transmitted by a stranger. You can call it intuition; intuition is a complex mechanism. On the other hand, if you see them again a week later, your experience and the way you think will only be a week old. Do you see what I mean?"

"No."

"I do like you."

"So do I."

The moment he set foot on the platform at Roma Termini, Nicolas wanted a drink; it was only twenty-five past ten. In the taxi, to stave off his impatience, he launched into a perilous eulogy on the architectural mixture of chalky stone and ochre stone, which, according to him, eased you from an imperial city to a tiny country town. Their bedroom window looked out over the Campo dei Fiori, and the one in the bathroom over a patio where a fountain tinkled. The fresh, orange autumn sunshine beckoned them outside, but they could not resist the temptation of closing the curtains and lying down on a large, motionless double bed. Huddled against each other, they relaxed their bodies wearied by the trundling of the train; a completely new energy gave them an urge for discovery. He opened the mini-bar, looked at his watch (too quickly to see what the time was), picked up a shot of whisky, impatiently unscrewed the metal lid and emptied the contents into a glass.

"Are you tempted?"

"I'll wait till lunchtime," she said, going into the bathroom.

Leaning out of the window with the glass in his hand, he looked at the Campo dei Fiori without seeing it, as if he were anywhere but there.

An hour later, they went into Saint Peter's Church, where Moses had been waiting for Loraine for five centuries, sitting there with his stern expression, turning to face her. She had the peculiar impression that she was late. Nicolas felt superfluous.

*

Their little tête-à-tête lasted an hour. When Nicolas's patience was running thin, he suggested that Loraine come and recover from her emotions in a trattoria.

"But first I'd like to stop by at a little wine cellar on the Via Cavour, it's very near here."

"You told me you didn't know Rome . . ."

"That's true, but I do know a bit about wine."

It was a *casa vinicola* shoehorned between a mini-market and a shop selling ceramics. Nicolas stood with his arms crossed, watching her scanning the shelves in silence, reading labels and picking up the odd bottle for the pleasure of touching it. The assistant managed to answer her questions and Loraine, once again, had found herself an ally in less time than it took to clink two glasses together.

"Is there a difference between *semisecco* and *amabile?*"

"No, they both mean slightly sweet, it's more the wines . . . *frizzanti?*"

"Sparkling wines."

The man invited them to taste a 1995 Chianti, which Loraine found *robusto* (although she did not know whether the word existed), and she asked: "Vitigno Sangiovese?"

"*Il* Brunello di Montalcino, *tutto* Sangiovese."

Nicolas understood only one thing: his glass was already empty. He had not had time to savour the bouquet, the tannins or all the subtleties held within that gulp of red wine, which had disappeared in under a second, while Loraine and her new conquest held the liquid high up in the air to see it in the light. He could not wait to get out of the little place to find himself in front of a whole bottle, and perhaps a second if the moment was right. In the meantime, he wandered round this house with walls of wine, with floors and ceilings of wine, dotted with furniture in wine. Loraine asked the salesman a thousand details about a bottle of *corvo bianco*, and he was amused to see a little French-woman so passionate about his shop. He congratulated Nicolas for "living with a woman who liked wine so much". Loraine asked for a price list. Nicolas shovelled her outside after two false departures, and they ended up, a few minutes later, sitting at a table in a small restaurant called Da Vincenzo near the Piazza del Popolo. According to Marcheschi, this was the place for "the best *melanzane alla parmiggiana* in the world".

The "best" was Marcheschi's real speciality. He waxed lyrical about "bests" in very diverse fields: he knew the best video repair man in Paris, the best Tonkinese soup in the Thirteenth Arrondissement, he listened only to Frank Zappa's best album, and he himself made the best *tarte au citron* in the world.

"I'll have the *melanzane alla parmiggiana*," Nicolas said casually.

"What's that?"

"Slices of aubergine layered like a lasagne, with melted parmesan."

"I'll have a hundred of them."

In one corner of the room Nicolas spotted a violin lying on top of its case, and an upright piano which looked well cared for. A Debussy tune came back to him.

"With your little performance in the shop back there, I'll let you choose the wine."

"Aubergine and parmesan, that must be quite strong on the palate," she said, picking up the menu. "How about a good solid Barolo?"

Nicolas relaxed when he saw the bottle, and drank two glasses straight away, quickly, as if he were thirsty. Now he knew how to smile and how to speak.

"I knew you liked wine, but it's a big step from that to knowing I'm sleeping with an oenologist."

"It takes quite a few years of studying to be an oenologist, and quite a bit of talent to be a good one – I don't have any of that. Wine's a friend, a real friend who gives me a lot of happiness and very rarely disappoints me. A friend I don't have to keep proving my

216

friendship to; we can even go for weeks without seeing each other, the friendship stays the same."

She raised her glass in the air, solemnly, and looked at it as if gazing into a crystal ball.

"Wine brings out the best in what we eat, it's a celebration. A couple of glasses of good wine at my table, I couldn't ask for anything else in life. It's our bodies and a big proportion of our souls. Our imagination."

Nicolas suddenly grasped something which had always been clear. He had had to come all the way to Rome to concede that he and Loraine would never be the same species, that they lived in completely different latitudes. Wherever he went, Nicolas felt he was in a hostile climate; but Loraine was at peace with the world. Nicolas was always afraid of what the next day might bring; Loraine agreed with the proverb "sufficient unto the day is the evil thereof". She had a gift for capturing happiness; Nicolas drove it away the moment he felt it nearby. She never tried to get drunk; Nicolas did as soon as he started drinking. She did not anticipate the end that comes to us all; he was sometimes tempted to precipitate it so that he need no longer worry about it. That was what their interlude in the *casa vinicola* had shown him.

"There's a story that we all tell in my family," Loraine said. "One of my mother's great-uncles inherited his father-in-law's wine cellar. A real prize, a dream collection with all the *grands crus*, all the best years, nothing but masterpieces. The problem was that he, bless him, had only ever known table wine and gut-rot in carafes. Just holding one of these bottles gave him a complex. Uncorking one for his guests was quite a drama. Choosing the right one, properly appreciating it, knowing how to drink it, remembering its name and its history, respecting its rituals . . . nothing but trouble.

Until the day when the cellar was flooded for long enough to soak all the labels off. There was no longer any way he could know anything about all those wines. He would uncork any old bottle as the fancy took him, and taste it. That was when he started to appreciate good wine."

Nicolas was hardly listening to her but watching himself drinking; he knew that his way of dealing with his feelings of helplessness could not go on, that fleeing like this was doomed to failure. And yet, the moment he felt the alcohol breathing through him, he regretted going for so many years without drinking, having lagged behind, bowing to everything without rebelling. Buried under his unhappiness, one thing was sure: he had been born one of those people who is happy when he is drinking. He did not try to understand this little miracle, he accepted it like a gift. As he brought the glass up to his lips, he imagined the child he could have been if he had had the chance to cheat as he did now. Another little boy, a happier and more reckless one, the sort of smart, rebellious boy people like. He would have spent his time inventing war machines and sniffing around the girls, intrigued by how implacably fragile they were. But he had never been that boy, he had sat motionless, waiting to grow up. He had dreamed of being an adult, when everything would change, everything would happen quickly, he would become a hero at last. He had made the most wonderful scenario of it in his mind, the most exciting adventure. It was that dream that – so many years later – he had rediscovered, still intact, in the bottom of a tiny little glass of iced vodka.

"It's that hint of freshly turned soil that I like in Barolo, can you taste it?"

"No."

"It doesn't matter, it isn't important."

"I'll never be an aesthete. I think I prefer quantity to quality."

"The two can go hand in hand, you know. The record for the most expensive drunken spree in the world is actually held by a sommelier. I heard about it from a friend who sells wine in New York, he was there at the time. It was about fifteen years ago at the Waldorf Astoria, they'd organized a very special wine-tasting for an American oenologists' society. The wines were from France, and they were all worthy of a place in the great-uncle's cellar, Pétrus '29s, Pommards '47s, all legendary – they were the sort of people who could afford them. The cases travelled from Paris with an escort worthy of a head of state, like a convoy of gold on its way to Fort Knox. The treasure was put into the cellar and only the Waldorf's sommelier had the key. When all the cases had been ticked off, the insurance company had registered their safe arrival, the organizers were convinced they were all right, and the transport company could wipe the sweat from their brows, the sommelier tugged sharply on the reinforced door to the cellar and locked himself in. Through the hatch he said: 'I'm going to go to prison, I know that. And I don't give a damn. My career's ruined, I don't give a damn about that either. I'm going to experience something that no one who loves wine has ever dared dream about. The most wonderful wine-tasting in the world, the time of my life, I'm going to have it now, on my own, until I'm completely drunk. I'm going to treat myself to the most incredible journey through the centuries. No one's done it before today, no one will do it again. Gentlemen, I'll see you in three days.' "

The wine was flowing through Nicolas's veins and warming him at last. He felt close to this wonderfully fanatical sommelier. He closed his eyes for a moment and gave a sigh which marked the boundary between this world and *that* one.

He had always known this world, it was the world of his childhood and of the passing years. A good old reality to which he was condemned like everyone else. This particular world was almost everything to him, it was the depository of the past and the guarantor of the future. It made you want to exist, if not to live. This particular world was not what men could make of it but what they did make of it. It would endure, men would not. It was made up of compromises, of stopgaps, a place where we looked for what little happiness each day could offer and where we soothed the pain of the moment. When we tried to flee, it became a prison; we could not live on the periphery of this world. It made anyone who had been weak enough to look towards *that* world pay a high price.

And that world was very different.

It was a place of asylum for anyone who might, occasionally, want to escape this world. An inn which was open day and night, a warm welcome at a modest price. Here, at last, all men were equals, all men could be proud. Who was not welcome in that world? Its door was always open, a brotherhood which took in everyone, from all walks of life: the happiest, the saddest, the strongest, the wisest. It was somewhere we could catch our breath, we could stay long enough to smile again. The most desperate took up residence there. The most lucid did too. All it took was a glass. And, above all, a sigh.

"For dessert, I'll take another plate of aubergine," she said.

He was far more fascinated by Loraine's gentle, impish smile than all the masterpieces in Rome. He put down his fork and watched her eating, drinking, smiling, amazed by her every gesture; he wanted to hold on to that brief moment of harmony, seeing so many qualities with one glance. Even though he knew that in a few seconds, an hour or a day all the troubles in the world would bear down on him again, at that precise moment his heart was happy. He ordered another bottle saying that, if he opened enough, he would eventually find a note from someone shipwrecked on an island, a treasure map or the secret of happiness.

"Shall we start with the Sistine Chapel or the *Pietà?*" she asked.

"We're going straight to the hotel to make love. If you want, I can work on the Renaissance style."

"You talk a lot of nonsense . . ."

"We'll go and see the *Pietà,* if you like. But promise me that once we're back in Paris you won't talk about Michelangelo for a fortnight."

At that precise moment, if Mephistopheles himself had appeared to grant one single wish in exchange for his soul, Nicolas would have asked to be included in Loraine's collection. He would never be an inventor, even a minor one, he was the very opposite; the Trickpack demonstrated a certain imagination which he allowed to express itself when he was half cut, but his creative abilities stopped there, with silly excesses which humanity could easily cope without. What was he left with to impress the woman he loved, to dazzle her eyes only, to feel unique? He would have condemned his eternal soul to find that breath of inspiration, the strength, the beauty.

A crazy idea came to him and he gave a little laugh, a laugh dredged up from way back in his past.

The piano, standing silently in the corner, reminded him of a scolded pupil.

No, you'd never dare.

He drank a whole glass from the second bottle, and looked at the backs of his hands stretched out in front of him, perfectly motionless.

It's been too long, Nicolas. You're going to make a fool of yourself.

No, he no longer needed his intrinsic shyness, it could no longer protect him. Trampling over it was becoming a source of pleasure.

You wouldn't know how to any more, it's the sort of thing you forget.

And yet . . .

How old had he been . . . Fifteen? Twenty?

The tips of his fingers were itching. He clenched his fists.

Loraine looked up when, without any warning, he headed for the piano. The waiters and other customers paid no attention, she was the only one to be surprised. He sat down like a real pianist, rubbed his hands together and toyed with the keys for a moment. Loraine watched him with her mouth open, her fork in mid air, amused, worried. The quiet hubbub in the room reassured Nicolas; he was alone with the keyboard, trying to remember a few moments stolen from his youth. Bent over the keys, he tried to identify them by association of ideas, as he had done at the time. *That one there over the lock is where the thumb goes, then a gap of three keys to the little finger. Now where was the right hand again? I had the first finger on a black key, somewhere to the left.*

Loraine crossed her arms; she loved surprises. She loved Nicolas even more.

What have I got to lose.

Had Debussy's notes ever rippled round this little trattoria on the Piazza del Popolo?

Nicolas remembered "Clair de Lune" from twenty years earlier.

The false notes were forgotten. The company fell silent.

Soon, there was nothing but the music.

*

The *Pietà* and the Sistine Chapel; they did not need to see anything else. After all, that was what they had come to Rome for; gorging themselves on art would probably have ruined it somehow. Nicolas could not wait to leave these marvels to go and drink, but settled for discreetly draining his flask. Alcoholism may have been gaining the upper hand, but he did not want to read it in Loraine's eyes. He wanted to be alone with her again, to get away from public places – even if they were sublime – and to mess around, to say and do whatever he felt like in a few square yards of space, so long as it had a mini-bar and curtains. She had absolutely no desire to go back to the hotel and wanted to make the most of Rome and of seeing Nicolas by the light of day. That was when he understood that he needed to drink to jam the cogs of his worrying, but also to ensure that the cogs of happiness did not get too carried away.

They had an aperitif on the Piazza Navona, like the tourists that they were, then wandered through the streets looking for places to take snapshots. Late into the night they went back to the hotel and threw themselves at each other. A full bottle of Wyborowa in one corner of the room would take responsibility for driving away Nicolas's demons should they threaten to come back in force. All he had to do now was to love, without thinking about anything else.

It would have been unthinkable for him to turn back into the unsavoury character he had always been, anxious for a thousand absurd reasons. From now on, at any time of day or night, he knew how to get in touch with his Hyde when he was Jekyll, so that he could take over the controls. His sense of the moment no longer betrayed him. He had learned to change gear as the fancy took him, to call on his double on demand. The *Other* knew how to make everything exciting: a conversation in a bistro, a journey on the Métro, reading a daily paper. He could make something magical out of meeting a woman in a lift, he could find the words to calm people who had got heated and re-enthuse those who had lost their enthusiasm. It was not the darkness in Nicolas which was set free but the very opposite: his benevolence towards humanity, his curiosity for everything outside his own little world, his gentleness which had been held in check for too long. In the rare moments when he let the *Other* drift away, Nicolas quickly felt a nostalgic longing for his escapades, his brilliant and peculiar ideas, his pride.

Be wary of the anxious, the day they lose their fears they will become the masters of the world.

The words which escaped in the night inspired him for the day ahead, and the simple fact of having written proof that this other version of himself existed gave him strength. He was no longer afraid of his shadow, his shadow was this *Other*, who protected him.

Beware those who confuse lighting with light.

Paul Vermeiren

He sat up suddenly and remained paralysed for quite a time, the newspaper in his hand, unable to react. Far away he could hear Julien Grillet's voice without grasping what he was saying. Paul took a few steps across his office, opened the window, let his gaze linger vaguely on the school playground opposite, and brought his hand up to his mouth to repress a retch. He desperately needed to get outside but he did not know where to go.

"I'm popping out for a minute. Can you field any calls?"

". . . Are you OK?"

Paul gave no reply.

"You're white as a sheet."

"I've got a meeting here in an hour, but I won't be here. Give some sort of excuse, suggest another time. I never do this . . ."

"I'll take care of it. Call me if you need to."

Julien followed him as far as the hall and closed the door gently behind him. At the foot of the stairs, drained of all his strength, Paul sat down on a step and opened the crumpled paper again.

> *The friends of Thierry Blin, who left us a year ago,*
> *are invited to meet on Tuesday, 16 May at 6pm,*
> *at 170 Rue de Turenne, Paris 75003,*
> *to have a drink in his memory.*

*

There must be some mistake.

It was the perfect crime.

He had committed it.

He had disappeared, this Blin, he was crossed off the list of the living. He was neither good nor bad, he was mortal: Paul had only precipitated the inevitable. And, God knew, a year after his withdrawal, Vermeiren had thought he was in the clear. He had enjoyed his impunity as if the screenplay for his crime and its incomparable execution had given him the right never to worry again. A year – it was longer than a statute of limitation. He deserved to be filed with the Pointless to Search cases, he had earned the right to exist, to live his life, to do his job, to see whoever he felt like seeing. He was not doing anyone any harm, he was even rather useful to the community; he paid all sorts of taxes, which should give an idea of how much society needed him. Paul Vermeiren had paid a high price for his place in the world and he would not give it up just like that.

Stay rational, analyse. The words "left us" could imply that Blin was considered to be dead. With a little luck, it meant that whoever had put the notice in had mourned their dear *friend*. Friend! Just the word itself, written in black and white in a daily newspaper, was unthinkable. Blin did not have any friends, not a single one to have *a drink in his memory*. Blin would almost

226

certainly have loathed having a friend who would use wording like that. Who wanted to bring Blin up like this? Who had noticed his disappearance? Who remembered him a year later? *Let him die! You bloody left him alone when he was here.* Blin had a right to be done with it, he had a right to demand that no one spoke his name ever again. All Vermeiren had done was help him.

This drink in his memory was to happen the next day; Paul had time to sniff around this 170 Rue de Turenne, an address which meant nothing to him. A bus dropped him on the Place de la République, and he went into the Grand Turenne café, where he passed himself off as a friend of Thierry Blin.

"I can't come tomorrow. Could you tell me who's organizing the gathering?"

The café owner often let out the first-floor room for various receptions; Paul managed to get the name of the woman who had contacted him: Mme Reynouard.

". . . Reynouard?"

His first reaction was to pick up the telephone to get Julien on the job. If he spent the day on it, his associate had a chance of tracking her down with just her name to go on. He changed his mind straight away, hung up, thanked the owner and left the area.

As he walked back to the agency, Paul pictured himself having that drink to his memory in amongst the ghosts who remembered the ghost of Blin. He went over all the bad reasons why he should go and the thousand opportunities he would have to give himself away. The most obvious was the risk of being surrounded by the only people capable of flushing Blin out from behind Vermeiren. All it needed was one insignificant detail that Paul could not have anticipated. This drink in his memory was a poisoned chalice.

But there it was. Was there a get-together in the world more fascinating than that one?

*

Twenty-four hours later, the temptation to play the living dead had got the upper hand.

He went into the Grand Turenne at 6.30. There was a slight hubbub from the room on the first floor, and Paul went up the stairs without a moment's hesitation. This evening he would find himself face to face with the devil. This was the opportunity he had dreamed of to hear the speculation about Blin's death, the follow-up to his disappearance, the results of the various searches. Some pieces of information might even help him avoid future mistakes. More than anything else, he would finally see whether Blin had any friends. Meet them. Measure their pain. Speak to them but, more importantly, listen to them. In less than an hour, he would have the confidence not to bother with him any longer. It was an ordeal by fire, but also the only way of shaking off the spectre of Blin once and for all. He was in fact going to put the nails in his own coffin.

He found himself in a little room off a larger one where a woman draped in a blue satin Chinese dress was uncovering aluminium trays of nibbles. She turned her head when she heard Paul arrive, and greeted him with a smile.

"Hello."

He looked at her questioningly.

"Did you see the ad?"

"Yes."

"It's this way, come with me. I'm Brigitte Reynouard," she said, holding out her hand to him.

. . . *Mademoiselle?*

How could he have forgotten that her name was Reynouard? This woman who knew Blin's social security number by heart, his account numbers, the little secrets of his daily life and his moods; he had not even taken the trouble to remember her surname. He had only ever called her "Mademoiselle". Brigitte wanted to take his leather jacket for him; still feeling dazed and awkward, he felt happier keeping it on. There she was, standing facing him, just as she always used to be, smiling whatever the circumstances. Blin could decode Brigitte's smile; she could express any emotion with those lips. *I don't know you, but thank you for coming, whoever you are,* she was saying now to this stranger. Her long straight hair in a synthetic black fell over her blue satin shoulders.

"Would you like to follow me? The others are already here."

Brigitte looked people in the eye, she shook hands firmly and kissed those she knew better with eager sincerity, as if she genuinely derived pleasure from brushing her cheeks against other people's. Greeting Vermeiren she had felt no particular emotion, apart from the happiness of sharing this gathering with yet another *friend.* Paul had just undergone the first test before he even had the wretched drink in his hand.

"These are people who were close to Thierry Blin, maybe I shouldn't be here."

"What matters is that you wanted to come. Can I ask who you are?"

He had prepared an answer and had rehearsed it out loud, as if playing a part.

"Paul Vermeiren, I'm a private investigator. He contacted me a couple of years ago to trace a drawing by a well-known artist which had been entrusted to him. A complicated business, but it turned out well for him."

"A drawing?"

"Yes, by Bonnard."

"He never mentioned it to me. But I knew everything that was in the shop, I did his accounts."

"He contacted me because he wanted to be discreet. I think it wouldn't matter now if I say he was hoping he could keep the drawing."

"That last year he would have done anything to get money."

"I only saw the ad by chance, yesterday morning. It gave me quite a shock, particularly the words *left us*."

"It gave us all a shock."

"Is he dead?"

She shrugged her shoulders, turned her palms up and sighed. "God alone knows."

"Was this get-together your idea?"

"Yes."

Mademoiselle . . . I wasn't thinking of you when I wanted to leave everything behind. Blin didn't deserve you.

"Come on, I'll introduce you to some of the people I know."

"I'd rather not talk about the business with the drawing. Just introduce me as a customer from the shop."

"I understand."

It was a large room, and there were about twenty people talking quietly, glass in hand. Like a good hostess, Brigitte introduced Paul to "one of Thierry's oldest friends".

Didier was still just as wet, just as blond, still wearing one of his many shimmering shirts with hidden buttons.

"Paul Vermeiren, a customer of his."

That was just the thing to say to Didier to stifle his interest in a new arrival. Didier liked nothing better than shaking the right hands; someone who was just a customer of Blin's was of little interest.

"Didier Legendre, a childhood friend of Thierry's."

They had met when they were in the fifth form; could you still call that childhood? Didier was one of those people who improved on the truth, not to pretty it up but to make the most of what little they had to say. He talked freely about going jogging in the Jardin du Luxembourg at 7 o'clock in the morning, summer and winter; in fact, he had done it exactly twice, in July, on the stroke of 10 o'clock. He boasted that he knew Barcelona "like the back of his hand" and forgot that Nadine, exasperated by how slow he was, had snatched the map from him to get them back to where they were meant to be. He said a dozen when he really meant eight, he said masses when he was talking about several, and he never failed to round reality up rather than down. Given who was there, though, Didier was actually the only one who could claim to be a childhood friend of Thierry's.

"Did you hear about this from the ad?" asked Paul.

"No, Nadine told me."

Paul could not see her there, but could not express his surprise to Didier.

"I don't know her."

"She was Thierry's girlfriend. One of the last people to speak to him."

He and Blin had lost touch: the lacklustre nature of their exchanges and Didier's determination to assert himself in any conversation had become intolerable. He was the sort of man who hogged the ball by tripping up anyone who came near, but never actually scored.

"The few times I met him, I felt I was dealing with someone discreet, always in control. Not the sort of man to disappear from one day to the next."

"There was something tortured about him, he was already like that when he was a boy. The fact that he disappeared is incredible in some ways, but if you knew him really well, it's not all that surprising."

"Really?"

"It would be difficult to sum it up in a few sentences, but when we used to stay up all night together, smoking our first cigarettes and telling each other about our first girls, he was already talking about who he was going to become. He was convinced he was going to bring the house down."

They had smoked, that was true, but they certainly had not "told each other about their first girls", those sort of conquests were still a myth in their young minds. As for "bringing the house down", that was just adolescent nonsense, a teenager's obsession with what the future held, dying to stand out from the crowd – so ordinary it was rather touching.

"We enrolled at the École des Beaux-Arts together. I'm still drawing, it's my job in fact, but using modern equipment: I create virtual pictures. Thierry wanted to be a painter and he ended up opening his framing shop."

At the time, you encouraged me to. You talked about the nobility of being a craftsman, a refusal to accept the world gone mad around us. Now, Didier Legendre made posters using circles and squares in every colour under the sun, creating an impression of relief which a child could achieve by pressing the right buttons. He had even unashamedly asked Thierry to frame some of them. Now, Blin had become Vermeiren, the man he had always wanted to be, and no one else had remained that faithful to their dreams.

"He felt he'd been robbed of a childhood that didn't measure up to his hopes."

Paul had to recognize that there was an element of truth in this.

"Do you know, I once went back to one of our favourite places, along the tracks near the station in Choisy-le-Roi, heading towards Juvisy. At one point there was a sort of hollow under the rails. You could get four people in there, hunched together, waiting for a train to go over. You can't imagine the violence of an experience like that, it went on for ten or fifteen seconds, it seemed like forever. We would scream with all our might to blot out the sound of the train and our fear, too. That's what we were like, Thierry and me."

Paul knew he would stoop pretty low, but not so far as to borrow other people's memories. Waiting for the train, kneeling under the rails – neither of them had done it, only someone called Mathias, who was afraid of nothing, and even let a banger off inside his fist once.

"I went back there because I was thinking of him. I didn't dare do it again!"

The hollow had been filled in two years later; the whole area had been inaccessible for a long time now, surrounded by high-tension fencing. Blin had been back there too.

"We saw less of each other in recent years. We didn't need to. I knew he was there, he knew I was there, that was enough. He would have set off straight away if I'd called for help at 2 o'clock in the morning, and vice versa."

God preserve me from needing someone like you at 2 o'clock in the morning. Blin had become critical of this friendship which had never really been one. It had all become too much one evening in a billiards room on the Avenue du Maine when Didier had spent the evening watching with delight as a group of beginners missed their shots. Thierry realized, too late, that Didier found other people's mediocrity reassuring. There was nothing to rival pleasure like that.

"Ah, do you know Anne?"

Didier used her arrival as an opportunity to slip away and not come back. Paul found himself trapped with the formidable Anne Ponceau, who looked more spruce than ever despite a tendency to portliness which was now irreversible. Ash-blond hair, hazel eyes, and still the careful poise in her voice. Nadine had introduced her to Thierry as her elective sister. They were bound to get on, except for the fact that Thierry was not the family-orientated type. *Anne, you came . . . You didn't seem to think very highly of me. Maybe I was wrong, maybe I mistook your discretion for indifference.* Anne had a lot going for her and just one flaw: psychoanalysis. She was one of those people who thinks that, just because they themselves have being lying on an analyst's couch for years, they can see into other people's souls.

"He never recovered from his father's death. Thierry always suffered from a fear of being abandoned, a lack of protection. For a long time he was looking for a father figure he could identify with."

What he had never been able to bear about Anne was the way she turned everyone into a child or, even worse, saw them as an interesting object of observation, which made her a sort of entomologist, passionate about these theories she put forward with such conviction. She could spend the whole of a dinner party, or sometimes even a weekend in the country, trying to find psychoanalytical explanations for the events of the day, from a plane crash to a mislaid pot of mustard. She could represent those around her as kindly little creatures betrayed by their merciless subconscious. Blin had enjoyed dropping deliberate Freudian slips into conversation – "fighting a liar" instead of "lighting a fire" – to see her go into a state of spontaneous combustion; the ensuing logorrhoea would have been

234

worthy of a minor publication in the author's name. Was this not the same Anne who had said one evening during the course of a sentence: "My mother was a Catholic, my other father a Protestant."

"And, actually, Thierry's mother never got over her husband's death. Nothing was ever the same again."

Interesting hypothesis. Anne had never ventured to say this in front of Blin himself. A strange situation having his own family dramas summarized when he himself had never been aware of them. Losing his father had been painful, but he had never felt that it had broken them, either himself or his mother.

"What matters is whether that can shed any light on his disappearance," said Paul.

"There must be a connection. Thierry was afraid of the process of analysis. It would probably have helped him get through this crisis."

Anne had tried more than once to urge him towards the psychoanalyst's couch; indefatigable preaching which was truly in keeping with her personality. *I went about it another way, Anne. It's still too early to say whether I've got myself right, but at least I've tried.* Paul would like to have seen the look on her face if he admitted it all to her now, that he had changed his face, his name, his job, his home, his girlfriend, that he had organized his disappearance and that he was there now, with her, listening to her making loud pronouncements like "Thierry was afraid of the process of analysis." Anne had absolutely no scruples about interfering with other people's lives or guessing what might become of them. She used a basic framework of ideas she had read about, and cobbled them together into the cast-iron certainties she could use till the end of her days. Trying to find predictable aspects in everyone was to deny the irrational element in each of them, the hint of poetry, absurdity and free will. Some kinds of madness were beyond any logic, and most – like Thierry Blin's – were not recorded in the great books on pathology.

Between sips of this drink in his own memory – a rather strong punch – Paul stopped to look at certain faces. With each pair of eyes, each turn of a head, each new arrival, he expected to be struck down by the wide-eyed astonishment of someone recognising Blin's shadow behind his features.

If they talked about him enough, they would end up seeing him everywhere.

In the meantime, he was passing the test with flying colours. His moment of truth had not yet come. Now that Anne had thrown herself into the arms of one of Nadine's friends – Mireyo, or some odd-sounding name like that, Blin had hardly known her – he could at last, slowly and methodically, tot up those who had bothered to get here to remember him.

He spotted, amongst others, the young framer who had taken over his boutique, standing talking to Mme Combes and various other customers from The Blue Frame. Paul was almost touched that they were there, especially the doctor, a kind, wealthy, brilliant man, who was extraordinarily polite and who had never actually paid for the display cabinet Blin had made him for his symposium on occupational medicine. Outside this little group, which was not mingling with the others, there was Roger, the man who had introduced him to framing at the Louvre. Paul wondered how he had caught wind of this gathering, and went over to him, saying hello as if out of pure courtesy, and held his glass out to clink it against Roger's. Roger was a real framer, the sort who sees it as an art to which a whole life can be dedicated. He was eloquent only in exercising his profession, the rest of the time he listened shyly, as he did now with Paul Vermeiren. His cousin Clément was there too, one of the last vestiges of a rather rootless family. Blin had never enjoyed a grandmother's jam or had rows with country cousins. Christmas dinner had never involved more than four people. Clément, the son of his mother's only brother, had lived in Vietnam until he was eighteen, then in Djibouti until the age of thirty-five; they had not spoken more than three times since his return. Paul noticed the completely unwarranted presence of Jacques and Céline, a couple who had been neighbours on the Rue de la Convention. Thierry had *left* them, and that simple word gave some sort of impact to the fact that they had known him; the little whiff of heresy made the trip worthwhile. Had Blin fallen into a crevasse? Had Blin been kidnapped, exiled, sequestered by some sect, bumped off by poker players with Mafia connections? Had Blin started a new life somewhere else? What cruel irony: he would live on in their memories because he had stepped out of their world with no explanation. Becoming a minor news item was the best way of ensuring you are not forgotten.

Oh look, the barber . . . the barber's come . . .

How could Paul have known that the barber was not the sort to bear a grudge. Once, when he had been walking past The Blue Frame, Blin had sworn at him for throwing his cigarette packet on the ground. He had flown into a blind fury: people who did that sort of thing were inferior beings with absolutely no thought for life or other people; they were condemned to remain puerile till their dying day, because they had a long way to go – too far – to change. The man had listened, speechless, and had made apologies which Blin, in his rage, had not wanted to hear. His anger swiftly turned to embarrassment; he never went back to the man's salon. Now, the barber was there with this drink to Blin in his hand. Paul could not resist the urge to go and talk to him.

"Hello, I'm Paul Vermeiren, I was a customer at Thierry Blin's shop but I don't live round there."

"Jean-Pierre Maraud, we were colleagues. Well, what I mean is, we both had businesses in the same area."

He took a handful of peanuts and swallowed them all in one go.

"What sort of business?"

"I have a hairdressing salon."

"I don't have much call for them," he said, stroking his smooth head.

Maraud was not particularly intrigued by Paul and was trying to listen to anecdotes from Mme Combes nearby.

"Did you cut his hair?" Paul persisted.

"A long time ago, yes, but there was a little incident, a stupid thing: I threw some paper down in the street and he never spoke to me again."

"He probably regretted it, you know. Perhaps he didn't dare go past your salon because he felt guilty."

"He was right to get so angry. It made me wonder why I chucked things on the ground. Was it because I didn't have any sense of the common good and I couldn't care less about keeping the streets clean? Was it because I could picture some dustbin man coming along behind me? Or just because it was forbidden here, wasn't that a good enough reason to allow myself to? I didn't manage to allocate myself to one of those categories, but I was frightened of ending up in any of them, and that taught me a hell of lesson. I had, as he said at the time, a long way to go. That business with the paper on the ground acted as a trigger, a moment of awareness. Now, when I see someone throwing

238

something away in the street, I feel sorry for them. I rate respect for the community pretty highly now. Thanks to Thierry Blin."

Paul Vermeiren suddenly felt very hot; the drink was going to his head. He would have liked to chat to all of them, to hear them talk about Blin, to learn a bit about him. All of a sudden he recognized a voice and turned round in disbelief. A little voice from the past, with an unforgettable ring to it which he had forgotten. He tried to find where it was coming from. *She was tiny, that girl.* A voice that matched her size perfectly. And her little face was always slightly screwed up, her way of coming over all sweet and innocent.

. . . Agnès?

Are you here, Agnès?

Her hair had faded a bit, but she had stayed faithful to the Louise Brooks bob. So like a little imp popping out of a box. Even when she was only sixteen she just wanted to have children and look after them, she even wanted to look after other people's, she wanted them all over the house. Blin had not yet known how to make them. Agnès had initiated him, barely older than him but so much more at home with all that. Her parents were divorced and she lived with her mother, who was the Blins' neighbour. One day Thierry and Agnès had taken the train to go and spend the weekend with her father in Rueil-Malmaison. They wanted to play lovers like in the films, all candlelight and fishnet stockings, fake champagne and genuine fear, all the elements of a fiasco in one go. They didn't actually make love until a week later, with no preamble or decorum, in the bedroom she had had since she was little, just a few yards from the sitting room where her mother was watching an episode of *Dallas*. Their relationship did not even make one complete revolution round the sun. How could he have guessed that, twenty years later, she would still attach any importance to it. There was a tall man with her, attentive and discreet. She had always dreamed of a giant to give their children a chance of being average. Slightly self-conscious, they were talking to one another to give an impression of belonging. They knew no one and no one knew them. Vermeiren went over.

"Hello, I'm Paul Vermeiren, I don't know many people. It seems you don't either."

"I'm Agnès and this is my husband, Marco. I read in the paper that Thierry was . . . well . . . he had left us. I wasn't even sure if it was the same Thierry. It was such a long time ago . . ."

Paul would have liked to hold Agnès's hand in his for a moment, just long enough to wind the clocks back.

"We were neighbours in Juvisy. How about you?"

Your bra opened at the front. You already knew how awkward boys were. You had a way of saying "oops . . ." when my hands ventured into still forbidden territory.

"We still live in the suburbs, it's better for the children."

I loved blowing on your forehead to mess up your fringe; you hated it. You let me watch you washing; I dried you, the towel wrapped right the way round you.

"We never saw each other again."

The two of us devastated one morning, and our tragedy had a name: thrush. There was a lot more about "always" than about love in what we said to each other. We didn't actually love each other, we just made a point of adoring each other.

"We've got quite a way to go and then we have to get the babysitter home. Tell me, do you mind my asking, is Thierry's wife here?"

Agnès wanted to see what she looked like, her

240

childhood sweetheart's wife. Paul had just experienced the same curiosity seeing the tall man on her arm.

"She was meant to come, but I can't see her here."

"Never mind. Well, thank you, Monsieur . . .? What was your name?"

"Vermeiren."

Her husband put their glasses down, looked for his keys and checked with Brigitte how best to get back out of the city to the south. Agnès took this opportunity to shake Paul's hand again; he felt a sort of caress in her palm. She looked him right in the eye and communicated her uneasiness to him.

"Shall we go, darling?" asked the giant.

Goodbye, little one.

Brigitte reappeared with a tray of canapés.

"Would you like me to introduce you to someone?" she asked him, attentive as ever.

She would never have guessed that he had something in common, however brief, with each and every one of them.

Nathalie Cohen, his sometime opponent in tennis. A far superior player to Thierry, her superiority more than compensating for his physical strength. Nadine and M. Cohen would watch them play for a while and then slip away to go and drink a Coke while she made him sweat as no other woman ever had.

Michel Bonnemay, his dentist, had come with Evelyne. Blin never paid for his treatment, reimbursing him with framing jobs. No one knew exactly how their accounts stood. They found the whole thing very funny and it certainly made the bookkeeping easier. Like Brigitte, Paul wanted to thank them one by one, all these people who had taken the trouble to come. Were they a mosaic of Blin, of his human interactions? Could they between them write the story of this dear friend who had left them? Mme Combes, who was very much making herself heard, would have been happy to take on a whole chapter.

"He was adorable, but you had to be careful – what a man he was! He liked to keep his customers in the frame, he really did!"

Blin had prompted her with that pun, and she had not got it at first.

"And I can tell you an anecdote. Oh, when I think of that day . . . You may remember, it was while I had that ear infection which wouldn't go away, but there were compensations! I can admit it now, I told everyone that I was deaf and most people believed me. That way I only heard what I wanted to. Well, one day, this was just for a joke, you know, I was in his shop to pick up a frame. He told me it came to 600 francs. Quick as a flash, I gave him a 200 franc note, thanked him and walked out. My God, it was funny! You should have seen him running after me and yelling '600 francs!' in my ear."

A few people smiled round her, the odd polite laugh. Paul remembered the incident; the night before he had seen a film in which the central character was a framer whom no one ever paid, not even a little old woman who pretended not to hear him and gave him half of what she owed as she thanked him with a beaming smile. Mme Combes had also seen it and had taken a good deal of inspiration from it; the scene had taken place just as she had described it except that Blin had not chased her along the street as she claimed, but had settled for letting her go like the hero in the film, saying: *You're very clever, Madame Combes.* He had lost 400 francs, but just for a minute he had seen himself as a character in a film, and it was cheap at the price. If Blin had been buried for real, Mme Combes would have

242

been the one making a collection for the wreath. *On behalf of all his friends in the street.*

One anecdote always raises another. Paul soon felt overwhelmed.

"I also remember a day when . . ."

"So do I, listen to this . . ."

Unable to catch them all, he missed half of what was being said, which was awful!

"And crafty with it . . ."

"Tortured in a way, you could tell . . ."

One at a time, for goodness' sake! Let me make the most of this, I do have a right!

"Well, I remember his shop better than I remember him," said the bookseller. "Going to the framer isn't like nipping to the butcher. Sometimes I would go for no reason, to chat and have a cup of tea, to listen to that strange silence punctuated by the sound of his rasp, to smell the varnish. In the summer, it was always cooler in there. Time passed in a completely different way from everywhere else in the area. And he moved slowly himself. While he was working we could stay like that in silence without either of us feeling embarrassed. It was like a serene backwater, cut off from the rest of the world, and when you came back out there was all the commotion of the streets of Paris."

"He liked encouraging people to do what they wanted. If you've always wanted to go to Nepal, do it! If you want to set up in business on your own, do it! If you want to lose twenty pounds, it's all up to you! He thought that everything came down to determination, and he was right. You only had to talk to him on the phone to feel better."

Paul was tempted to believe them but he tried to think it through: these people were meant to say nice things about the friend they had lost, that was just the point of the gathering. There was nothing exceptional about Blin; anyone else would have been entitled to the same treatment.

"He had a strange combination," said a voice which carried over the others, "of sensitivity and a sort of distance from things."

The man was very talkative and his baritone's voice gave resonance to his charisma. A solid little body, deep set eyes, a very lined face, an unfamiliar figure who had intrigued Paul since the beginning of the get-together.

"Setting such high standards for himself that he could do the same with other people."

It was definitely the first time he had ever seen this man in his life.

"The word 'ethical', which is so bandied about nowadays that it doesn't mean anything any more, still meant something to him. The word 'honour' did too."

Isn't someone in this room going to get around to asking him what the hell he's doing here, in God's name?

"I'm sure I can tell you this now that he's no longer here, he always used to say: 'You see, René, I feel nostalgic for the existence of God. Life would be so much simpler if I were a believer. I wouldn't stop to think about so many things.'"

How long are you going to let him hold forth like this? This man's an impostor! He's never met Blin in his life!

"Once, by chance, I saw him at the cemetery in Montmartre, standing thinking over Stendhal's grave."

Madman! Murderer! Brigitte, turf him out! He must do this every day, it's a hobby, a skill, a perversion or something like that. He reads the deaths column in the papers and comes and puts on his little performance! It's not even the word "drink" that motivates him, it's the word "memory"'!

Nadine's arrival attracted people's attention, and

they lowered their voices. Even the impostor. On her own, looking pretty good, dressed rather extravagantly to show that she was anything but a widow. Here too, Paul would have paid a high price to see what the new man in her life looked like, or the man in her new life. Like his clients at the Good News Agency, he was curious about his successor's face. Nadine kissed almost everyone, poised between smiles and seriousness. After all, she had a part to play. He wanted a real test and here she was at last, in the flesh. He was going to have to face this woman he had lived with for five years, a woman who had cried in his arms, who had cared for him when he was ill. Brigitte introduced her to the few guests she did not know, including Paul.

"Nadine Larieux."

"Paul Vermeiren."

She said hello and moved onto the next person, just like that, taking him in her stride. He would never have guessed that she had such a firm handshake.

. . . Nadine? Tell me it's not true . . . Nadine, it's me!

"Hello, Michel, hello, Evelyne."

Yes, me . . . the guy who took off all your clothes in those deserted woods, in broad daylight, because he liked the idea. And you did too, I have to say. Hey . . . Nadine?

"Hello, you."

"Hello, Nadine."

The one who asked you to wear those leotards which opened between the legs. Yes, it's me, come on, have a look at me for goodness sake!

"How are you, Didier?"

The one who used to gag you with his hand when you sometimes made too much noise. Doesn't that mean anything to you any more?

"Well, are we going to have this drink, then?" she said.

Another round of drinks was served while everyone chatted and laughed. Paul Vermeiren had just found what he was looking for: the right to exist, to put together his own memories without needing Thierry Blin's. Feeling very reassured, he was about to leave when Brigitte asked for a bit of quiet.

"I'd like to thank you for coming here today for Thierry."

People reacted, raising their glasses towards her. She shook her hand to show that she had not finished.

"To be absolutely honest, that's not the only reason I asked you to come here this evening. As you may know, the investigations into Thierry's disappearance have officially been closed, for want of clues. I've spent hours talking to the police about it, and they have to follow procedures. But I'm not satisfied with that version of the truth. I can't accept it."

Everyone was caught on the back foot. The punch had barely awakened their consciences, the mood of reflection had given way to a warm ambiance, the witnesses to a life had become guests looking forward to an evening together. And then Brigitte had drawn their attention to a tragedy.

Hers.

"I thought that, if I assembled everyone who knew him, we could piece together what we know and get information the police don't have. If we all try to remember the last days before he disappeared, we might be able to pick up some clues, even tiny ones, which could reopen the enquiry. There's not much left to hope for, but I've got to see this through. I wouldn't forgive myself for the rest of my life if I didn't try."

There was silence in the room.

Brigitte looked at them expectantly.

No one knew how to respond to what she had said and

246

the silence persisted, disturbing and uncomfortable. Paul felt overcome, and went and sat down by himself for a moment.

So it was her.

Brigitte.

She had been the one to contact the police, she had waited for the results of the enquiry, she had given and hoped. There was no doubt now that she was the one who had reported Blin's disappearance. Why had she done so much? Blin was nothing more than a client of hers. He did not remember one single ambiguous moment, not one of those looks that inadvertently passes between a man and a woman, like a tacit code. He did not remember looking at her legs once, or peering down her blouse. Or dreaming about her. He had no memories of any little play of seduction. To him, Brigitte was charming, adorable, attentive and radiant. That was quite a lot, but that was all.

*

Before leaving, each of them said what they could to help Brigitte, even the impostor. Even though she did not admit it, or even formulate the idea, Anne did not like to think that Blin was alive. Too irrational, too unrealistic. Blin did not have the makings of one of those news stories. Paul felt almost hurt. Luckily, the general tendency was to be pessimistic, as if people wanted to dampen Brigitte's hopes and prepare her to accept the worst. She had become the sailor's wife, still waiting for a miracle even after the shipwreck had been announced. A woman who would have given anything just to be sure. Blin meant that much to her. It was almost touching seeing even Nadine come over to comfort her.

"He'll go on living in our memories."

"If he's dead, may he rest in peace," said Didier.

"If he's alive, let's respect the choice he's made," ventured Michel.

Paul crossed his fingers in the hopes that it would stay at that. When the last of them had left the room, Brigitte had a false air of widowhood about her. Paul picked his leather jacket up from the back of a chair, and she ran over to him.

"Stay a bit longer, I'm going to see the others out."

An order. Gentle and shy but still an order. Right up until the last handshake and the last thank yous, Paul felt his heart beating in his chest fit to burst. He was afraid that Vermeiren's mask had not stood up to scrutiny from a woman in love.

Paul had almost believed in Blin; Agnès had kept a place for him in her memory, the barber felt a better man thanks to him, even the impostor had managed to describe him as a pure spirit. And had this marvellous man really been so blind that he failed to notice Brigitte's affection?

Now they were alone in the large room, which suddenly felt very quiet and empty.

"I was afraid this gathering wouldn't do much good," she said, "but I couldn't not do it."

"I understand."

"Are you in a hurry? Shall we have one last drink? Not to remember, I don't mean that."

He was not sure what she did mean, but he agreed, hypnotized by eye contact from this woman who had managed to hide her love like some romantic heroine. She took out a bottle of whisky and immediately poured two glasses. Blin used to do it for her to celebrate finishing the tax return and other forms like that; a ritual she had kept up.

248

Mademoiselle . . . How could I have guessed what you felt for me? You should have given me some sign. It might have changed everything, who knows?

"How could he have done this to me, after everything we went through? I wasn't just his accountant you know . . ."

Paul listened expectantly.

"Well, I can tell you, we had a relationship."

He swallowed hard.

"No one ever knew anything about it, not even Nadine. We were discreet . . . we were brilliant!"

Still, he said nothing.

"More whisky?"

"Perhaps you should slow up."

"We used to make love in the workshop, he would lie me down on the long table, near the bench, in amongst the wood shavings and the pots of varnish. Unforgettable!"

"Brigitte . . ."

"In his arms, I felt like . . . it's hard to say . . . I saw myself as . . . 'Mademoiselle'. A woman who existed for his eyes only, the woman I became when he came near me . . . I want to be 'Mademoiselle' again . . ."

He watched her in silence.

"Find him for me."

". . . I'm sorry?"

"I know he's not dead. I'm absolutely convinced. I can tell he's there, not far away, that he's played a dirty trick on us."

Paul waited anxiously.

"I'd like to hire you officially. That's your job, isn't it? Where the police have failed, I'd like you to make it your mission."

"Don't you think the others are right, that it's better to forget him?"

"I can't help it. Until I'm given formal proof that he's dead, I'll look for him. When he sees everything I've done for him, he'll fall in love with me."

"If he's still alive, it could take years!"

"If you won't do it, I'll take on someone else, and someone else after that."

Panicking at the thought of this, Paul tried to find a definitive argument, and only came up with a pathetic: "It's going to be very expensive!"

"Never mind that. Will you take it on or not?"

He closed his eyes and searched, deep inside himself, for the strength not to break down in tears.

Nicolas Gredzinski

This *Other* him was emphatic: *leave her alone.* The notes that he left for Nicolas in the early hours of the morning were beginning to sound like dictates. *For once you've met someone who's not asking for anything except that you don't ask her anything – don't go and ruin it all.* The reasoning sometimes changed, but the message remained the same. Nicolas was offended by it: while his double was writing these fevered words, Loraine was close to him, warm and beautiful, devastatingly present, just a caress away. It was easy enough for the *Other* to beg him to be patient, he did not have to live with the unbearable doubt which dogged Nicolas all day long. If she was hiding something too shameful to mention, he had a right to know; a right because he was in love and he was suffering. Why go on with this extraordinarily cruel game? The *Other* came back time and again to the word "trust", but did Loraine trust Nicolas? Surely the poor man had successfully passed all the tests? Surely he had been patient enough? As time went by, he interpreted Loraine's silence as suspicion, and this suspicion took on an air of contempt.

Nicolas no longer hid in front of Muriel when she came in to give him his mail at the stroke of 10 o'clock. With the whole range of Trickpacks on his desk, he no longer even felt he had to hide his beer. The device had been conceived from a feeling of shame which he had now shaken off; he drank beer because it was what his body wanted and his conscience had no problem with that. From time to time the *Other* would lash out with a comment on the subject: *Drink as much as you need, drink so long as it helps you get on. Steer clear of aniseed derivatives and spirits made from fruit. Your first try was a stroke of luck, stick to vodka. You can mix with it so long as you don't lose sight of the pleasure of the taste. And remember to drink lots of water between glasses of alcohol. I know it's not easy, but do your best.*

"Shall I leave the newspapers that came while you were away?"

"Thank you, Muriel."

He used his daily review of the papers to emerge from his hangovers, which were getting worse and worse. He opened a second Heineken and chose the Trickpack of another brand of beer to disguise it, amused by the absurdity of what he was doing. Amongst the latest range of Trickpacks offered by Altux Ltd, there was a design with black capitals on a white background stating something along the lines of: *Excessive drinking can damage your health.* There were the designs for couples, *His* and *Hers* – with options for personalizing them by inscribing names or printing photographs on them. There were subversions of canned foods, including Popeye's famous can of spinach. There was the *Trichloroethylene* Trickpack, but also the ones saying *Arsenic, Strychnine* and *Holy Water.* And, to crown it all, slogans about drunkenness, and extracts from famous film dialogues. Nothing surprised Nicolas any more, especially before his first beer of the day, the one he tasted with every last taste bud. The rest of the day he had the choice of a variety of poisons, depending on the circumstances. At a particular time in the evening, the beer called quite irresistibly for vodka, and then, late at night, the vodka would call for the chill of beer. And Nicolas threw himself into this spiral without a shadow of remorse. Some day soon, eaten away by alcohol and at death's door, he would still have the delicate memory of the bitter taste of beer in the morning.

> *The friends of Thierry Blin, who left us a year ago,*
>
> *are invited to meet on Tuesday, 16 May at 6pm,*
>
> *at 170 Rue de Turenne, Paris 75003,*
>
> *to have a drink in his memory.*

In between two articles he barely glanced at: Thierry Blin.

Looming up from another life.

The tennis match at the Feuillants Club. Borg and Connors.

Such a small paragraph, such an aberration.

Now that was one drink that Nicolas would not be having: he had been in Rome on Tuesday, 16 May.

Any doubts about the name did not stand up to the "who left us a year ago". This was the same Blin, the one who had thought of the drunken challenge. They had arranged to meet three years later, on June 23rd to be precise, in less than a month in fact.

His beer suddenly tasted like sparkling water and was no longer any use to him at all. To register the shock, he felt he had to put his hand to his flask in his left inside pocket. The swig of vodka was taken almost before he realized it; he needed to concentrate without awakening his fears. What did that "left us" mean? Dead or missing? How could he guess what the madman was up to? Had he carried on with his ridiculous idea of becoming someone else? What for? And at what price? Had Blin died because he'd wanted to become this other person? One thing was sure: neither of them would be at the rendezvous they had arranged. Nicolas would never forget that lunatic who wanted to be someone else and who, without realizing it, had introduced him to vodka. So he raised his flask to the memory of Thierry Blin, his unwitting benefactor. That was his way of drinking to his memory.

The newspapers and magazines spread out over the table had just lost all interest. For reasons that he did not yet understand, Nicolas took back out the notes left by the *Other* the night before. All that really mattered was written there on those little pieces of paper, the rest could be forgotten. The monster was becoming more and more precise with his wording and now even took care with punctuation and made proper sentences, though still in the same spirited – sometimes threatening – tone, as if bellowing from the very depths of darkness.

Before, if someone made you wait more than twenty minutes for a meeting, you would worry that they had died. From now on, you should hope they have!

Some passages were more cryptic. Nicolas kept them carefully in a drawer and cast his eye over them from time to time to decipher the enigma.

Tell Garnier to piss off with his restructuring plan. It improves things only for his department, even if he's claiming otherwise.

Rereading these words, Nicolas instantly dialled Garnier's direct line.

"Guy?"

"Hello, Nicolas."

"You know, I've been thinking, and I'd prefer it if our departments stayed separate, at least for now, but thanks for thinking of it."

There was a stunned silence on the other end.

"Goodbye, Guy."

254

Nicolas did have to acknowledge that the *Other* was right about almost everything, except on one point: Loraine's secretiveness. If she did not make up her mind to share her secrets, Nicolas was going to have to do without her consent. He could already hear his double screaming like some voice of doom: *You'll ruin everything, you idiot. Remember the Orpheus myth!*

"I'll take the risk."

She must have her reasons.

"I want to know what they are."

Aren't you happy with what you've got, living from one day to the next? Do you want more? How much more? And at what price?

"That's just it, it's not *from one day to the next*, it's only ever nights. I love this woman, I *love* her, I can't go on not knowing what she does when I'm not there, it's driving me mad. At first, the game was fun, there was a whiff of heresy to it, but the smell of it's become unbearable. I want to know because I have a right to."

You have no right at all.

"What do you know about it? She's always with you, you don't have to suffer her not being there."

What she's giving you is already so good, if she needs more time, let her have it.

"I'm not going to wait one more night."

He had been mulling it over for a few weeks and everything had come to a head when they got back from Rome. He had to know. Right away. All he had to do was open the yellow pages at the letter D.

Detective, Investigations, Tailing, Discretion . . .

As simple as that.

Paris Association of Detectives . . . BU Detective Agency . . . Cabinet Latour, enquiries . . .

In amongst all of these there was bound to be one which could tell him who Loraine was.

APR, missions . . . Anticipating, Deciding, Instigating, commercial and private cases . . .

She would know nothing about it.

Surveillance and Research . . . Detective since 1923 . . .

He would know for sure.

Surveillance in radio-cars, close to Chaussée-d'Antin . . .

He had the right to know.

Consultant Detective . . . Security audits . . . Counterfeiting . . . Debtors . . . Missing persons . . . Data protection . . . SOS Detectives . . .

Which one? These men would do anything, you just had to pay the price. He tried to find a name which inspired him in the listings and the boxed ads, but they were all as good as each other, they all made him suspicious. He took another swig of vodka to give him courage, and looked through each address, each name. Without realizing it, he could not get over the shock created by Blin's reappearance: a reappearance announcing a disappearance, it was all happening too quickly. The words "left us" had disturbed him for reasons that were now becoming clear. And what if, by remaining so anonymous, Loraine disappeared too? And what if she had said as little as possible with the sole intention of facilitating her exit, some time soon? And what if her silence was protecting Nicolas from some threat? Somewhere behind Blin's disappearance, he had become afraid for Loraine. He emptied his flask without even knowing he was doing it.

Private cases . . . Discretion . . . Good News Agency . . .

Why not the Good News Agency? The name was both absurd and naive. This one or one of the others, what did it matter in the end. Having run out of vodka, he resigned himself to finishing his warm beer in one go. He was drunk, he knew that, he had tried hard enough to get there.

"Hello? I'd like to talk to a detective."

"Monsieur Vermeiren is on a case at the moment, but I could arrange a meeting for you."

"I need someone straight away."

"Try BIDM or Paul Lartigues's company, they're big organizations and they can get things going quickly, but perhaps not within the hour."

"I'll sort something out, thank you."

Actually, why did he need to use that lot? What was the point in pouring his life out to some stranger? It wasn't rocket science, after all. With a bit of application and guesswork, he would have it all worked out in less than an hour. He missed the burning of the vodka, he could not wait to get out of the tower and go into the first bar he could find to fill up his flask – he had tried all sorts of other spirits, but none of them could get the *Other* to appear in broad daylight.

"Hello, Loraine? I can't hear you . . ."

"The reception's not very good here. I haven't really got time to talk."

He wanted to give her a chance to tell him everything. Perhaps that was what she was waiting for.

"Where are you?"

"I've just said I haven't got time. Anyway, we're seeing each other this evening, aren't we?"

"I've got to see you now."

"What's the matter?"

"It's important. I wouldn't ask if it wasn't. It's the first time I have, isn't it?"

She did not answer.

"Well, isn't it?"

"Yes."

"Tell me where and when."

She would not commit herself.

"Loraine!"

"The Petits Carreaux Brasserie at the end of the Rue Montorgueil."

"When?"

"One fifteen."

If her secret was too heavy he would help her carry it. If it was too heavy for two, at least he would know for sure and he would know what sort of decision to make.

"Hello, Muriel? I'm going to be out for the rest of the day. Could you cancel everything I'm doing this afternoon?"

"All right, Monsieur Gredzinski. There's just a meeting with the Rhônes-Alpes local council people who are in Paris until Saturday. I'll find another time."

"Thank you, Muriel."

"Monsieur Gredzinski? There is something else . . . Someone's just arrived for you, he'd like you to see him."

"Now? Who is it?"

". . . He says he won't keep you long."

"Who is it, Muriel?"

". . . It's Monsieur Bardane."

"Don't send him in."

He picked up his flask, put it away in his inside pocket and left his office, heading for the lifts. Bardane was there, sitting on a chair like a courier waiting for his package. The last person in the world that Nicolas wanted to bump into. Loraine was waiting, it could be that a whole life was going to be decided in the next hour, and the prick had chosen that precise moment to resurface! Why could the words "left us" not be reserved for people like him?

"Hello, Nicolas."

Bardane held out his hand and forced a smile. Gredzinski did not take the same trouble.

"Your timing's not great. I can't see you now."

There he was, the former client director, looking somehow neglected and dressed up to the nines at the same time. Tired, red-faced, eyes downcast – everything about him looked desperate.

"Just two minutes, please, Nicolas."

The most arrogant will all be servile one day. But why the bloody hell did it have to be today?

Since Bardane had left, Nicolas had felt something close to remorse, but it was a sporadic, low-grade remorse, a decorative remorse, a safety-device anxiety which vanished with the first mouthful of alcohol. This man had tried to humiliate him at a time when he was not yet the Gredzinski he was now, when he was frightened if someone raised their voice in front of him, frightened of his own shadow, of life, of everything: easy prey. Now he had every right to give his resentment full sway.

He was waiting for the lift. Bardane was close behind him, his efforts to catch up as grotesquely pathetic as his every move had been since his redundancy. Nicolas ostentatiously ignored him but there was nothing for it: they ended up alone in the lift.

"I know I made a lot of mistakes with you, Nicolas. I shouldn't have inflicted that meeting on you. I know that that's what you resent me for the most, and you're right."

"I didn't want your job, I was handed it on a plate. If you miss it all that much, take it back, I don't need it any more, I don't even need to work again in my life, I'm getting ten or twenty times my salary every month – and, incidentally, my salary was raised after you left, anyway. I'm only doing this job because it's been quite fun until now, but it's over. They'll be recruiting soon, put yourself in the running."

"Stop making jokes like that. I lost my sense of humour a long time ago."

Did he ever have one? Nicolas wondered as the doors to the lift opened onto the atrium.

"I came to apologize. I'm responsible for everything that happened."

"I'm in a hurry, can't you see?"

"No one wants to take me on, given my age. I thought I'd be able to find work straight away and . . ."

They had reached the paved entrance. The faster Nicolas walked, the more ridiculous the situation became.

"Broaters only sees things through you, just one word from you and I could have a job again – anything, I'm quite happy to be demoted."

"You *have* been demoted."

"Take me on in the department. I know the workshop by heart, I could be an asset."

Nicolas was almost running along the footbridge. He was going to be late, Loraine would not wait. He loved her, he had to tell her right away and convince her that he could take whatever she had to say. Bardane would not give up now and was in danger of ruining everything.

"When the time comes for the Final Judgment," said Nicolas, "and I stand before the Eternal Father, I'll confess all my sins: 'I stole a Transformer toy from someone younger than me when I was six. In the second year I told everyone in my class that Clarisse Vallée was in love with me, and they all made fun of her. I once kicked a cat incredibly hard when it woke me up miaowing for food.' And when the Good Lord asks me how I redeemed myself, what good I did for mankind, I'll tell him: 'I broke Bardane.' "

Nicolas launched himself into the Métro station

and, as he reached the ticket machine, he glanced over his shoulder.

No one.

*

He looked round the café. It was a bad time, with customers trying to grab lunch and looking for a little corner to sit down, and highly charged waiters far too busy to deal with him. He forced his way through the comings and goings and found room to stand at the far end of the bar, which was cluttered with empty glasses and coffee cups. Why had she not told him to meet her in a place they knew, a back-street bar, a park? How could they play out their moment of truth in all the hurly burly of a bistro? She came in, came over to him and gave him a furtive kiss on the lips.

"What's going on?"

"Don't you want to go somewhere else? There must be somewhere quieter round here."

"Nicolas, I've only got ten minutes. I only came because I thought it was an emergency, and emergencies don't take hours, otherwise they wouldn't be emergencies."

"We've got to talk about us."

"Oh shit! I deliberately said I'd meet you here because I saw this coming."

"Don't you think I've waited long enough?"

She raised her eyebrows questioningly.

"I love you, for God's sake!"

"I do too, and that's exactly why I think you should forget about seeing me here now, and we should meet at about 9 o'clock at the Lynn, like we agreed. I'm perfectly capable of doing that, how about you?"

To avoid making the situation any worse, he felt he

had to say yes. After everything they had been through, she still knew how to put him in his place, as she had on the evening they first met.

"Well, till this evening. Give me a kiss, you idiot."

He hated her, he loved her. They kissed. The *Other* was right: he would have to be mad to threaten what they had. She left the bistro; he watched her leaving, she waved to him and went off down the Rue Montorgueil.

He would have to be mad.

Why had she chosen that café?

After all, it didn't matter at all.

Why quarter past one?

Nicolas wondered where all his wonderful determination had gone. The barman wanted to serve him, so he ordered a double vodka and downed it in one, making his eyes water. Did this café mean something in Loraine's life? In her work life? Or her private life, the one he felt excluded from? He went back out onto the street on an impulse, set off in the direction he had seen her taking and stopped on the corner of the Rue Étienne-Marcel. He could see her in the distance, heading for Les Halles.

It was for him to decide, and quickly.

Should he obey the *Other*'s lecturing, go back to the office like a good boy, drown himself in work instead of vodka, meet up with Loraine in the evening and spend the night with her? Or play detectives even though he did not know where that might end up?

He did not have to follow her for long.

Loraine went into a shop with a blue and white frontage.

Through the window, between two posters offering cod fillets for 64 francs for a 1lb bag and Cajun chicken portions for 22.80 francs, Nicolas could see a woman buttoning up her white overall near the till.

262

Loraine froze when she recognized Nicolas's face.

A smile he would rather not have seen crept over her face. She waved to a colleague to take over for her, came out to him, stood squarely in front of him and crossed her arms.

"My name is Loraine Rigal, I live in a studio flat at 146 Rue de Flandre, I'm single and I don't have any children. I was born in a little village near Coulommiers, my parents ran the farm. They weren't very rich, but I got as far as the *baccalauréat*, which wasn't much use to me when I moved to Paris when I was nineteen. I had a little garret room on the Rue Madame with a gas stove and a beige saucepan next to my bed; it had a nice view, I thought it was very bohemian. I went from one little job to another and one little studio to another for a few years until I got a job here. I make sure the departments are properly restocked, I run the till and, given how long I've been here, I run the place without anyone getting on my back. Just like everyone else, I always thought I'd have some great love affair. A waiter in a restaurant put me in the 'weekend' category. He had a girl for one night, a girl for a month and the woman of his life. Just for me, he created the special 'weekend' slot. Then there was Frédéric. I met him in a bookshop, he was a sound engineer in films. I thought he was beautiful and he seemed to like me. Over our very first cup of coffee, he asked me what I did for a living. When I told him that I worked in a frozen-food shop, I felt everything got faster and – without realizing there was a cause-and-effect connection – we were very soon lovers. I was crazy about him. It was one of those situations when you tell yourself that this time it's *for real*. One day he invited me to a huge film gala. It was the first time I'd seen celebrities so close up. That evening I noticed a strange phenomenon: when any man came up to me, it took less than a minute (you could have timed it with a watch) for him to ask me who I was and what I did for a living. When I bravely told them that I worked in a frozen-food shop, it took them less than a minute (you could have timed it with a watch) to find someone else to go and ask the same question. But what else can you say except for 'checkout girl in a frozen-food shop' when you are a checkout girl in a frozen-food shop? What do you say? I work for a large distribution chain for a range of food products? I'm a technician for a chilled-goods chain? So many friends asked Frédéric what he was doing with me that he ended up asking himself the same question. It took me nearly a year to get over it. Then there was Eric. Like all married men, he didn't like us being seen together in public places. We would meet at my apartment and he never stayed after two in the morning. He eventually left his wife to marry an editorial director from a publishing company. And I won't mention Fabien, who knew what I did because we met when he was shopping here. When we had our first argument, he couldn't help himself telling me that he wasn't going to have 'some frozen-foods salesgirl telling him what to do'. I don't see any shame in doing what I do, but for a few years now I've had a different ambition in life. I want to live a real dream: to deal with wine. I got to know wine all on my own, in Paris. I would go into wine bars for the pleasure of discovering it. To learn more about the subject, I read guides and magazines. It's impossible to develop a palate on your own, so I started joining cellarman's associations, and going to wine seminars and tastings. In the more upmarket places I managed to get them to take me on as staff, and I was allowed to taste the *grands crus*. I listened to the professionals and took notes. Then I signed up for a wine tasting course, it helped me differentiate between the flavours and classify them. It was all becoming more and more serious, I saved enough money to go on my first course with trips to vineyards. That's when everything started. I was given time off without pay, and I did the training to get a diploma from the National Federation of Independent Cellarmen. I learned to manage stocks, to buy and store wine, to explore new possibilities. I may have met someone who wants to form a partnership and try to get this going with me. My plan would be to open a little shop for ordinary people with bottles at twenty or thirty francs, sometimes fifty. To do that, you have to trawl up and down France looking for small vineyards which still show a respect for wine in their work, you have to explore the regions that aren't as sought after as others, the Luberon, Corbières, Cahors, Anjou, Saumur, Bergerac, etc. There are still wine producers who know not to make too much, to wait till the grapes are ripe, they take real risks to try and rival the cheap plonk from the co-operatives, the kind you get in Paris in all the big stores with labels showing estates that don't exist. I want to open this shop for the people who'll never try a Talbot '82, to give everyone a chance to taste good wine, because everyone has a right to.

"While I'm waiting to become this other version of me, this *Loraine who gives a good bottle of wine even to the poor,* I promised myself I would never say that I was *Loraine, the checkout girl from a frozen-food shop* again. The journey from one Loraine to the other is exciting but it's long and difficult, it wouldn't take much to bring it all crashing down. So, in order to look after myself, to keep my strength up, to stick to my convictions and to make sure I wasn't infiltrated by other people's doubts – even people who meant well –

265

I've become *Loraine who never answers any sort of personal questions.* Until today it wasn't going too badly. But you just had to know. And because of that, I never want to see you again."

Paul Vermeiren

If he refused Brigitte's case, Paul would be exposing himself to serious danger: having another private detective set on Blin's trail. A charlatan would rake in all her savings and an experienced private detective could follow the trail to Vermeiren.

She had dreamed about Blin so much that she had invented a relationship with him – what a cruel declaration of love! – and this blindness frightened Paul. Her determination to find the beloved man she had lost put him in danger. He had to get out of this and he had to set her free from this passion which had turned *Mademoiselle* into someone who now believed her own fabrications.

So Vermeiren set off to look for Blin, but before starting he could not resist the temptation of asking her about the man.

"Did he have any hobbies, what was he interested in?"

"He liked tennis, but he was too proud to lose a tournament, or even a match. He was what people call a 'bad sport'."

He raised an eyebrow to encourage her to elaborate.

"If he started playing poker, it would only have ended badly. You could try looking in that direction."

"Without knowing what connections he might have had in those circles, it's not going to be easy. Anything else?"

"I don't know if it's significant, but there is one detail

I never mentioned to the police. I didn't want to breach professional secrecy, even if it was a useful clue."

Again he waited for her to explain.

"An accountant is like a doctor or a lawyer. You see what I mean, there are the same restraints of confidentiality."

"Go on . . ."

"When I went through his cheque stubs, I would find three or four payments a year to a 'Barbara', with no other details. 'Barbara 800 francs', 'Barbara 300 francs', those sorts of amounts, never more. I thought it must be a mistress. I got quite jealous of her, but nothing's turned up to support that hypothesis. I never found out who this Barbara was. Could that be any use to you?"

Barbara had a red nose, green hair and size 25 shoes; Blin had never seen her real face. Barbara was a clown. In a long interview in *Nouvel Observateur* she had described how she spent her days in hospitals making children with cancer laugh, weekends and bank holidays included. Especially public holidays. Over the years she had managed to find a handful of voluntary helpers; at the end of the article there was an address to which to send donations. Blin gave the money, sometimes wondering whether it was buying him a clear conscience, until he realized that the answer did not really matter. He could have helped so many other organizations, charities and support agencies, but he had chosen Barbara because the photographs published in the press had not revealed her real face. She could have been a neighbour from his apartment block, he would never have known.

"Did he have foibles, habits?"

"Not really. Or just weird things."

". . . Weird?"

"There was one thing he liked more than anything

else. When it was raining really hard he would secretly watch through the shop window as the street emptied and people ran for cover. Without fail, there was always someone who took refuge in the phone booth on the pavement opposite. Thierry would ring the number and the guy would look a bit disconcerted but he'd always pick up eventually. And that . . ."

And that what? It was just a schoolboy prank, an overgrown teenager's dirty trick.

"Thierry would pretend he was this disturbing, dangerous character, as if he wanted to get the poor man out of there. It would be things like '. . . Hello, Étienne? I could only get 6 kilos, but I won't go below 600 a gram, is that OK?' The man would say something in reply and Thierry would say: 'You're not Étienne! Look, are you in the phone booth opposite the stationers in the Rue Raymond-Losserand?' The poor man would slam the phone down, go out into the rain and disappear round the first street corner. Thierry played lots of other characters: Russian spies, jealous husbands. I thought it was a nasty little game, and he would tell me that he'd just injected a dash of excitement into someone's life when they were bound to have been a bit short of it. You can't imagine how unfair it was."

"What if there was a woman in the phone booth?"

"That was different. Thierry would make a point of trying to make her laugh. He sometimes succeeded."

That was what Paul wanted to hear. Even if hundreds of times Blin had felt like putting on a lugubrious voice and saying: 'That little red skirt really suits you.'

"Can you think of anything else, Brigitte?"

"I found a few pages from his memo pad, but they don't say anything."

"A few pages of what?"

"It was a little notepad, he would put everything he had to do on it, so he wouldn't forget."

". . . How did you get hold of them?"

"I would pick them out of the bin as he threw them away."

Paul had to bite his lip to hide his surprise.

"I know that makes me look mad, but . . ."

Yes, ripe for locking up; he could not believe his ears.

"I've brought a few for you, to show you, but they may not be any use to you."

Absolutely none, but Paul wanted to see them with his own eyes.

Order 50 sheets of plywood from Rossignol
Tuesday evening, chicken. Or veal, Juliette likes veal.
01 55 24 14 15, possible client for the Combes (watercolour)
Tell Nadine she looks good in that dress she doesn't dare wear.

"Is it any use, Paul?"

Annual drink at Parshibi, Sunday (Efferalgan)
Record the film on Channel 3 tonight.
95C? Get an explanation.

"Is it or not?"

"None at all. Are you going to keep them?"

"Of course. I've got so little left of him."

Even if Paul had nothing to fear from these notes, he felt somehow despoiled and he resented Brigitte for being capable of this. Dream chaser, fetishist, what else? Did one-way love push people to these extremes?"

"Did he ever talk to you about suicide? I know the question's a bit abrupt, but we have to consider everything."

270

"He could sometimes seem absent, opaque, distant, but never depressive. The only time I ever heard him use the word suicide, it was in connection with the 'Little Archimedes'."

Vermeiren knew exactly what she was referring to and he found it quite entertaining asking her to explain.

"He quite often told me the story of the 'Little Archimedes', and I would pretend I'd forgotten because he liked it so much. I can't remember where he'd got it from, the papers, a book, a film, it doesn't really matter. It was about a boy of four or five who was an incredibly gifted musician. With no teaching at all, he mastered his scales and could play any instrument without any lessons. His parents were dazzled and they bought him a piano and paid for a teacher. They had a mini Mozart, it was the most amazing luck. But the child's enthusiasm quickly petered out, he refused to play and his parents – who had fostered all sorts of wild hopes – forced him to practise his scales, which made him absolutely miserable. One morning the child threw himself out of the window. In his room, well hidden under his bed, his parents found masses of sketches, geometric figures, calculations, mathematical equations. They discovered, too late, that their child wasn't a little Mozart but a little Archimedes. Like all great mathematicians, he could decipher the language of music, but it was just a diversion. His passion, his true calling, was algebra, geometry, calculus, the laws that govern the universe and shapes. Thierry was fascinated by this story. He couldn't bear the thought of a thwarted vocation."

A shiver ran down Paul's spine as he finally understood why Blin had so liked telling this story.

"Do everything you can. Don't hide anything you find from me. I can cope with whatever you have to tell me."

"Are you sure of that?"

"Yes."

It was perhaps this certainty which encouraged Paul to fulfil his dearest wish: a fortnight later he asked her to come and see him at the agency late one afternoon. He made her wait for about ten minutes, until his associate had left.

"Come in, Mademoiselle Reynouard."

Like other clients, she looked round the room, looking for some typical thing in there, an atmosphere. Then she sat down and crossed her arms, tense, ready for the worst. Paul waited until Brigitte's eyes finally came to rest on his.

". . . What's happened to you, Monsieur Vermeiren!"

"Do you mean this?" he asked, pointing to the bandaging on his face – a wide band of gauze under his left eye, which was bruised and almost closed, and a plaster at the corner of his mouth. On the scars front, Paul had seen much worse than this: these would disappear in less than a week. In the meantime, they were having the intended effect.

"Was it your enquiries which. . .?"

His response to Brigitte's surprise was a long silence.

"I'll come back to that later, let's start at the beginning. I thought about it for a long time before agreeing to this case. The simple fact that Thierry Blin was a client of mine meant that, theoretically, I shouldn't have undertaken any enquiries about him; besides, he knew my face, which would make tailing more risky. You managed to persuade me, and what then happened proved that you were right to."

Paul felt almost jealous as he wondered how Blin could still put that glow in a woman's eyes.

"Despite your best efforts, Blin's own friends and acquaintances didn't give us very much. So I set off on the only trail I had: the job he'd given me with the Bonnard drawing, trying to find its owner. Do you want the details about how I traced him?"

"Have you found him?"

"Yes."

He saw her cheeks flush in a moment, could sense her body tensing, her breath quickening. Blin had never noticed any of this when Brigitte came close to him.

"Where is he? Have you spoken to him!"

He put his hand on a blue file.

"It's all in here, Mademoiselle Reynouard. Thierry Blin lives in Paris, his face has changed and he's now called Franck Sarla."

She listened in stunned silence.

"It took me six days to track him down, four to find who he was in his new life. And it's those four days that are recorded here. Before you read the report, I would like to warn you: what you read will probably shock you. You could still just leave it. I know how determined you are, but you may give up a memory you hold dear for a truth which could be a burden to you for a long time. Think it over!"

"I've thought!"

It was bound to happen.

He picked up the blue file and handed it to her.

She settled herself in the chair, took a deep breath and started to read while, at the back of the room, Paul took a cigarette from a packet that he kept for very rare occasions.

Confidential

Not to be divulged to any third party.

SURVEILLANCE REPORT

Purpose: Surveillance of M. Thierry BLIN, known as Franck

SARLA (and hereinafter called by that name), on Monday, 28 May, starting from his home at 24 Cité Germain-Pilon, 75018 Paris.

0800 hrs: Mission begins.

0830 hrs: Set up surveillance equipment opposite 24 Cité Germain-Pilon.

1025 hrs: M. SARLA comes out alone, wearing trousers and a heavy leather jacket. He walks to the Mont d'or Brasserie, on the corner of the Boulevard de Clichy and the Rue André-Antoine. The staff and *patron*, M. Brun, seem to know M. Sarla. M. Brun comes to greet him and they sit down together at a quiet table to talk.

1150 hrs: End of conversation with M. Brun. M. Sarla leaves the Brasserie and goes into the Métro station.

1205 hrs: M. Sarla comes out of the Métro at Brochant and goes into the Cercle Batignolles, a gaming establishment located at 145 Rue Brochant. This is a club governed by the 1951 law, so only proposed members have access to the card and roulette gaming rooms. The surveillance continued from the billiard hall adjoining the gaming rooms.

1330 hrs: Brief reappearance of M. Sarla wearing a jacket and tie clearly leant to him by the establishment. He visits the toilets and goes back to the gaming room. From information gathered, it can only have been in the room used by poker players.

1550 hrs: M. Sarla leaves the club, alone.

1555 hrs: M. Sarla goes into the Brochant Métro station.

1605 hrs: M. Sarla comes out of the Métro at Place-de-Clichy and heads for the Rue Blanche.

1610 hrs: M. Sarla goes into a municipal crèche at 57 Rue Blanche.

1625 hrs: M. Sarla comes out of the crèche carrying a baby. He takes a pushchair from a shed and puts the baby into the pushchair. He leaves.

1630 hrs: M. Sarla pushes the pushchair towards the Rue

274

Notre-Dame-de-Lorette to the Saint-Georges bus
stop for the No. 74 bus. He waits.

1635 hrs: The bus arrives. A young woman gets off the bus
and comes to meet M. Sarla. She appears to be
20–25, is wearing a short skirt and a Perfecto-style
leather jacket. She kisses M. Sarla on the lips and
picks up the baby in a motherly way.

1655 hrs: M. Sarla leaves the young woman and the baby,
and walks back up the Rue Notre-Dame-de-Lorette,
then the Rue Fontaine and stops at a shop selling
tailor-made fur and leather garments at 17 Rue
Duperré. He tries on a very long sort of tunic in
beige leather with black embroidery; the tailor
adjusts the sleeves (which are very wide, bat-wing
style), asking M. Sarla to try the tunic on several
more times.

1720 hrs: M. Sarla comes out of the shop and goes into the
Pigalle Métro station.

1745 hrs: M. Sarla comes out of the Métro at Sentier and
heads for the corner of the Rue Réaumur and the
Rue Saint-Denis.

1750 hrs: M. Sarla waits at the street corner.

1755 hrs: A prostitute (aged 40–45) comes to meet M. Sarla.
They speak for a while, then step into the porch of
148b Rue Saint-Denis and enter the dilapidated
building. From information gathered, the prostitute
is known by the name Gisèle and works mainly on
the Rue Saint-Denis.

1945 hrs: M. Sarla and the said Gisèle come back out of the
building and part company. It is important to point
out that part of the prostitute's face is swollen
(signs of blows, bruising), she has clearly been
crying and still has a handkerchief in her hand.
As she goes back to her usual work area,
M. Sarla walks towards the Porte Saint-Denis
and goes into the Strasbourg-Saint-Denis Métro
station.

2005 hrs: M. Sarla arrives at the Place Vendôme and goes into the Alibert restaurant on the Rue de Castiglione. This being a top gourmet restaurant, all tables must be reserved in advance; the surveillance continues from outside, in the Café Balto opposite.

2305 hrs: M. Sarla comes back out of the restaurant with two men, both in their fifties and well dressed. They talk for a few minutes then both men get into chauffeur-driven cars, a Mercedes registration 450 CZH 06 and a Safrane registration 664 DKJ 13. The man getting into the latter invites M. Sarla to join him. He refuses.

2310 hrs: M. Sarla leaves the Rue de Castiglione.

2350 hrs: M. Sarla has walked home to 24 Cité Germain-Pilon.

2355 hrs: The surveillance equipment is kept in place outside 24 Cité Germain-Pilon.

Paul was waiting for the exact moment before she turned the page.

"I felt I should stay there, even if it meant spending the whole night there. Bearing in mind what he had done so far, I thought he might have nocturnal activities. And I was right."

The pink had drained from Brigitte's cheeks, leaving them much paler.

SURVEILLANCE REPORT

Purpose: Surveillance of M. Thierry BLIN, known as Franck SARLA (and hereinafter called by that name), on Tuesday, 29 May, starting at his home at 24 Cité Germain-Pilon, 75018 Paris.

0240 hrs: M. Sarla leaves his home in the same clothes he was wearing the day before. He sets off down the Boulevard de Clichy.

0300 hrs: M. Sarla parks outside the disused cinema, Le Royal, on the corner of the Rue du Delta and the Rue du Faubourg-Poissonnière. He rings a bell outside the sliding metal shutter, and waits. He repeats this procedure several times and shows signs of impatience.

0310 hrs: An elderly man opens the inside door of the cinema, then the metal shutter, and lets M. Sarla in.

0540 hrs: M. Sarla comes out of the cinema with four women, aged between 25 and 40, smartly dressed and very made up. They wait on the doorstep in silence.

0545 hrs: Three taxis stop level with them. M. Sarla sees all the women into the taxis. They shake hands. The taxis leave. M. Sarla goes down the Rue du Faubourg-Poissonnière while making a number of different calls on his mobile.

0615 hrs: M. Sarla goes into the Holiday Inn hotel on the Boulevard des Italiens. From information gathered from the concierge, M. Sarla took a room, alone, and asked to be woken at 1430 hrs.

1510 hrs: M. Sarla comes out of the Holiday Inn and goes up the Boulevard des Italiens. He stops at the Deville & Charron chocolate shop to buy some s*arments à l'orange*, which he eats as he heads back towards Place de l'Opéra.

"Those were his favourites!"

Moved, Brigitte smiled.

"Sometimes he would do a detour of three arrondissements to go to Deville & Charron to buy them. The best in Paris, according to him."

She sighed and went back to her reading. Paul, still leaning against the window, waited patiently.

1535 hrs: M. Sarla goes into the FNAC store. On the books floor he spends most of his time in the "Esoterica" department.

1550 hrs: He comes back out having bought several books including: Rémy Grangier's *A History of Sects*, Carina Lorajna's *A Guru for Life* and Mark Selmer's *Forbidden Minds*.

"Monsieur Vermeiren . . . Do you think there's some connection with the extraordinary tunic he tried on at the tailor?"

"There's no way of knowing."

1555 hrs: M. Sarla goes into the Café Marivaux opposite the shop. He sits at a table and orders a *croque-monsieur* and a glass of beer.

1620 hrs: As he eats he looks at the books he has bought.

1630 hrs: He receives a phone call, speaks for a moment, ends the call and asks for the bill.

1635 hrs: M. Sarla comes out of the café and walks to a workshop which does alterations (but has no sign) situated at 61 Rue Bachaumont. He speaks to the owner. They are alone.

1655 hrs: A police van stops outside the workshop. Three uniformed officers – two men and a woman – get out and go into the workshop. They are greeted enthusiastically by the man and M. Sarla. They engage in conversation while the man goes into the adjacent café, La Chope, and comes back out with a teapot and some cups.

1700 hrs: The three police officers, M. Sarla and the man from the workshop have a cup of tea.

1710 hrs: The officers leave and get back into the van. M. Sarla stays in the workshop a little longer.

1720 hrs: M. Sarla comes out of the workshop. He makes for the Rue Saint-Denis by cutting along the Rue Saint-Sauveur.

1730 hrs: He stops on the corner of the Rue Réaumur and the Rue Saint-Denis, and waits.

1755 hrs: The aforementioned Gisèle comes to meet M. Sarla. They go to the Surcouf *café-tabac* on the corner of the Rue Réaumur and the Rue de Palestro.

1800 hrs: They sit at a table with a glass of beer each and talk. M. Sarla has his hand on Gisèle's knee.

1810 hrs: They part on the doorstep of the café-tabac. M. Sarla catches the Métro at Strasbourg-Saint-Denis.

1830 hrs: M. Sarla comes out of the Métro at Bastille and heads for the Faubourg-Saint-Antoine. He goes into a furniture shop called Alain Affaires situated at number 51. He meets the young woman in the Perfecto jacket to whom he handed over the baby in the pushchair the day before. The young woman has her child with her, and M. Sarla picks the child up and kisses it.

1835 hrs: M. Sarla and the young woman walk round the shop accompanied by a salesman. They seem to settle on a rustic-style wooden wardrobe, and a foldaway double bed. M. Sarla sits down to place the order and to write a cheque.

1855 hrs: The Rue du Faubourg-Saint-Antoine is very busy, and M. Sarla, with the woman with the pushchair, is trying to find a taxi.

1910 hrs: M. Sarla puts the pushchair into a taxi, kisses the young woman and the child, and walks back up the Faubourg-Saint-Antoine. He goes into the Bastille Métro station.

1935 hrs: M. Sarla comes out of the Abbesses Métro station and goes to the Le Poussah hostess bar on the Rue d'Orchampt. The surveillance continues from outside the bar.

2245 hrs: M. Sarla comes out of the bar and goes back towards the Place des Abbesses.

2250 hrs: M. Sarla stops when he reaches the square and turns back the way he has come. He comes over to his tail, whom he has spotted, and – without a word – drags him into the small lawned area in the middle, which is completely deserted. The tail is struck violently on the back of the neck and loses consciousness.

"... He hit you?!"

Paul turned away. The bandaging on his face was the best answer. "I'd been following him for too long."

". . . And what happened to you?!"
"Read on."

Approximately 2330 hrs: The tail regains consciousness in a
            very damp, bare cellar. His hands are tied behind his
            back. Franck Sarla is facing him, they are alone. He
            destroys the film containing the photos taken that
            day and the day before, then he tries to get the tail
            to admit how long he has been following him and
            who hired him. When the tail resists his
            interrogations, M. Sarla beats him violently about
            the face.
Approximately 2345 hrs: The tail gives the name Brigitte
            REYNOUARD to M. Sarla.

". . . How did he react?"
"When I said your name? He seemed very surprised.
He was expecting it to be any number of other names,
but not yours. I'm sure you'll understand that, given
the situation, I didn't ask who the others were."

Approximately 2350 hrs: After a long silence, M. Sarla leaves
            the room.
Approximately 0010 hrs: Wednesday, 30 May: M. Sarla
            reappears with a pad of paper and a pen. He starts to
            write a letter.
Approximately 0030 hrs: M. Sarla puts the letter in an envelope
            and asks the tail to give it to Brigitte Reynouard, then
            he lets him go. The tail goes up a flight of stairs and
            finds himself in the central courtyard of a dilapidated
            building on the Rue Véron. From information
            gathered, the cellar belongs to the jointly owned
            apartment building and is not used by them.
            M. Sarla's name does not appear anywhere in
            connection with it.
0040 hrs: M. Sarla leaves in the direction of the Rue
            Lepic.

280

Holding the sheets of paper limply in her hands, with her arms hanging by her sides and a faraway look in her eye, Brigitte let a tear roll down her cheek. Paul lit another cigarette and put the pack in his drawer. There was something delicious about every drag of it.

". . . He's a monster . . . this man's a monster!"

"He threatened me if I didn't stop tailing him straight away. I don't need to tell you that I took his threats seriously. I didn't know Thierry Blin well, but I can tell you, Franck Sarla has enough influence to get rid of whoever he likes. Personally, I wouldn't take it any further."

". . . And the letter?"

He opened a little drawer in his desk, took out an envelope and handed it to Brigitte.

"Would you like me to leave you alone?"

"No, please stay, Paul."

Mademoiselle,

It seems such a long time . . . such a long time since that makeshift little office in the corner of the workshop. You knew how to be part of the furniture, forgotten even. Perhaps too much so. You could have lived this affair instead of dreaming about it, who knows? We were never lovers, try to convince yourself of that instead of convincing the rest of the world we were. You were the opposite of a mistress, you were my confidante. You were the woman I could tell everything, even my heartaches and salacious jokes. I liked the thought of talking to a woman about another woman. But you were never the one I talked about. We will never be lovers. Thierry Blin is dead, leave him in peace, and forget him, even the memory of him. The man I am now doesn't have much left in common with the man you knew. It's a shame you felt you needed that detective on my tail to realize that.

Do you remember the day when you asked me where I was on a scale of one to twenty in relation to McEnroe? I'm now at twenty on the scale of my own life and I don't want any other, however strange and wrong it may be. I don't know where it will take me, but it's what my life is now. Blin used to cheat. I don't cheat.

I've destroyed all the photos taken by your investigater, I don't want you to know what my new face looks like. Don't ask him about it, in your own interests and his. Leave me in peace. Don't try to find me again, Mademoiselle, I'm too good at taking advantage of women, I'd turn you into something that was no longer you.

With your salary, you can't afford this M. Vermeiren's services. I have paid him, and he shouldn't ask you for any more. Try to be happy, Brigitte, you deserve to be. If there's one person in the world who deserves to stay the way they are, then it's you.

Never turn into someone else.

FS

It had not been easy going back to Blin's cramped and barely legible writing. Brigitte was one of the few people who could make sense of it. She had had to be, after hours spent deciphering his accounts, his notes, all the scribblings in that workshop. Nowadays, Paul Vermeiren's handwriting was more rounded, more fluid, smoother. Just another form of gymnastics.

"I'm so sorry, Paul," she said, holding back her tears.

"Would you like a cup of coffee? Something hot? or a little glass of brandy? I must have some for emergencies."

She did not reply. He went to prepare some tea and left her to stew in silence. Something told him that

Franck Sarla would not be haunting Brigitte's memory for long.

He handed her a cup of scalding hot tea, and she came out of her daze.

"Salacious jokes . . . That was what he used to say. 'A little salacious joke, Mademoiselle?' I hated them but I would listen, and sometimes I'd smile just to please him. 'This is the sort of thing I can't tell Nadine.' It's all in this letter, the way he repeated himself, his spelling mistakes, even the word 'makeshift', which he used to use all over the place. There's so much of him in this letter . . ."

After a moment's silence she picked a lighter up from the desk and lit the corner of the letter. They watched in silence as it burned, until the ashes scattered.

"Do I owe you anything?"

"Sarla gave me enough to cover my charges and the bandaging."

"And there I was thinking I knew him better than anyone else . . ."

Paul Vermeiren had spent the whole night typing out the report. With the first light of dawn, Franck Sarla had started to exist. Paul could hear him starting up the stairs, ready to come and punch his face in if he did not stop referring to him.

"Could you destroy the report too?" she said. "The fewer traces of this bastard there are, the better it'll be. Thank you for everything you've done. I've got my answers at last. Everything will get better now."

She headed for the door very quickly.

"Goodbye, Monsieur Vermeiren."

"Brigitte . . . I wondered . . ."

"Yes?"

"I was going to suggest we could meet again when all these ghosts have disappeared."

She smiled again. Surprised and probably slightly flattered.

"There's something about you that I like, Paul. I would even say that I'm drawn to . . . something I can't put my finger on . . . But you live in a world of Franck Sarlas. There's too much violence in that world. Thierry was from my world. You're not. I'm so sorry . . ."

She put her arms round Vermeiren and kissed him as if saying goodbye to a friend.

"Goodbye, Paul," she said with a nod of her head to emphasize the finality.

She disappeared into the stairwell.

He went back into his office, picked up the Sarla file and burned it.

The *Other*

Since he had discovered that, in Russian, vodka meant "little water", Nicolas could see no reason why he should not have it in the morning. When he woke he would get out of bed and drink a cold beer in the kitchen, then he would go back to bed with an iced vodka in his hand, and he would sip at that until he was fully awake. His despair no longer had time to set in; he had sworn that he would never let it gain control again.

He definitely did not miss anything about the days when he was sober, apart perhaps from the energy of the first few hours of the day. The only true enemy of the drunk was not cirrhosis of the liver, the worrying, the possible cancers, the hangovers, the redundancies or the sideways glances: it was the tiredness. Even first thing in the morning he had trouble overcoming the weakness in his limbs; he had to wait till that "little water" had done a whole circuit of his organism, till the beloved molecule had set its chain reactions in motion, and till his brain found a good reason to set the body to work. Then he had to run the gauntlet of the mirror.

Gredzinski's mask had fallen and the *Other*'s true face had finally appeared. He expected to see the face of a depressive or the distorted features of some other-worldly creature; he found only dark rings under the eyes, blotches with red highlights, sagging eyelids and patchy stubble. So was this the face of his double, then? Something about it was similar to him, but there was something sad about it as well, like the bloated, decomposing body of an older brother. Seen in the cold light of dawn, this *Other* – who was so eloquent, so dazzling when he was a creature of the night – had the sickly expression of someone who already knows their fate. He would die blind drunk, with a bottle in his hand and oblivion in his head; which was still better than dying praying to whatever spare God might be knocking about. Nicolas may, without realizing it, always have been afraid of death, but to the *Other* it was a distant promise of deliverance. He found it reassuring that all this could come to an end one day. And if life was a shooting star across some dark eternity, each of us was free to make it shine in their own way. Nicolas still remembered Loraine's words, the tone of her voice, the little blue twinkle in the depths of her retina which gave a malicious edge to everything she said: *You're so lucky . . . You've got a liver like a baby's.* She was right, this predictable death could wait a while yet. Major-league alcoholics had been known to drink right to the end of their life expectancy without missing a single drop.

But on that particular morning, Nicolas was in the grips of an uncomfortable feeling of foreboding. An unpleasant impression which was very different from the dying notes of a night laden with dreams or the first mists of intoxication. An indefinable threat which he tried to drive out with a good mouthful of vodka.

He always ended up going to the office. He still found the little performance of his daily life amusing; this masquerade would soon come to an end, but he preferred the decision to come from above. In the meantime, he kept testing the limits the way children do to see just how powerful they are. He could see he was going too far, he could feel all of them trying to contain themselves when he came near them.

"They're all there for the departmental meeting – they're only waiting for you now."

"Thank you, Muriel."

He did a detour via his office, dived straight into the bottom drawer to check that he had something to fill up his flask with; the bottle of Wyborowa had barely been touched. His tiredness had evaporated in a downward movement, releasing first his head, then his arms and finally his legs. He took a swig of vodka in preparation for the Friday meeting, strode through the corridors in a beautifully relaxed way, and stepped into the workshop where everyone was waiting for him round a long trestle table.

"You look tired, Nicolas," said Cécile.

"Tired? Are you sure that's the word you want? Don't you mean 'depressed' or 'plastered'?"

Cécile was too embarrassed to reply.

"It doesn't matter. Let's get on with the catalogue of complaints. Who's going first?"

Now they were all embarrassed.

"Well, that's what I'm here for, isn't it?"

"Perhaps you should get some rest, Nicolas. We've been under incredible pressure these last few weeks."

"What do you lot know about *pressure*? You, Valerie, you spend the best part of the day stretching text to fit the space and choosing typefaces, and that's when the computer's not doing it for you. And you, Jean-Jean, the biggest tragedy in your life is that you've lost your Rotring pen. Last time I borrowed it from you, you looked like someone had disembowelled your little sister. You, Véro, you deserve a special mention for your arsy vocab, your *de-stressing* holidays, your lunch *slots* and your *debriefings* round the coffee machine. And then with you, Cécile, everything's always *massively urgent* because you're only any good up against a *deadline*. And Bernardo, incapable of doing simple division without his IBM computer, and Marie-Paule, queen of the Internet, of faxes and phones and mobiles, always so keen to *communicate*, yet the only things you can say are 'Where are you? Can I call you back?' "

There was a painful silence round the room.

Which went on.

And on.

"All that would be bearable if you didn't spend your time – my time! – complaining. Are you wishing you were dying slowly in some factory so that you only survived for three weeks of your retirement? Do you want to have a chat about redundancy and all the horrors that go with it?"

"Nobody told us we were on trial. What is this?" said Bernardo.

"Well, if everyone took that line . . .!" added Cécile.

"No one's asking you to take a particular line, but just to stop listening to yourselves all day long. I'm not saying this for me, or even for the work or the Communications Department or the whole Group. In the long run, what do we actually do all year? We dress up merchandise, we give a bit of colour to other people's profits, a little logo here, a metal plaque there, no one gives a damn but it keeps us alive. I'm only telling you this for your own sakes, because if you take everything that happens here seriously, you're heading for trouble."

He stood up and disappeared off to the toilets, where he locked himself in, put down the seat and sat down. Blue-grey metal, immaculate white china, halogen lighting. Swig of vodka. Big sigh. He liked these moments of ultra-modern contemplation.

*

The company restaurant only ever had one free space at the busiest time, right opposite Gredzinski. He had not had lunch with the others for weeks now. Another paradoxical effect of alcoholism; he had become very particular about subjects of conversation. Any apparently banal chitter chatter was "deadly" according to his criteria; his barometer of mediocrity had an almost instant tolerance threshold. Nicolas no longer had the strength to play-act politely while waiting for his dessert, and one fine day he announced that he would be considerably less bored on his own.

The afternoon slipped by so calmly he should have been suspicious. His feeling of foreboding had been with him all day.

"Hello, it's Alissa, how are things?"

"What's the news?"

"Could you nip up to see my boss later?"

"Broaters wants to see me in person?"

"Just for a couple of minutes, if you've got time, at about five-thirty."

"That's not going to be easy today," he said, to be sure about how serious this was.

"Can't you try?"

"So I'm being summoned."

"If you want to see it like that."

It could not go on forever, after all. His relationship with the Group had come to term. Good! He had other territories to explore, other worlds to conquer. He promised himself he would buy a ticket to New Guinea the very next day, and would be playing cricket with the natives within a week. He would even be the first Westerner in the world to be accepted as part of a Papuan team. After that, life would go on to set him other impossible tasks.

"It's good of you to find the time, Nicolas. Rumours are just rumours, but I do have to deal with them and find out how they started. Did you have some sort of problem this morning, during your briefing?"

"The same problems you have every day, Christian. By the way, we can call each other by our first names, can't we?"

Broaters was surprised and replied with a slight nod.

"Reports have come back to me. Are you having problems in your private life? Or a disagreement with Lefébure?"

"He's a prick."

"Please. He's a close collaborator, and I respect him as a person and in his professional capacity."

"Do you want to know if I drink? It's true."

Broaters said nothing.

"Vodka. It's a love affair."

Still Broaters said nothing, and Nicolas looked at him steadily.

"I'm sure you'll understand that we can't keep you any longer. Your behaviour, the friction you've created because of your . . . condition. I'm sorry to be so blunt. You're an intelligent man, I expect you already see what I mean."

"It's not so much the fact that I drink that bothers you, the results have been much better since I've been heading up the department. I sorted the sheep from the goats; I'm a useful ally, and you know it. The problem is you've got to get rid of someone who's no longer frightened. The Group can't cope with some-one who's not afraid of leaving the Group. Even if it gets results, my independence isn't acceptable. You're like Dobermans, you can smell when people are afraid. Like here, right now, in this office, you can smell that I'm not afraid of you, or of your decisions. Under all your gentlemanly airs and graces, you look at the staff with a very clear message in your eye: *It's cold outside.* It's cold outside the Group, and anyone might find themselves outside from one day to the next, even someone like Bardane, who thought he was untouchable. But I'm not cold any more. It must be the vodka, they used to give it to Russian soldiers. How much do you get a month, Christian?"

Broaters was too surprised to answer.

"Two hundred thousand? Two hundred and twenty? Let's say two forty, we shouldn't skimp. That's way below what I make when I'm asleep. It's not especially glorious, but it means I can stand in front of you without shaking – with fear or with cold. I didn't need to go to some swanky college and be ragged as a new boy, I didn't have to swear allegiance to any brotherhood or play watchdog to anyone's profits, I haven't made or broken any marriages, or made anyone redundant or dallied with power. I just had an idea, a stupid, pointless invention, I put it down on paper and found a use for it in minutes. I exploited the absurdity of the whole system – like you do every day – and the system paid me back very nicely. It sheltered me from itself. Thanks to that, I'm highly likely to die an extremely rich man."

Broaters, who did not understand a single word, stood up and headed for the door to be sure that Nicolas left his office.

". . . I've still got a lot to do today, I have to justify this salary, which, sadly for me, is way below what you think. I will, therefore, have to ask you to leave, Monsieur Gredzinski."

"So, what are we going to do about my compensation?"

Broaters looked at him in speechless amazement.

"As a matter of principle."

"You'll have to see Alissa about that."

"No hard feelings," said Gredzinski, holding out his hand.

Broaters could not avoid shaking it. As he left the floor, Nicolas wondered whether the gesture had been a sign of fair play or rather pathetic. He went back to his office and sat slumped in his chair for a long while. Oddly, his feeling of premonition still dogged him.

*

Usually, someone who had been made redundant left his office with a little cardboard box full of his personal effects. A couple of files, a sweater, a photograph of loved ones, a mug, an umbrella, a few headache pills in a box. Nicolas could find nothing to take except for his complete collection of Trickpacks, a fob watch he had found in the corridor, and a postcard Jacot had sent him from Kauai. The latter had gone back to his barrister's robes and his speeches for the defence now that the doctors had officially announced that he was in remission. He had rediscovered his will to fight; Nicolas could leave with a clear conscience.

He left the premises with his head held high, not before emptying what was left of the bottle of Wyborowa into his flask. He would have liked to know how other people would tell his story, later, in the corridors of the Group. *Grezinski? He started drinking after his promotion, he always turned up drunk, he'd hide in the toilets to drink on the sly, he was kicked out in the end.* That would be all they would remember. My God, collective memory was unfair. In the evening rush hour he took the lift with all the people who would be there again the next day. The atrium opened up before him; he strode across it imperiously. He was so impatient to do battle with the world that he had pushed himself to the point of being thrown out, and now there was nothing that would make him backtrack. He passed the Nemrod, knowing they would be there having their aperitifs. Something persuaded him to go and say goodbye to them. As he drew closer to them he could hear them falling silent.

"I've come to say goodbye."

The girls prayed that José or Marcheschi would say something but neither of them could make up their mind to.

"I know what you think. Why's he coming to drink with us when he's already drunk?"

"No, that's not what we think," said Régine rather sadly.

"And don't go putting words into our mouths," José added. "No one here has ever judged you."

"Come and sit down and have a drink with us, what does it matter if it's the first or the last?"

To reinforce what he was saying, Marcheschi took a chair from a neighbouring table and everyone moved up to make room for Nicolas. Arnaud waved to the waiter, who brought over a beer. The embarrassment gradually faded, and the conversation picked up again.

"Apparently everyone working on 4.99 is going to be entitled to an improvers' course," said Régine.

"Where?"

"In Nîmes."

"Doesn't bother me. I love that cod dish they make down there, *brandade*."

"Does *brandade* come from Nîmes?"

Nicolas realized that these volatile little moments would never happen again. From now on he would not have the same references, the same preoccupations, the same reflexes. He would have to find his way on his own, in a great anonymous crowd. Vodka excluded any other company.

"I won't be joining you here next week," said Marcheschi. "I'm off to Seattle."

"For work?"

"I'm signing a deal with Slocombe & Partridge. I won't go into details but it's huge."

"Well the drinks are on you, then," said Arnaud.

Marcheschi did not stop at that. Nicolas regretted coming to say goodbye.

"I had Europe, Africa with Exacom, Asia with Kuala Lumpur, Oceania with Camberoil, and I've just hooked the only continent I was missing!"

It was too late to leave, too late to backtrack, to pretend Marcheschi had not said anything.

"Marcheschi, you're not a saint or a sinner, you're neither good or bad, brilliant or stupid, attractive or ugly. You're there in that worrying middle ground of people always trying to prove how individual they are. The affection you feel for us is quite touching, it's a love story which always has a happy ending. You're not a genius, but don't get upset, no one's a genius, almost all of us have managed to accept that. Even the statue you raise in your image is far from being a masterpiece. You'll never have the effortless class of Cary Grant, Billy Wilder's humour, Lucky Luciano's nerves of steel, Marie Curie's determination or the bravery of . . ."

Marcheschi did not even take the trouble to hear him through to the end; he stood up, took Nicolas by the lapels and head butted him. The impact of their foreheads made a dull thud which surprised them both; before they even realized it, they were on the ground, taking the table and glasses with them as they fell. Marcheschi fell on his shoulders and stayed motionless for a few seconds, while Nicolas brought his hand up to his nose which was bleeding all over his shirt. Terrified by the red stickiness on his fingers, he was overcome by instinctive fury and hammered punches on Marcheschi's face. For those few seconds he struck him with supernatural glee and strength, as if suddenly shaking off all the fears he had felt since his childhood so that the beast in him could reign over the world at last. Amid the cries and commotion, Arnaud and José tried in vain to stop him, and they all stood rooted to the spot, petrified and impotent in the face of this violence which seemed to come from so deep inside him. Eventually, José managed to trip him so that he fell to the ground, and Arnaud picked Marcheschi up. It should all have stopped there, but, forgetting his own fear and now also furious at the sight of his own blood, Marcheschi threw himself down onto Nicolas with all his weight, knocking the breath out of him. He grabbed him by the hair, lifted up his head and bashed it against the ground several times. In spite of the screams, everyone heard the bones in his nose cracking and his cheekbones caving in. Marcheschi stopped of his own accord when Gredzinski's face was nothing more than a blur of red.

And then silence fell.

Uncoordinated flapping gestures from Arnaud and José, panic from Régine, the waiters and the *patron*, who had no idea what to do. Marcheschi stood up, leant against a wall for a moment and, ignoring the blood still dribbling from his nose, wiped his tears with the handkerchief that someone handed to him. Nicolas was no longer there.

He was in a school playground in blazing sunshine. He was lying on the ground, bent double, completely unaware of the pain. He was reduced to pure humiliation. The boys who had beaten him up were standing round him and looking down at their feet at the little bundle of shame which no longer dared stand up. That was probably his baptism of fear, it had taken up residence in him and would never be driven out again.

"We've got to call a doctor!"

Marcheschi walked shakily out of the café followed by Régine. Everybody's eyes had come to rest on Nicolas. He refused to see a doctor.

"You're bleeding. We've got to get you to hospital."

He repeated himself, only much louder, and everyone left.

"José, if you want to make yourself useful, bring me some vodka, a glass filled to the brim."

"But . . ."

"Quickly, or I'll just have to do it myself."

Nicolas was holding a napkin to his face. Sober, he would probably never have recovered from such a beating; but protected by drink, he was still conscious and holding out. He wanted to cry, to laugh, to calm everyone else down, to pretend it was nothing, to keep his dignity. There would be time enough to suffer tomorrow. José held out the glass of vodka and he drank it down in one slow draught, like medicine. That was what it was. His whole body was plagued with countless dull aches. He had lost the use of certain muscles, but, in spite of everything, he tried to stand up. The little drink had barely gone down his oesophagus and it was restoring the use of his limbs. It felt to him as if it had replaced the blood and all the other fluids in his body, from head to foot. Soon he experienced that feeling, so often described but hard to believe, of being somewhere else, outside this suffering body, far removed from this shame which should have made all his inner wounds bleed.

He was drunk.

"Do you really not want me to . . ."

"No."

He headed for the door. The courtyard was empty and the Group had melted away. He took a few steps towards the guardrail to the car park, and leant against it for a moment while his battered face tried to identify the early summer breeze.

He hobbled over to the newspaper kiosk. Every step took several hours. There was blood trickling down his sleeve. What would the next stage be? Getting to the door of that building over there on the left? No, he was going to go for the big one, all the way to the beginning of the footbridge, then down it to get to the taxi rank. None of the drivers would open their doors to him, that was for sure. So he would take the Métro, at worst he would be taken for the tramp he had now become: unshaven, splattered with blood, blind drunk and out of work. He found the strength to step onto the footbridge, and walked along it slowly, his legs obeying him. The embankment of the Seine was deserted, he was alone dragging his carcass along it, and it was better that way.

But when he thought about it, he was not completely alone on that footbridge.

Right at the bottom he could see a small motionless figure.

Waiting.

The nasty premonition, which had survived every insult the day had thrown at him, suddenly felt more acute.

The stiff, rigid figure was looking towards him. This

was not some illusion. His battered cheekbones were not clouding his view, his concussed brain was not distorting his senses, the little guy was there waiting for him, stiff as a poker, at the bottom of the footbridge. The image was still a long way off, but already familiar.

He made out the features without daring to recognize them.

He would have been so much happier for this to have been a hallucination, some evil creature surfacing from his worst nightmares. The little guy had small eyes, small hands and probably a small heart beating in his chest.

The little guy definitely was someone, and he had every right to go wherever he liked in the city. So what was he doing at the bottom of this footbridge, as if the fate of the man he was waiting for had no choice but to come past him.

When he drew level with him, Nicolas was exhausted and damp with his own blood. He turned to face him.

"What do you want, Bardane?"

Alain Bardane gave no reply. He was wearing a dark suit, a white shirt with several buttons undone and no tie.

"I expect you can tell," said Nicolas, "I'm not feeling great . . . I'm still just about getting by because the vodka's acting as an anaesthetic but soon . . . I . . ."

Bardane still did not break his silence, so Nicolas tried to get round him and continue on his way, but Bardane, thrusting his hand into his jacket pocket, did not give him a chance.

"Stay where you are."

He took his hand back out clutching a small black metallic object which Nicolas could not immediately identify . . . for the simple reason that it was the first time he had seen one so close up.

"Is that a revolver you've got there?"

Bardane was silent again as he held up the tiny revolver, no more realistic than a child's toy. Not something to be afraid of. Nicolas tried to control himself. The alcohol was still fuelling the fire in his skull. Was it tiredness or the hazy veil woven by the vodka that was coming between him and reality? He was not frightened yet. It was all so unthinkable. Nothing made any sense.

"I'm tired," he said. "I want to disappear. Not be here any more. To be out of the picture. Let me pass and I promise no one will ever hear my name again. I'm going to take a plane to some impossible place and I'll never come back. Give me a bloody break."

"It was the friends who left first. My wife won't stay much longer. I've had to sell everything that could be sold. The word that keeps cropping up is 'depression'. As far as doctors are concerned 'decline' doesn't really mean anything, but 'depression' does."

"They're right. Depression can be treated."

"I didn't realize everything would stop so quickly, I wasn't ready. The children could fend for themselves, I thought I was in my prime. I've never done anything but work. It's what I do. I could have gone on another ten or fifteen years. They told me I couldn't be recycled. Like most rubbish."

"Put that gun away and let's go and talk about this somewhere."

"At first, I thought it was to do with money, to do with living standards, but that doesn't actually matter very much, I can cope without all that, but I've got nothing else to live for except my work. It must be my fault."

"Put that gun away."

Bardane started to sob. Nicolas could feel the effects of the vodka seeping away and he knew that soon he would be left alone and more terrified than ever.

"I've been sacked too," he said. "The position's vacant. Broaters might take you back." Nicolas was backing away as he spoke and Bardane was furious when he realized.

"Don't move, Gredzinski!"

"Go and talk to him, he'll understand . . ." said Nicolas, taking another step back, then another, unable to stop himself.

"Don't move, I said!"

Nicolas thought Bardane was going to drop his arm and point his toy at the ground.

Instead, he heard a bang and his chest buckled with the impact.

Winded, he brought his hand up to his heart.

Fell to the ground.

His eyes closed involuntarily.

There must have been some logic to all this, everything made sense. He had never had any talent for living. As a child, he had watched others live.

What a shame . . .

Everything could have been so different.

All he had to do was to get over that footbridge, and then, straight after that, the world.

But it was getting dark, far too early for the time of year.

His cheek against the tarmac.

The greatest fear, the thing he had been so afraid of for all these years . . . is this all it was? Just this?

In a few minutes Nicolas Gredzinski would no longer be afraid of anything, he had all eternity to recover from this practical joke. No one would be able to get to him there, the little coyote was not allowed in, nor were any of the other pains . . .

A warm liquid, oozing from his heart, ran down his neck.

Is this all it was was? Just this? I've spent so long being frightened of . . . this?

A slick of liquid wet his chin and lips.

He would know the taste of his own blood before dying.

The tip of his tongue found a drip at the corner of his lips.

Hot and sharp at the same time.

Yes, it was hot.

But why sharp . . .?

Why was his blood sharp?

It wasn't blood.

It wasn't blood . . .

He knew that taste.

I know that taste . . . It's . . .

It definitely was what he thought it was.

Is it vodka . . .?

It definitely was vodka.

His heart was oozing vodka.

Heaven? Hell? What was this place where he had vodka instead of blood?

He checked through every part of his body; his arms, legs, lungs, head – everything was working. Laboriously, broken, smashed, dislocated, but working. He could even try opening his eyes.

It was light.

It was a long time until nightfall.

He managed to stand up and found he was at the bottom of the footbridge. There was no one now to stand in his way.

He looked at his chest and could find absolutely no traces of blood. He thrust his hand into the inside pocket of his jacket and took out his dripping flask, which had a hole pierced through it.

Alcohol had been killing people since forever. But,

amongst the millions of lives it took, it occasionally happened to save the odd one.

*

He pressed his forehead against the shop window as he waited for her to turn round.

She eventually came out and looked him up and down to assess the full extent of the damage.

". . . I miss you, Loraine."

She did not say anything alarming. Or anything amusing either. Just: "Let's go back to my place."

Epilogue

They had said 9 o'clock.

Nicolas remembered, in spite of the state he was in
that evening. How could he forget that feeling of taking his life into his own hands, like a freed slave, utterly
surprised by the sudden freedom. In the three years
since that night of June 23rd, he had experienced the
drunken thrill of the peaks and the troughs; he had
unleashed his own strengths which had been held back
for too long, he had even looked death in the face. All
of this could have encouraged him to miss a rendezvous
he had not believed in anyway.

The announcement in the newspaper about Blin's
disappearance had persuaded him to go. The words
"left us" seemed to him to be a confirmation, a logical
conclusion to a sequence of events for which he had
been the pretext. Only a dead man, returning from the
dead, could respect the terms of their bet.

Nicolas arrived with plenty of time to spare and this
was intentional: he wanted to have a look round the
Feuillants Tennis Club. Half pilgrimage, half nostalgia trip – nostalgia for his own physical fitness, which
he might never see again. The alcohol might not have
made his hands shake or taken his legs from beneath
him, but it had slackened his reflexes and his general
mobility. However much his doctor reassured him,
his good old habit of worrying had regained the
upper hand, he could already see himself as a breath-
less old man who would soon not manage just one

flight of stairs. Coming back to the Feuillants, he wanted to see players moving, having sudden bursts of speed and playing winning shots. Perhaps the magic of tennis would reawaken something in him and give him a taste for physical exertion again. He spent a few minutes watching a mixed doubles match where the combined age of the players was around the 300 mark. Septuagenarians dressed all in white exchanging vicious shots and making jokes about the more litigious points. Exactly what he needed to watch. Then he walked all round the club hoping to see a dash of true brilliance, which he did here and there on the various courts. He felt the urge to play again.

His watch said twenty to nine. His rendezvous, even if it was only a symbolic one, was in no danger of being late. He got his car and went to the infamous American bar, which had not changed one iota; he paused in the doorway to look all round the room so as not to miss a single person. He might have drunk a lot these last few months, he might have gone a bit too far off the rails, scrambled his memory and forgotten who he had always been, but he still remembered Thierry Blin's face. A little round face with dark, sly eyes, smothered by a beard and neglected looking hair. Here in this bar, at five past nine, there was no one who looked like that. He settled himself on a bench seat and crossed his arms, happy to be there although he could not have said why. No one asked him what he wanted to drink. New faces appeared, office workers, couples, a few tourists, nothing that looked like this Thierry Blin who had "left us".

At twenty to ten he eventually resigned himself to the fact that the ghost would not appear and it was better that way; there are some mysteries that gain nothing by being explained, and some secrets it is better not to know.

The time had come to go back to the woman he loved. He stood up with a feeling of resignation, perhaps a little disappointed, and cast one last glance round the room. He would never set foot here again, in the place which had turned his life upside down in the space of a few hours; that was a long time ago now. His gaze lingered on one man's head, or rather the nape of his neck, quite hairless and motionless, and set on shoulders dressed in light-coloured linen. The man had been there since he arrived, leaning over the counter, with his fingers around a huge orange and blue cocktail. As he approached him from the side, Nicolas recognized one of the members of the Feuillants that he had been watching an hour earlier.

"Excuse me, my name's Nicolas Gredzinski, I watched a few of your rallies earlier at the Feuillants."

". . . And?"

Gredzinski did not recognize anything about this face, not even the sly little eyes.

"I had a strange impression when I watched you hitting the ball. Would you mind if I told you what I really thought?"

"Please do."

"Your shots have quite good flowing style, you never miss an easy shot, but it's clear that if things speed up at all, you have a slightly delayed reaction."

"Well, that was very honest."

"In a word, you're an honourable player, but you wouldn't get a ranking higher than fifteen."

"I've never tried, that way I've never had to face the evidence."

"All the same . . . there is something unique about your game: the backhand down the line."

The other man raised his eyebrows questioningly.

"A wonderfully tactical shot, startlingly fast and with unbelievably straight action. A champion's shot."

Gredzinski paused, but got no response.

"There are only two people in the world capable of mastering a trump like that. There was Adriano Panatta, particularly during the 1976 Roland-Garros tournament. And there was someone, who's not with us any more, called Thierry Blin."

Paul Vermeiren said nothing. Holding back a smile, he gestured for Gredzinski to sit down on the stool next to him.

The waiter came over without being called.

"I'm going to have a vodka in a well chilled glass," said Vermeiren. "How about you?"

Nicolas thought for a moment, and let the temptation wash over him. Later in the evening he had planned to open a bottle of some unknown wine discovered by Loraine; he had decided he would now drink only when he was with her; from now on she would be there to share in his moments of euphoria, and perhaps she would be for a long time to come.

"Nothing, thank you."

They sat in silence until Vermeiren's drink arrived.

"I thought I'd won the bet," he said. "I fooled everyone who knows me, but then my mask falls in front of a complete stranger!"

Nicolas smiled, flattered.

"Do you remember what was at stake?" said Paul.

"Of course."

"Bad luck on the loser. You can ask whatever you want of me."

Nicolas had never thought about it. To his own surprise, he heard himself saying: "A revenge match on the tennis court."

Paul burst out laughing but quickly contained himself. "When?"

"Why not straight away, then it's done with."

"The club will be closed soon, it's almost dark," said Vermeiren looking at his watch.

"The number four court has floodlights for tournaments. With a good enough tip, Maurice will pull out all the stops for us."

Paul raised his glass, there was no need to say anything else.

Half an hour later they were warming up. Nicolas was back on the court much sooner than he had imagined. He had learned to grab opportunities, and this was one which would never present itself again. After the toss, Paul chose to serve. They each swore to themselves that they would win.

HOLY SMOKE

Tonino Benacquista

"An iconoclastic chronicle of small-time crooks and
desperate capers, with added Gallic and Italian flair.
Wonderful fun." *Guardian*

"This prizewinning novel is guaranteed to keep you up late at
night, driven to discover the ending. It's exciting, funny and
bizarrely even includes tips on cooking Italian food; it makes
you glad they decided to translate the novel into English."
Coventry Evening Telegraph

Some favours simply cannot be refused. Tonio agrees to write
a love letter for Dario, a low-rent Paris gigolo. When Dario is
murdered, a single bullet to the head, Tonio finds his friend
has left him a small vineyard somewhere east of Naples. The
wine is undrinkable but an elaborate scam has been set up.
The smell of easy money attracts the unwanted attentions of
the Mafia and the Vatican, and the unbridled hatred of the
locals. Mafiosi aren't choir boys, and monsignors can be very
much like Mafiosi. A darkly comic, iconoclastic tale told by
an author of great verve and humour.

Tonino Benacquista, born in France of Italian immigrants,
dropped out of film studies to finance his writing career.
After being, in turn, a museum night-watchman, a train
guard on the Paris–Rome line and a professional parasite on
the Paris cocktail circuit, he is now a highly successful author
of fiction and film scripts.

"An entertainingly cynical story. I read it in one sitting."
Observer

"Much to enjoy in the clash of cultures and superstitions, in a
stand-off between the Mafia and the Vatican. And a tasty
recipe for poisoning your friends with pasta. Detail like this
places European crime writing on a par with its American
counterpart." *Belfast Telegraph*

£8.99/$13.95
Crime paperback original, ISBN 1–904738–01–X
www.bitterlemonpress.com

HAVANA RED

Leonardo Padura

Winner of the celebrated Café de Gijon Prize, the Novela Negra Prize and the Hammett Prize.

"So many enchanting memories, sultry Cuban nights and music in this novel that you let the author take you by the hand, impatient to find out what comes next." *Lire*

On 6 August, the day on which the Catholic Church celebrates the Feast of Transfiguration, the body of a strangled transvestite is discovered in the undergrowth of the Havana Woods. He is wearing a beautiful red evening dress and the red ribbon with which he was asphyxiated is still round his neck. To the consternation of Mario Conde, in charge of the investigation, the victim turns out to be Alexis Arayán, the son of a highly respected diplomat. His investigation begins with a visit to the home of the "disgraced" dramatist, Alberto Marqués, with whom the murdered youth was living. Marqués, a man of letters and a former giant of the Cuban theatre, helps Conde solve the crime. In the baking heat of the Havana summer, Conde also unveils a dark, turbulent world of Cubans who live without dreaming of exile, grappling with food shortages and wounds from the Angolan war.

Leonardo Padura was born in 1955 in Havana and lives in Cuba. He is a novelist, essayist, journalist and scriptwriter. *Havana Red* has been published in Cuba, Mexico, Spain, Portugal, Italy, Germany and France and is the first of the Havana quartet featuring Lieutenant Mario Conde, a tropical Marlowe, to be published in English.

"A magnificent novel. An author haunted by the tragic story and the passion and emotion of his characters." *Magazine Littéraire*

"Padura is among the most translated and acclaimed Cuban authors. The crime element in his novels, as in those of Le Carré and Graham Greene, serves only as the key to a deeper labyrinth." *Corriere della Sera*

£8.99/$13.95
Crime paperback original, ISBN 1–904738–09–5
www.bitterlemonpress.com

THE RUSSIAN PASSENGER

Günter Ohnemus

At fifty the good Buddhist takes to the road, leaving all his belongings behind. His sole possession is a begging bowl. That's fine. That's how it should be. The problem was, there were four million dollars in my begging bowl and the mafia were after me. It was their money. They wanted it back, and they also wanted the girl, the woman who was with me: Sonia Kovalevskaya.

So begins the story of Harry Willemer, a taxi driver and his passenger, an ex-KGB agent and wife of a Russian Mafioso. In an atmosphere of intense paranoia *The Russian Passenger* follows their flight from the hit-men sent to recover the cash. This is not only a multifaceted thriller about murder, big money and love, but also a powerful evocation of the cruel history that binds Russia and Germany.

Günter Ohnemus, born in 1946, lives in Munich and writes novels, essays and translations. He has written three collections of short stories and a best-seller for teenagers. This is his first novel to be translated into English.

£9.99/$14.95
Crime paperback original, ISBN 1–904738–02–8
www.bitterlemonpress.com

THE SNOWMAN

Jörg Fauser

"A gritty and slyly funny story. About the life of the underdog, the petty criminal, the fixer, the prostitute and the junkie. With a healthy dose of wit." *Cath Staincliffe, author of the* Sal Kilkenny *series*

"German author Jörg Fauser was the Kafka of crime writing." *Independent*

Blum's found five pounds of top-quality Peruvian cocaine in a suitcase. His adventure started in Malta, where he was trying to sell porn magazines, the latest in a string of dodgy deals that never seem to come off. A left-luggage ticket from the Munich train station leads him to the cocaine. Now his problems begin in earnest. Pursued by the police and drug traffickers, the luckless Blum falls prey to the frenzied paranoia of the cocaine addict and dealer. His desperate and clumsy search for a buyer takes him from Munich to Frankfurt, and finally to Ostend. This is a fast-paced thriller written with acerbic humour, a hardboiled evocation of drug-fuelled existence and a penetrating observation of those at the edge of German society.

"Jörg Fauser was a fascinating train wreck: a fiercely intelligent literary critic who also wrote the occasional nudie-magazine filler; a junkie who got clean in his thirties only to become an alcoholic; a tragic figure who died mysteriously at 43 in a 1987 Autobahn accident. Oh, and along the way he managed to crank out one of the most indelible crime novels in German history. Fauser writes with a gimlet eye and a black, acerbic (so, German) wit, creating an unflinchingly brilliant tale of a perspective – the outsider among outsiders – he knew all too well." *Ruminator*

£8.99/$13.95
Crime paperback original, ISBN 1–904738–05–2
www.bitterlemonpress.com

IN MATTO'S REALM

Friedrich Glauser

"Glauser's second novel involving the dour Sergeant Studer,
a Swiss Maigret albeit with a strong sense of the absurd.
Studer investigates the death of an asylum director following
the escape of a child murderer. A despairing plot about the
reality of madness and life, leavened at regular intervals with
strong doses of bittersweet irony. The idiosyncratic
investigation and its laconic detective have not aged one iota.
Who said the past never changes." *Guardian*

"Glauser was among the best European crime writers of the
inter-war years. This dark mystery set in a lunatic asylum
follows a labyrinthine plot where the edges between reality
and fantasy are blurred. The detail, place and sinister
characters are so intelligently sculpted that the sense of
foreboding is palpable." *Glasgow Herald*

A child murderer escapes from an insane asylum in Bern.
The stakes get higher when Sergeant Studer discovers the
director's body, neck broken, in the boiler room of the mad-
house. The intuitive Studer is drawn into the workings of an
institution that darkly mirrors the world outside. Even he
cannot escape the pull of the no-man's-land between reason
and madness where Matto, the spirit of insanity, reigns.

Translated into four languages, *In Matto's Realm* was originally published in 1936. This European crime classic, now
available for the first time in English, is the second in the
Sergeant Studer series from Bitter Lemon Press.

Friedrich Glauser was born in Vienna in 1896. Often
referred to as the Swiss Simenon, he died, aged forty-two, a
few days before he was due to be married. Diagnosed a
schizophrenic, addicted to morphine and opium, he spent
the greater part of his life in psychiatric wards, insane
asylums and, when he was arrested for forgery, in prison.
His Sergeant Studer novels have ensured his place as a cult
figure in Europe.

"*In Matto's Realm*, written in 1936 when psychoanalysis
was a novelty to the layman and forensic science barely
recognized, makes gripping reading as Studer questions both
staff and patients and tries to make sense of the inscrutable
Deputy Director's behaviour." *Sunday Telegraph*

£8.99/$13.95
Crime paperback original, ISBN 1–904738–06–0
www.bitterlemonpress.com

BLACK ICE

Hans Werner Kettenbach

"A beautifully translated thriller, not a drop of blood on its pages. The nastiness takes place off-stage which makes it all the more threatening." *BBC 2 "Culture"*

"A natural story teller who, just like Patricia Highsmith, is interested in teasing out the catastrophes that result from the banal coincidences of daily life." *Weltwoche*

Erika, an attractive local heiress, is married to Wallmann, a man with expensive tastes. When she falls to her death near their lakeside villa, the police conclude it was a tragic accident. Scholten, a long-time employee of Erika's, isn't so sure. He knows a thing or two about the true state of her marriage and suspects an almost perfect crime. Scholten's maverick investigation into the odd, inexplicable details of the death scene soon buys him a ticket for a most dangerous ride.

This beautifully crafted thriller set in a European world of small-town hypocrisy was made into a film in 1998. It is written by an essayist, scriptwriter and best-selling novelist whose work is now available in English for the first time.

"*Black Ice* isn't just a class crime novel. It is one of the most beautifully told stories of our years, in which humorous *noir* dialogue and poetry flourish side by side." *Stern*

£8.99/$13.95
Crime paperback original, ISBN 1–904738–08–7
www.bitterlemonpress.com

ANGELINA'S CHILDREN

Alice Ferney

"A wonderful portrait of a woman both imperial and bruised, a greying ravaged mother-wolf that still controls all those around her. A novel of rhythm and grace, a beautiful voyage with the gypsies." *Le Monde*

"Few gypsies want to be seen as poor, although many are. Such was the case with old Angelina's sons, who possessed nothing other than their caravan and their gypsy blood. But it was young blood that coursed through their veins, a dark and vital flow that attracted women and fathered numberless children. And, like their mother, who had known the era of horses and caravans, they spat upon the very thought that they might be pitied."

So begins the story of a matriarch and her tribe, ostracized by society and exiled to the outskirts of the city. Esther, a young librarian from the town, comes to the camp to introduce the children to books and stories. She gradually gains their confidence and accompanies them, as observer and participant, through an eventful and tragic year.

Alice Ferney's distinctive style powerfully involves the reader in the family's disasters, its comic moments and its battles against an uncomprehending, hostile world; in the love lives of the five boys, the bravery of the children, and, eventually, in Angelina's final gesture of defiance.

"A beautifully feminine and fertile book . . . Ferney's prose at its most powerful." *Le Figaro*

WINNER OF THE LITERARY PRIZE
CULTURE ET BIBLIOTHEQUES POUR TOUS

£8.99/$13.95
Crime paperback original, ISBN 1–904738–10–9
www.bitterlemonpress.com